DAUGHTER OF THE BLACK FLAG

SONJA DEWING

PIRATE CREW

Thank you to my early adopters/supporters!

Katheryn Wagoner AKA Ironwheel Kate

Andrew Berry AKA Captain Berry the Merciless

April Pfeifer AKA Barrel-Blast Pfeifer

Christa Rumage AKA Rum Runner Rumage

John Emmerich AKA Stormhand Emmerich

Ronin Magnussen AKA Mad Ronin of Tortuga

INTRODUCTION

This story is based on some characters created by Robert Louis Stevenson in *Treasure Island*. In his book, it refers to Captain Flint and his crew having sailed the seas, but we never meet Captain Flint or learn how the treasure was captured.

In Part I, I've created that backstory, as well as added Chen, a young woman who becomes a pirate. She's based on an amalgam of the real pirate women who sailed the seas for freedom and treasure, and replaces the character Long John Silver.

Part II is my interpretation of *Treasure Island*. The original has only one female character - Jim Hawkin's mother, who faints when things get too exciting. This version includes a couple of female characters (Chen and Andy). Women of that time had few life choices.

Andy and Chen are examples of what freedom meant to women and what they had to do to keep it.

In Part III, you'll find suggested nonfiction reading on women pirates. Most of them I've read. From a team of women pirates to one of the most successful pirates in the world (a woman, of course). Keep in mind, the only women pirates that were written about were those that became famous, and even then, they were written about as if they were unique, but we know that if there's one, there's more.

ACKNOWLEDGEMENTS

As always, writing a story takes some work, writing a great story takes teamwork. Thank you to Jim for helping with the sea-faring terms. Thank you to my critique group of awesome writers who helped frame some important story ideas. And, thank you to the women who led the way as pirates.

And thank you to my new editors: Christine Chronis and Crystal Chronis.

SHIP CREW MANIFESTS

S hadow Serpent

Captain Flint
Billy Bones
Chen
Black Dog
Isreal Hands
Dirk
Pew
Nails Boone
Gibbet Hayes
Iron Tom
Ezra
Weisel Fitch
Ben Gunn
Rage Reg
and others..

Night Sky

Captain Chen
Ty
Meg
John
Cuddy
Prosperity
Quill
Caitiff
Micajah
Will
Will D
Fate
Levi
Alexander
and more...

HISPANIOLA

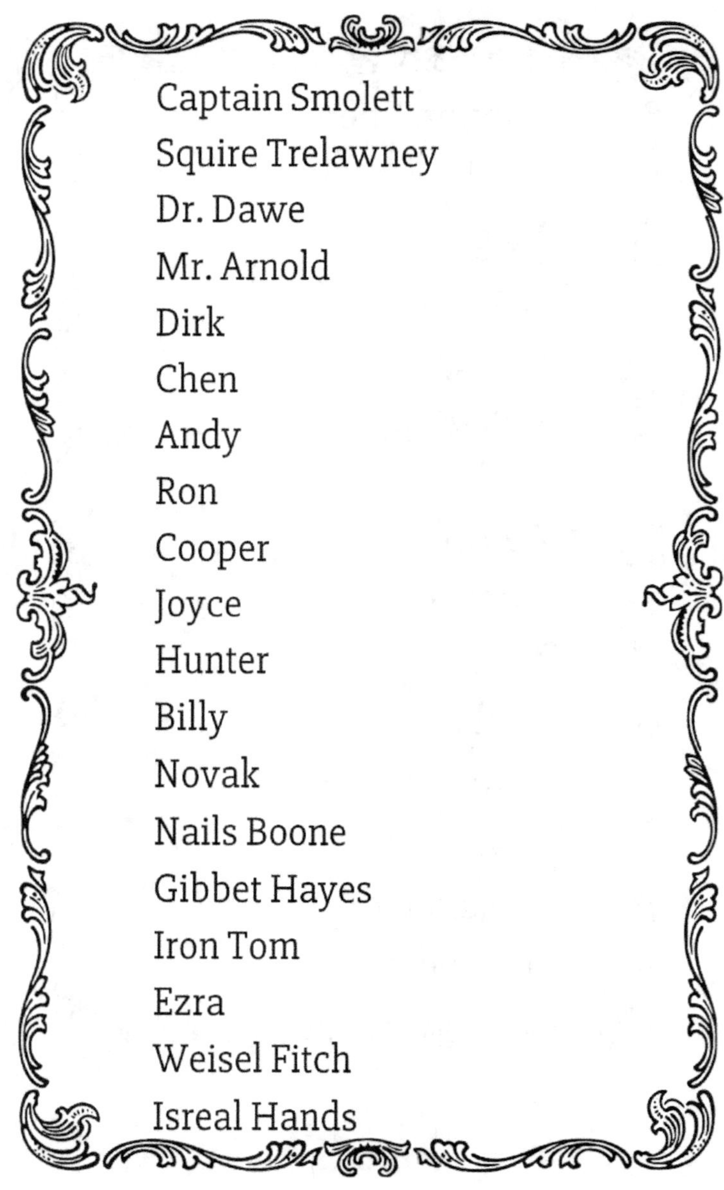

Captain Smolett
Squire Trelawney
Dr. Dawe
Mr. Arnold
Dirk
Chen
Andy
Ron
Cooper
Joyce
Hunter
Billy
Novak
Nails Boone
Gibbet Hayes
Iron Tom
Ezra
Weisel Fitch
Isreal Hands

PART ONE

CHEN

Iwent down to the docks, my only activity in the early morning that got me away from my boring life. Where the rest of London was still waking up, here it was teeming with activity. Fishermen just coming in with their first load, a ship docking with passengers waiting to enter London, and merchant ships either loading or unloading. But there was one ship in particular that drew me to it.

Could they be pirates? No one dared fly the Jolly Roger at the docks, even if they were working for the king, but they had that way about them. The men were chanting as they unloaded. The colors of their outfits and the things that were unloaded for sale were always food for my dreams.

The captain was standing on the deck of the *Shadow Serpent* and giving orders. His bright red coat was in contrast to the dark blue of the sailors on the military boats or the many passengers disembarking from the other ships in their dingy greys.

The ship itself had an air about it with two large masts that stood taller than the other ships. The shine of the wood hull was bright even on this dreary morning. Last time it was in port I had asked around and found out it was a Spanish made ship. This question then started a whole argument between passersby on what ships were the fastest, but I had lost interest.

The next thing I knew I was on the ground on my knees. My hands had stopped my face from smashing into the grit of the dock. The push had come from my backside.

"Look! It's Little Miss Pigtails."

I rolled away from the voice and jumped up, mad at letting my excitement get away from me. I knew better than to let anyone get close, especially one of the snotty girls from the local etiquette school.

The girl, surrounded by her friends, reached out to tug on my long black hair that I had tied back on both sides. I smacked her hand away.

She gasped. "You can't touch me like that! I'll tell the magistrate. You and your mother will go to jail, little Chinese girl!"

I worried if that were true, but I wasn't going to back down now. No one was going to touch my hair. I put up my hands as my father had taught me in order to fend for myself.

"What's going on here then? Ladies, brawling in the streets. What has London become now?" A voice broke through.

We all turned to stare at the ship's captain, his hands on his hips, his dark hair sticking out under his black hat. "I have some children about your age. I don't think you should be fighting."

I turned and ran, my heart pounding with the pace of my feet. I couldn't let myself be caught by anyone. I had no idea if the captain was going to be kind, but I couldn't take a chance. Life was hard enough without the suffering that being in jail would cost my mother and me.

When I had turned several corners, I looked behind me to make sure no one was following, then shimmied up the building to our window and climbed in. Mother was standing at the front door and shook her head at me. "Chen! Why are you climbing through the window? There's a perfectly good door. Besides, we need to go to work." Even though she was mad at me, her heavy Chinese accent gave English words a softer, almost musical quality.

I nodded and grabbed my knapsack for the day. On my way out, I stopped at the hand-drawn image of my father. I bowed to him and hoped he would see us all well today.

As we exited the building, I looked over at the one open hallway door. Mr. Dolines was in his sitting room, watching us walk by—always watching. I could feel his stare follow me everytime. I much preferred climbing the building than waiting for some nosy neighbor to see me come and go.

The two-mile walk was always slow with my mother, but I didn't let that bother me. Every slow step of her bound feet was a reminder to me why we were here in London and that I was the reason.

We walked past the tenements that my mother had moved us out of recently, then into the neighborhood of the tall, grand houses. As my mother walked in her tiny steps, I would zigzag and look at all the wondrous things I could find to bide my time. My mother walked in her special shoes, made by one of the best shoemakers in London. It was the only way she could walk, even though it was still painful for her.

We turned at the tallest house and walked around to the side entrance to a tiny door that my mother almost had to stoop through.

I stood as tall as I could at 16 years. Still not as tall as my mother, not tall enough to stoop through the servant's door.

We changed into the fancy maid uniforms that were waiting for us and then waited in the servants' hall for the housekeeper. We weren't allowed to do anything until she checked us over. Then she'd send us to cleaning.

Most of the kitchen servants and maids lived here full-time in the basement. Elizabeth, the scullery maid, had shown me her space once. It was so dark and cold, I couldn't imagine living there.

The only reason that we had been hired as walk-in maids was that we were 'exotic'. No one in all of London had a Chinese maid. It made me feel more like a collection, like all the fine art on the walls.

We gathered buckets, rags, and everything we would need for the day. I could smell beef stew in the air and my favorite, fresh bread rolls. Not that we were allowed to eat them. We had to eat what we brought with us.

The butler grunted as a welcome when we walked past him in the kitchen. As we walked by the cook, she slipped me two rolls. I thankfully palmed them into my pocket and walked tall with my mother into the grand entrance of the house.

After a long day of cleaning, I began to daydream. I was captain of my own ship, my mop was my sword. I lifted it in the air and parried and caught another's sword before it could strike me. I danced around the room to keep it at bay, glancing into the mirrors and pretending I was wearing a tricorn hat instead of a maid's cover.

"Chen!" My mother walked into the room. She

berated me in Chinese, words I knew were abrasive but didn't know exactly what they meant, although, now that I thought of it, it could be complete babble for all I knew. "Are you trying to get us dismissed?"

I put the mop back down, and the dream faded. I sighed and followed her out to the back of the house. We changed out of our maid outfits, put on our street clothes, and walked outside into the deep darkness of the city night.

"Mother, is this all life will ever be?"

She was quiet for a whole three blocks until she finally said, "For us? We would have had an easier life if I had obeyed my family, but now we must work very hard to support ourselves. Many women must marry in order to get by."

I wondered how much longer my mother could work with her feet hurting her with every step.

By the time we reached home, I felt like a lead weight. This would be my life forever. That or end up like the flower girls near Covent Gardens, staying out late and selling more than just flowers. I pushed that horrible thought away.

Mother made rice and vegetables.

I added the rolls to the table. "From cook."

She smiled, "I have my own surprise." She set an apple on the table.

I gasped. We so rarely had fruit.

"The cook also slipped this to me today." Mother

carefully sliced it and handed me a quarter, and she took a quarter. The rest was tucked away for tomorrow.

The sweet taste made me smile.

Mother nodded as she bit into hers. "I like the apple, but oh how I miss dragon's eye from home. If you ever go to China, you should try dragon's eye. It was always my favorite growing up."

I nodded, not sure if I would ever go.

I stretched out on my bed of cushions on the floor and looked up through the window into the night sky. I closed my eyes and dreamed of being free under those stars.

DAILY LIFE

A bird singing outside the window woke me in the early morning. I stretched and climbed out and down to the ground. When I reached the docks, I searched to see if the *Shadow Serpent* was still there. This time, they were loading cargo. I wandered around some of the barrels, trying to decide what might be inside. The markings on the outside were black Xs.

"Gunpowder," the voice came as if reading my mind.

It was the captain, his red coat looking newly clean and tidy. I backed up a few steps, and he shook his head. "You need not be afraid. You're welcome to check out the barrels. Just don't set any of them on fire." He smiled, his green eyes kind.

He pulled something long and yellow from his pocket and offered it to me.

I stretched out my hand and took it. "What is it?"

"A banana. You peel it and eat the inside."

I looked at him uncertainly. "What?"

He pulled another one from his pocket and showed me how to peel it. I followed suit and then bit into the flesh. The explosion of flavor was unlike anything I had ever known. Much better than an apple.

A member of his crew walked up, a man with a scar across his leathery face, his brows knitted together. "Why ya spending time with this mangy gal?"

"Flint, you know damn well that I'll do what I want."

"The men want to be leaving, Captain."

"Well then, they need to get this gunpowder loaded, don't they? And we still haven't been able to hire a cook."

Flint nodded and walked away, a grimace on his face.

"A cook?" I asked.

The captain nodded. "Even we need to eat, and sailors don't always make the best cooks."

I don't know what came over me. "I can cook!"

The captain laughed. "Sorry, but women are considered bad luck on a ship."

"Why?"

The question seemed to stump the captain. He shook his head.

"What if I dressed as a man? I could wear a hat and bind my figure."

The Captain's mouth hung open for just a second. "What's your name?"

"Chen."

"Chen, life at sea isn't kind. There are storms and danger at every turn. I lost a lot of my own men from fever just last week and had to hire some new ones. I don't know if they can be trusted. Besides-" he glanced around him before he continued, "we're pirates. We take what we want. I have my rules, we don't kill anyone unless it's during a battle, but we still kill men who try to stop us from taking their ship and what we want from it."

I nodded; I didn't like the idea of killing anyone, but my dreams were calling to me. "My life is endless toil. At least at sea, it would be of my choosing."

He rubbed his beard. "It will take the day to load the ship. Be here tonight, dressed as a boy, and I will hire you on. Otherwise, I'll make one of the new shipmen a cook, which might in itself be a disaster. That will give you the day to think about this, Chen."

I nodded, a thrill going through my soul all the way to my toes. I turned and ran home, climbing up the wall to the window in the blink of an eye.

My mother was waiting at the door. "Chen! Hurry. It's time to leave."

That day I embraced every cleaning chore, knowing that it would be the last time that I'd ever have to sweep, mop, and clean the rich people's home.

"I'm glad we had that talk yesterday," my mother said as we were putting away our things at the end of the day. "You have a newfound love of our life."

Then it hit me, what would she do without me? Could I send her money? How often would I be back? These thoughts went round and round as we walked home.

As soon as my mother was sleeping, I opened the crate that held our precious things and laid out my father's clothes. I considered cutting off my hair, but I really did love it. So instead, I twirled it on top of my head, used my mother's fancy comb to keep it up, and then put my father's hat over the top. His pants were too big, so I used my mother's sash to tie them.

In the crate, there were also strips of fabric. My mother had said they were to remind us all of why we were on our own. She and my father had refused to let anyone bind my feet, taking a stand against it. They had taken me out of China so that I wouldn't feel ostracized. The fabric would have been wound around my feet after they broke my big toes and warped my feet to look small. I would have hobbled like my mother my whole life. Climbing would probably have been impossible. A shiver went down my back.

I still had so many questions for my mother about why she made the decision to go against tradition and break from her family, but she would never answer direct questions. Finding out any answers would have to wait.

I used the strips of cloth to bind my breasts, then put on my father's shirt, also too big. We had no mirror but I imagined it made me look even younger.

As I shimmied down the building, I hoped my mother wouldn't notice the missing items for a long time, at least, not until I was able to start sending her money.

THE COOK

I ran to the dock, worried that maybe they had left, but there she was, a fine ship.

As I walked up the plank, I felt off balance as the ship was rocking in the water. Walking fast, as I made it onto the ship, I caught the wall to stop me. In the light of the lanterns, there were men of every nationality making ready to sail. The captain was nowhere to be seen.

I glanced back at the city and could see the girls' school building, a place I'd never be welcome.

"What do ya want here?" It was Flint from earlier. He stood with his hands on his hips, like he was the captain. His graying hair curled out under his red bandana. His hand was sitting on the hilt of his cutlass, and his coat was missing buttons.

I took a breath, but stepped back and coughed from

the rough smell of rum, tobacco, and other horrible things emanating from him. I tried again and spoke low and strong. "I'm the cook."

He laughed, hearty and long, while I stood there.

I sighed and finally walked around him, looking around. "Where's the kitchen?"

Flint made a snorting sound and, between more laughs, said, "It's a galley, you landlubber."

"Galley, then."

He pointed toward a square hole in the deck of the ship. "Below decks," was all he said.

"And where's the captain?"

At this, he finally stopped laughing and pointed at the bridge. "The helm. Keeping watch, like he always does."

And there the captain was, pacing the upper deck at the back of the ship. Hands clasped behind his back. He glanced down at me and yelled, "Welcome aboard, Cook Chen. You'll find everything you need in the galley. After we set sail, come see me in my cabin."

Flint grunted and walked away. I headed toward that dark square, my heart thumping.

At the bottom of the ladder, I found the galley, and through another door was obviously where the men would eat; there was a line of tables and chairs. Back in the galley, I stored the few things I had brought with me and began exploring.

The stove was much like the one from the fancy

house, although smaller. I had seen the cook feed a lot of wood into it to heat things up. The pile of wood in the corner gave off a forest scent.

The shelves were covered with containers, a few of which were labeled. There were barrels around the room. I opened one to find a pile of dried meat. I wandered up the ladder to the next level. This was obviously where the men slept. There were some hammocks, but a lot more cushions lying on the floor. I held my nose against the stink that permeated here. I'd sleep in the galley before I'd ever consider sleeping in here. Not to mention, I knew I needed to keep separate from these men.

I could feel when the ship began to set sail; the wind pushing at the sails was rocking the ship. It was a lot like dancing with its movements to and fro. I would have gone back to the galley, but I knew I needed to do as the captain had asked.

I worried that maybe I had made a mistake. Had this all been a lure to get me here, to take my virtue? I dashed down to the galley and pocketed the sharpest knife and then made my way to the captain's cabin.

I figured the captain's room had to be the only one above the deck, and found I was right. He was standing at his window.

"Welcome, Chen. You'll need to sign the articles."

I picked up the documents and shuffled through

them. The words on the page looked like a bunch of scribbles to me.

I slapped them down on the table. "I can't read." I hoped he wouldn't kick me off the ship for that.

He laughed, and my face flushed as I lowered my eyes to the planks. This was a short-lived adventure.

"No one can read on this ship. Except for Ben Gunn."

I looked up at him as he continued. "In the pages, it says that you are required to follow the rules in order to remain employed on this ship. The penalties for hoarding food are death. The penalties for killing another man, whether a crew member or another, without provocation, are death. We do not torture any captives, they are held for ransom. If they aren't ransomed, we leave them somewhere they can be found. Understood?"

"Even you can't read?" I asked incredulously.

He shook his head. "I never had much time to learn myself. I had these drawn up by Ben Gunn."

"But don't you have documents to read?"

He nodded. "Ship manifests, that sort of thing. Those I know from experience. Now I need you to acknowledge the rules with your signature here." He pointed to the last page.

I picked up the feathered pen, but wasn't sure what to do with it.

"Dip it in the ink, carefully. It's the only ink I have."

I did as he asked, then hovered over the page.

"Just sign with an x, that's what all the men do."

I nodded and marked the page with an x.

The captain took the pages and set them aside. "You'll probably want to sleep in here. My door has the only lock on the ship, and you are safe here from the men." He pointed at a wooden bench along his wall.

I nodded. "Thank you. And what about you? What makes you safe?"

"You remind me of my daughter. I would never harm you." He continued, "But you've also signed up for a lot of work. You'll need to get up before dawn to start breakfast."

"What should I make?"

He shrugged. "A cook has to be creative. Whatever food we have is in the galley and the storehouses around the ship. Get to know what we have and come up with something."

I nodded and curled up on the bench, using the blanket as a pillow, and put the knife under it, just in case. I felt like I was somewhere I belonged. That no one else could read was somehow a welcome feeling.

Meanwhile, I was glad he had never asked me if I could cook. Certainly, I would have to learn fast.

DEVASTATING NEWS

I woke up, not sure what time it was. The captain was snoring loudly.

I made my way outside. One man was standing watch at the helm.

"Welcome to the quarterdeck, are you the new cabin boy?" he asked.

"No, I'm the cook." I walked to the edge and looked out over the sea. The breeze was warm, and I realized that there was no scent of garbage or coal fires like home. The stars were so bright, and they were all mine. For the first time in my life, I felt happy and free.

I closed my eyes and for a moment pretended I was the captain. That I could sail and go anywhere I wanted at any time.

I heard whispering voices and noticed a group of

men on the deck, collected together, talking quietly. I suddenly worried that I was late in starting breakfast.

"When is dawn?" I asked the man at the helm. He was big, twice the size of any of the other men on the ship.

"Three ship's bells." He didn't look at me, but kept glancing at the ocean, the stars, and then at the group of men.

"Bells?" I asked.

He sighed, "Two glass turns of sand equals a ship's bell."

That still didn't tell me in terms of time, but I had more pressing matters. "How long does it take to cook oatmeal?" I asked.

He looked at me wide-eyed. "Oh, boy." He shook his head. "Once the water boils, watch it until it looks cooked. I don't know the time, maybe one glass turn. If that's what you're making for breakfast, make sure to put out the dried fruit and some of the salted fish."

"Okay. Thanks."

I lit a candle to find my way down to the bottom of the ship and followed his instructions. In the galley, I started the wood fire in the stove and inspected all the available food. When I found the bananas, I snatched one up, ate it, and put another one in my pocket.

Unfortunately, as the stove warmed, I began to sweat. I wished I could remove my hat, but that would reveal my hair. I prepped the oatmeal, stirring it, not sure what it should look like when cooked. And what did I do to announce breakfast? I had set everything out in the dining area, and yet no one had come down yet.

I walked back up the stairs. The bunks on the tween deck were nearly empty; most sailors were up top. I could hear yelling as I stepped out to the cooler air.

They were having some sort of party. Flint was standing tall, his cutlass in the air. I stopped mid-step when I realized it was half covered in blood. A drip fell from it and seemed to slowly hover and then plopped onto the deck.

Who was dead?

"You can call me captain now, and those of you that don't can find yourselves with the former in the sea."

"No." I ran to the captain's quarters. His bed was empty. My one and only ally was gone and I didn't even know his name.

Outside the captain's quarters, two men were squabbling over the captain's coat. There was a gust of wind and the coat flew into the air. I gasped, hoping it wouldn't fall into the sea, but then it hung for a moment in the air then came straight at me. His coat hit me hard, pushing me back a step.

The men who had been arguing gave me a grudging look and then nodded. Did this mean I got to keep it? I held onto it as I went back down to the kitchen to think.

There was no way that Flint would let me sleep in the captain's room, and I wouldn't want to, not if he was the captain of this ship. I was petrified that he'd make me sleep in the room with the other men and that meant it was only a matter of time before I was found out as a girl.

Plus, I figured there was a way to make it seem more like loyalty than a lie.

I put on the captain's red coat that was five sizes too large for me and stepped outside to the party. If this didn't go well, the ship couldn't be that far from home. I would leap over the side and try to swim. Drowning was preferable to what else might happen.

GOOD LUCK CHARM

As I stepped up to the quarterdeck, no one seemed to care about me and what I was doing. Boldness, it was what this new captain might appreciate.

I walked up to Flint and held my kitchen knife in the air. "I'll follow you, Captain Flint, as long as you keep all hands off me."

He and the crew laughed.

I pulled off my father's hat and my mother's comb that held all my hair. The wind took it as if it were flying like a flag. "I'm Chen, daughter of Immura and Haitao Tiande! I trusted the old captain with this secret; I'm choosing to trust you."

Flint sat down on the steps to the bridge and laughed harder.

A dark man with a scar across his cheek pointed at

me with his grubby dark hands. "Captain Flint! She'll bring us bad luck!"

Flint shook his head. "If'n that were true, this mutiny would've gone bad. Hold tight Billy Bones. She's okay, I've never laughed so hard in my life. As long as she can cook, she's safe on this ship." He looked at every single man on board; his eyes were steel.

"That's right, Captain Flint. She's our lucky charm!" Someone chimed in.

Another yelled, "She's got hair black and blue, she's our own sapphire!"

I felt honored. A sapphire was considered a precious gem and very good luck.

However, I didn't feel comfortable with all these eyes on me and changed the subject. I repeated words I had heard the butler say to the master of the big house. "Breakfast is served." I walked back to the galley with my head up high.

When I reached the galley, I sank next to the stove, held the coat tight around me, and cried. The one nice man I had ever met was dead. I hadn't even asked for his name. Would anyone else mourn him? And, what would happen to me? Would they keep their word?

As I heard the men clomp into the room next door, I wiped my tears away and hoped that they liked their breakfast.

As they sat with their bowls of food, I looked over at the men. Most wore smiles on their faces. How could they be so happy over the death of someone so kind? My blood boiled at their happiness.

The man who had been at the helm earlier nodded at me. "I'm guessing you've served the officers?"

I opened my mouth but wasn't sure what to say.

He pointed at the door across the way. "Officer's mess."

I rushed to the pot of oatmeal and stopped short. It was empty. I hadn't made enough. I was a dead woman.

The helmsman was standing next to me, nodding. "Our new captain is still up top celebrating. You might have time to make more."

I ran into the galley. Thank goodness I hadn't let the stove get cold. I put the water to boiling and cooked up the oatmeal. As soon as I felt it was done, I dashed out into the mess and took the door the man had pointed to.

Captain Flint and Billy Bones were walking in another door.

The captain smiled. "Smart gal. I do like it when the oatmeal is hot."

I could feel the muscles in my stomach relax a little. I set out the oatmeal and ran back for the fruit and salted meat.

As the two took food, they ignored me.

Billy Bones was saying, "How much ya think the captain has?"

As I turned to walk out, I heard Flint say, "There's enough gold in there for us to live high off the hog, Bones! One more strike and we should set it somewhere only we can find it. A perfect retirement for men of fortune!"

On my way to the galley, I stopped at the man from the helm. "What's your name?"

He swallowed a piece of fruit. "Ben. Ben Gunn."

I nodded. "Thank you, Ben." I was glad to know his name, just in case he didn't survive the day. Of course, I didn't know if I would survive the day, but for now, it seemed that things were settled.

I spent the next few hours roaming the ship stores and memorizing all the food I could find. I was thrilled to find a barrel of rice; I'd use that and some of the pickled vegetables for lunch.

I was walking through the empty mess hall when a man stepped in and moved into my path. "Hello, Missy."

I took a step back, but put my hands on my hips in an attempt to look tough. "The name's Chen."

He smiled, nodded, and took a step closer. "Chen. You know, there's some here who could use your femininity." At that word, he looked me up and down.

I had an urge to vomit.

"It's refreshing to have a young woman aboard." He leaned in, his face coming closer to mine.

I pulled out the kitchen knife and held it up. "You heard the captain. I'm to be left alone."

He leaned back and put his hands in the air, laughing. "I was just making conversation." Then backed up and headed up to the deck.

I moved into the kitchen and sat next to the stove, closing my eyes and letting my heartbeat slow to normal. I was not going to become like the desperate flower girls. I was going to be a pirate, an untouchable pirate.

While Flint was wandering the ship, I slipped into the captain's quarters and pulled out scraps of paper as well as the quill and ink. In the kitchen I drew two pictures. One of my father and one of the captain. I secured them to the wall and thanked both my father and the captain for their protection and the hope that they would continue to guide me. Then hid the pictures and the writing implements behind a pot.

I stood and got down the pots I'd need for rice and vegetables, hoping that it would be good enough to keep me alive.

A MERCHANT SHIP

Lunch and dinner had been a success, or at least they had eaten the food without complaint. We had anchored the ship in a small cove and the sun was setting on the horizon.

"Captain!" The call came from the crow's nest. "There's a Spanish ship out there weighing anchor."

Flint walked closer to the nest. "Oh, and?" he yelled back.

The man in the nest climbed down quickly, the rest of the men gathering around. "It looks to be a good one. She's probably stopped to fix something. We should hit her before mornin'."

"You heard him, boys." Flint smiled. "There's loot for the taking. Be ready to hit them at midnight."

The men seemed happy for a fight. I was glad it wasn't me.

As the captain walked past me, he said, "You'll have your chance."

"My chance?"

"To prove your worth. We attack the blaggards at midnight."

"But I'm the cook."

He laughed. "The old captain might've had a soft heart, but not I. You'll take on the battles, same as any other pirate on this ship, woman or not."

I went back to the galley to think about this. I needed to live long enough to get off this ship. I imagined that if we went over as a crew, even in this dark of night, the Spanish ship would certainly spot us and fire on us. If we made it on board, it would be a hand-to-hand fight that I had no business being in. I would be dead.

But if I went over and talked to their captain, warned him about the pirates, maybe he would take me with him. On the deck, I found Billy Bones and the captain whispering about something, but I interrupted them.

"Give me a boat."

"What, girl?"

"Give me a boat. I'll signal you when you can come over."

Flint laughed again and shook his head. "You're going to take out the whole crew and then send for us?"

I nodded.

He shrugged and pointed at some of the men. "Black Dog and Pew, get the lady a boat."

I climbed into the boat and took a few minutes to get the hang of rowing while the men laughed up on deck. At least I was entertaining them.

As I rowed away, I could hear Flint say, "At least we're rid of her."

What did he think would happen to me?

I pushed that thought aside and focused on figuring out how to row. Once I had control, I quietly rowed out of the cove and to the merchant ship. I tied the boat to the anchor line and crawled up the rope. It wasn't as easy as climbing a building, and I wasn't a fan of the deep sea beneath me.

When I had reached the top of the rope, I used the small opening as a foothold and pulled myself up to the ship's railing. There was one sailor in sight, and his back was to me.

I wasn't quite sure how I was going to get to talk to the captain of the ship. Would they listen to me?

I pulled my leg over the side of the railing. The wind tore my father's hat off; I caught it with one hand, and my hair started flying in the wind. That lone sailor turned toward me.

"Dios Mio, sirena!"

The rest was unintelligible as he backed away quickly. He fell backwards over something and then he was silent.

I climbed all the way onto the ship and ran to help him up. Only, that wasn't going to happen. He had fallen over a rope and cracked his head on the deck. I closed his eyes and cursed my luck.

While I wrapped my hair back up, I considered my next step. Would the rest of the Spanish crew believe it was an accident? Probably not. I was going to die in a Spanish prison.

I looked back at the land that hid the cove and the pirate ship. I didn't want to go back there either, but I had no other choice.

From below, there were men singing. For the moment, I was undiscovered. I moved silently around the ship and found no one else on duty. Did they think they were safe here? Idiots.

I moved to the ladder that led downstairs and peeked around a corner. A large group of men was singing and drinking. What was left of a cake was being eaten.

Back at the top, I locked the door to the ladder from the outside, then I found the other door. There wasn't a lock, so I pushed several heavy barrels onto it.

Then I grabbed a lantern, took another moment to think about it, but then went ahead and signaled to the pirate ship. I wasn't sure if they could see me, but I kept it up until I thought I could see the sea ripple with the movement of the boats. Then I found the rope ladder and tossed it down for them.

I sat down and leaned against the railing. Looking up into the sky, I wished on the stars that I would get out of all this alive and in one piece.

Flint and crew came barreling over the side with weapons raised, ready for a fight.

Ben asked me, "Where are they?"

"They're trapped in the tween deck."

Flint kicked the dead body and laughed. "Chen, we should have you fight all our battles. Easiest ship we've ever taken."

Some of the men snarled, obviously disappointed in the lack of a fight.

The men below had found out they were locked in and were pushing on the door blocked by barrels. One of the pirates tapped another and they grinned, moving toward the door with unnecessary stealth.

One pulled the barrels away, and as the Spanish crew emerged, the biggest of the pirates raised his sword. The Spanish men at the front fell backwards, knocking others behind them down and ended up in a heap of bodies at the bottom of the ladder.

"Bunch of cowards," Flint snarled. He stalked to the door and yelled down, "Stay below if you know what's good for ya'." He slammed the door down. "Israel, move those barrels back. We have plenty of bodies to ask for ransom." He walked over to me and slapped my back, knocking me forward. "Lass, I'm proud of ya'."

Later that night, I was exhausted as I curled up in

the galley. But the cushions I had taken from the merchant ship would allow me to sleep comfortably. I reached out to touch the small bag full of coins Captain Flint had given me. It was more money than I had ever seen in my life. Billy Bones had looked daggers at me.

Flint had been so happy to see so many people for ransom and a ship in good shape, with not one shot fired. The rest of the men had looked at me again like I was some sort of mythical creature.

When we got back to the ship, they had asked me to tell the tale, but Ben Gunn had interrupted and made up his own story of how I had snuck on the ship and cut the throats of every Spanish man I had seen.

The men laughed, knowing that wasn't true, but everyone liked a good cut-throat tale. They had raised a glass of celebratory drink to me. To me!

I asked Ben, "What's a sirena? The sailor on the Spanish ship called me that."

Ben nodded his head. "It means a siren. A woman who calls men to their deaths. That's perfect."

Ben hit his metal cup against the mast for everyone's attention. "We have a seafaring name for our cook. The Sapphire Siren!"

There were whoops of agreement and men nodding.

I was elated, even if I was being honored by a bunch of bloodthirsty pirates.

There was talk among the men as to whether we would take the new ship as our own, sell it, or offer it as a gift to the English king. Captain Flint quickly decided that we were going to sell the merchant ship, ransom the men, and take whatever else we could get off the ship.

I curled up in my captain's jacket and dreamed of my mother's face when she would receive some of the money. And I wondered how much longer until I could get off this ship.

The next morning, I got through breakfast, and each finished meal made me feel just a little more secure in my position. But then, oatmeal now seemed easy after the first time. I went up to the deck to take in the sun and look out over the ocean.

Not long after being up top, a man walked up to my side. "The Sapphire Siren, is it?"

I glanced over at him, the question strange as everyone knew me and there was no reason to ask my name, real or newly minted. "Yes."

"I'm Rage Reg."

"Rage?"

He nodded. "Long story. Want a sip?" He thrust a wine skin into my hands.

I could smell the alcohol, whether from him or the skin, I wasn't sure. He looked out over the water and I followed his gaze.

I turned a bit and raised the wineskin and saw in

my peripheral vision, the man who had called me Missy earlier.

He was looking at Rage, and Rage gave him the slightest nod. It was like some sort of agreement between them and I already knew I didn't like the other man.

A chill went through me and I paused with the wineskin. "You know, I'm not really into wine. Besides, I must cook lunch soon." Then handed him back the skin.

He smiled and took it back.

As I walked back to the kitchen I looked around. There were no others watching us. Perhaps Rage and the other were the only two that seemed interested in my 'femininity'. From now on, no drink unless I had poured it for myself.

GRIMWOOD ISLE

It had felt like months, but by my count it had only been a few weeks. The plunder of the merchant ship collected and partially distributed to the crew, I was curious about what would happen with the rest of it.

We had sailed to Grimwood Isle and moved the ship into a bay. We were surrounded by land. There were high hills and tracts of tall trees that blocked much of our view.

I thought that perhaps I could sneak ashore. If there were a town, I could pay for passage back to mother.

As we anchored, I saw Ben cross his heart and I asked him why he did so.

"This place, Grimwood Isle. It's haunted, it is. This is where no man wants to live or die."

"Is there no one who lives here?"

He shook his head.

"So why are we here?"

He nodded toward the captain, who was having the men move the chests of money down to the boats. "The captain likes this place for his loot. He says there's only one sure way to approach the island and it keeps it safe."

I felt disappointed at learning there was no one here. I'd have to wait to get home again.

Rage Reg raised his sword into the air. "Captain Flint. We've yet to sign a new article. This loot you're putting away also belongs to *us*." He stepped toward the captain with the last word.

Captain Flint nodded, all eyes were on him. "I know it Rage. When we hit land next, we'll draw up all new articles for you and the crew. For now, we'll put the money here and divide it up when we are in agreement."

There was grumbling but it soon stopped when Billy Bones walked among them and glared. "You heard the captain. We'll make some decisions once we have a new agreement."

As the boats lowered with Captain Flint, Billy Bones, Ben Gunn, Rage Reg, four others, and several chests, one of the men standing next to me grumbled. "Taking most of the loot for himself, he is."

"But he said he'd share it later. You don't think he

will?" I asked. The man, Pew, had eyes that creeped me out with their milky film.

He growled at me and then said, "If'n he was goin a share, he would have split it. And a capt'n that doesn't share equal isn't a capt'n that lives long." He turned and walked slowly away, obviously having a hard time seeing.

Ben and the others in the boats were rowing hard, the treasure making the boats heavy. When they reached the beach of the island, they used wheelbarrows and two men each to pull the chests along. They soon disappeared into the trees.

It didn't make sense to me to hide the money. Why not spend it, or share it more equally among the crew now?

I imagined that the money in those chests would set my mother and me up for life. We could buy one of those fancy houses, or maybe move somewhere warmer where we wouldn't have to go outside in the cold. I'd buy my mother her own carriage so she wouldn't have to walk anywhere.

I went back to the galley and checked on my own stash of coins hidden behind the stove. As soon as we docked in civilization, maybe I'd get my own ship. However, I would definitely take some of the money to my mother.

I took out the drawings I had of my father and the captain and asked them to help me get home soon. I carefully tucked them away and went through the food stores to decide on the next meal. I was beginning to enjoy this part of it. It was like fitting together a puzzle, only you had to figure out what the pieces were.

I set the potatoes and meat cooking for a stew. While I had some time before dinner, I wanted to continue to learn about the ship. With Ben gone for now, one of the few men who talked to me, I picked out Dirk.

Dirk always seemed to be cordial with me. Whereas the other men would move to sometimes stand in my way or throw their bowls on the floor after a meal to make me clean more, Dirk would step out of my way as if he were a gentleman and I more than a cook. There was even that one time when the ship had lurched in a wave and he had grabbed me by the back of my shirt to keep me from falling overboard.

He was in the crow's nest keeping lookout, so I climbed the rope ladder. I had never been up here before— the scene laid out before me was a mix of land and a little ocean. I could see the tops of the trees on the island, but there was no sign of where Flint and the other men had gone.

"Wow." I couldn't stop looking at the ocean.

"What's the cook want in the crow's nest?" Dirk asked.

"I don't want to be just a cook. I want to know everything about the ship." I looked over at him and was surprised to see that he had moved to the opposite side and was giving me that look that men reserved for when they spoke of sirens and mermaids.

I glanced down at the deck and there were several crew members looking up at us. Didn't they know I could climb? I wasn't quite sure what was so odd about a woman climbing.

"What do you want to know?" Dirk asked.

"Is there always someone up here, even in rough seas?"

He shook his head. "If it's a rough sea, not much to spot except the next wave, which any man can see from the deck. Not much use losing a man to sit up here for that."

"And, does everyone have to come up here?"

He made a short laugh and shook his head. "Nah. There are some men that would rather jump in the sea with sharks than come up here. Afraid of heights and all. And then there's Pew. He's been losing his sight for a while. Him up here would be as useful as a lubber on deck."

He glanced at me. I knew what he was thinking. I was the newest addition to the crew, I was the closest to a land lubber than anyone else, yet here I was.

I spotted men appearing on the beach and pointed them out to Dirk.

He took a breath and said what I was thinking.

"Them's not good signs. Only two men when eight went in."

Each of the men boarded a boat, and as they came closer, I could see it was only Flint and Billy Bones.

I had a bad feeling in the pit of my stomach, but I crossed my fingers that Ben was okay. I climbed down the rope and made it to the deck as the captain was brought on board.

I asked, "Ben Gunn and the others?"

The captain shook his head as the rest of the men gathered. "There are some locals here on the island. They didn't take too kindly to us and they didn't make it."

Billy Bones had a smirk on his face and I knew that it was all a lie. They had killed them all to protect the location of the loot. I wasn't sad about the loss of Rage. One less lecherous man to worry about. But Ben had been the closest thing to a friend I had.

I went back to the kitchen and drew Ben's picture as best as I could. I put his next to the captain's.

In the galley, I set out the biscuits as well as some of the butter we had taken from the Spanish ship. I glanced at the chair that Ben had often sat in. I touched the chair and sent good thoughts to him and hoped the captain would look after his spirit.

That night at dinner, Flint walked around the officer's mess with a bottle of rum in his hands, talking to Billy Bones about all the things they could do with their money. As I walked back and forth, cleaning the dishes, I thought about how he didn't deserve that money and how no one had been there for Ben.

The next morning, Captain Flint had his next wild idea. As I served breakfast quietly so as not to disturb the captain's hangover, he whispered to Billy Bones, "I think we should go to the colonies."

Billy laughed, grabbed his head and groaned, then shook his head at Captain Flint. He spoke softly, too, "Why in the ocean blue would we do that?"

"We have that stock of items from the Spanish ship and that would be the perfect place to sell it all."

Billy leaned back and seemed to consider the move.

I slipped out of the room and pulled out my pictures. I prayed to the three that they would stop Captain Flint. I didn't know a lot about sailing, but I knew enough to know that to get to the colonies was a long sail. It would be hard and take many days.

I went back to clean up the dishes and kept my hopes up that we'd be going home.

ACROSS THE OCEAN

That day it was announced we were on our way to the colonies. I felt deflated but went through the motions of my work and kept learning as much as I could.

Days later, an English ship was spotted, and a plan was drawn up by Flint. Luckily, he wasn't expecting me to go over on my own and take over the ship.

"Replace the Jolly Roger with the English flag. Hurry, Black Dog! Let's trick these lubers into getting closer. Israel, ready the cannons!" he yelled.

While the men got ready, I went to the kitchen and practiced fighting with my knife. In a head-to-head fight, I didn't expect to be able to take on someone with a sword, but I was going to stay low and out of the way as much as I could. The knife would only be for defense.

I jumped when the cannons fired. I ran up to the

foredeck into a cloud of smoke. A cry went up from the men as the smoke cleared and we could see the English ship had sustained damage to the mast and there was even an open wound in the side of their ship. High enough to be out of the water, but also where we could see men scrambling to reach their cannons.

The English were just now opening their cannon turrets. If they fired, would I get hit? Where would the cannon shots go? My heart was pumping fast with excitement.

As the English lit their cannons, Captain Flint called, "Hard to stern!"

The men seemed to be expecting this. In an instant, the sails were changed, the ship turned, and we showed them our bow as the cannons were shot.

Several of the shots went wide, one went too high and right over the ship, but one landed mid deck,

Dirk yelled to me, "Sapphire! Go below and let me know if we start to take on water. "

I hated to leave the scene, but ran down the stairs to see the damage. The cannonball had gone through the tween deck, destroying a good section of floorboards, hammocks, and anything that had been within range of the crash.

I went down to the kitchen. Nothing here. I moved back to the storage area where there was always a few inches of water sloshing around. The cannonball was sitting in the water, waving back and forth with the ship.

Thank goodness it hadn't gone through.

Our cannons shot again. I ran back to the upper deck and reported to Dirk. "It didn't go through the bottom."

Meanwhile, a line of men was standing near the rails, weapons ready.

Billy Bones pushed me forward. "Get in the line, Chen."

I lined up and took out my knife. I felt wholly inadequate.

Israel Hands glanced over at me and laughed. "See you in Davy Jone's locker, Chen."

Hooks were thrown over to the other ship. Some of our crew leapt from one ship to another. Dirk swung over on a rope, Israel waited until the ships bumped, and jumped over the railings. I followed behind Israel.

There was a loud clash of steel on steel. The English were at least putting up a fight. I ducked around fighters and stepped below decks.

Israel was right behind me. "Smart move, kid. Maybe you'll survive after all." He moved past me down to the hold, and I followed.

There were barrels stacked high but no idea what might be in them. Worse, though, was that the ship was taking on water.

Israel snarled. "Go tell Flint, the ship is sinking!"

I ran up to the upper deck and looked around in the melee for Flint. He was on the quarterdeck, gleefully sparring with an English officer. I skirted the fights until I made it to him.

"Captain Flint! The ship is sinking!"

The officer looked over at me with wide eyes, and Flint cut right through his chest. Flint kicked him in the stomach and the man fell off his sword and back into a heap. My stomach lurched a little, but I held it together.

"Then we better act fast." Flint walked through the crowd of fights, helping his men kill each Englishman. From there, the fight quickly turned in our direction.

Minutes later, bodies lay strewn on the deck and our crew went to work, no celebrations yet. Everyone grabbed something from storage, barrel after barrel was brought up to the top, and men started moving them to our ship.

At first, a few men were able to toss a barrel over to our ship, but now the Spanish ship was several feet below ours. Men were starting to move over to our ship and stay.

"Hurry!" Billy Bones yelled. "Get those stores moved!"

There was a loud crack and a scream. A mast had fallen, pushing a few barrels along with it, right into Nails Boone.

Dirk went running to help him. I ran over as well.

We both tried to move the barrels, but they were pinned by the mast.

The Spanish ship made a groaning noise and now Billy Bones changed his tune. "Time to heave ho, mates! Get what you can."

Nails screamed and more men were leaving us behind for our ship.

"Get an axe!" Dirk shouted.

But there was no time. I looked around wildly—there, a broken spar was wedged against the rail. If I could use it as a lever...

I jammed it under the mast and threw my weight onto the other end. For a heartbeat, nothing. Then the mast shifted.

"Get him!" I screamed.

He pulled Nails free. I let go, and the mast collapsed down with a crash.

As we rushed to our ship, the deck below us shuddered. We grabbed onto ropes hanging. Someone had thrown down a rope ladder and Nails was holding onto it for dear life.

The men pulled up Nails. Dirk and I made it up to the deck as he was pulled in and collapsed. They carried him down to a makeshift bed.

My ribs hurt from throwing myself on the spar and my hands were turning a deep red.

"She saved Weisel's life," Dirk yelled as he watched his friend be carried.

Some of the men seemed impressed; others shrugged.

Later, after dinner and the men had gone back to work, Dirk came down to the kitchen. "Sapphire Siren, I don't know how you did it, but you came back for my brother, and I appreciate all you did." He handed me a short sword. "This has been in my stash for years. Never had a need for it."

"Your brother? I'm glad I could help." The sword felt light and just the right size.

WINDLESS DAYS

Eventually, the days all began to mix together and there wasn't much to do.

I wanted to learn more about everything but at other stations, most of the men treated me like I was a mermaid and shied away from talking with me. So, I learned what I could, watched people at their work on the sails and the helm.

I finally pleaded with Ezra to tell me more about how the sails worked.

He shook his head. "You're too important to be talking to the likes of me," Ezra told me. "You're the best cook I've ever had on a voyage and besides, there's something commanding about you."

I laughed. "Fine, then I command you to teach me about the sails."

He laughed as well and finally let me in on some of the workings.

I also wanted to learn more about navigation, but Captain Flint took pride in his knowledge and didn't want to share. Although, as the days wore on, I thought that maybe he was guessing the whole time.

As the days continued, Captain Flint swore we'd reach land soon, but there was a lot of grumbling among the men. Many were concerned that he didn't know the way and that we'd all starve to death before we reached the colonies. The food from the English ship helped, but it wouldn't last forever.

Then one morning we were dead in the water. There was no wind, not even a current, just an endless ocean of calm in every direction. There wasn't even a cloud!

"It's a curse," Israel muttered. "We're cursed for having a girl on board."

If Dirk and many of the others heard the grumblings, they quickly stood up for me, but a few others were starting to agree. After all the things I had done and suddenly being considered a curse by a few of the men who had never liked me, it seemed unfair.

I could feel the mood shifting, dangerous and superstitious. I did not need a quarter of the crew coming after me with thoughts of getting rid of a curse.

On the second night, I went up to the bow. I didn't know if anything I did could make a difference, but my life could be in danger and the least I could do was try. I closed my eyes and reached out my hands toward the ocean, just like the ship's figurehead calling to the sea, to the winds, to the moon, to help us on our way.

"Please," I whispered. "Just a little wind. Just enough." I thought of wind, of movement, of sails filling, and the ship cutting through water.

A chill spread from my chest to my fingertips.

Then—a breeze. So soft that I barely felt it. Then it grew stronger. The sails rippled, then filled.

The ship lurched forward.

I opened my eyes and took a deep breath. I turned to find half the crew staring at me. Iron Tom's eyes were wide. Even Flint looked shaken.

"Just a lucky wind," I said, my voice shaking.

"The Sapphire Siren has saved our hides!" Weisel Fitch cried. This had been one of the men who had been grumbling along with Israel. Hopefully, I had won over a few more. I didn't want anyone to hate me.

She's got Neptune's favor!" Black Dog exclaimed.

Flint bowed at me, Billy Bones gave me a withering stare, and Israel Hands shrugged. It was definitely a mixed bag.

COLONIES

As the days wore on our stores grew empty. I had to start serving dried fish and pickled vegetables for every meal. On the sixth day of fish and vegetables, the men grumbled even louder. I left the kitchen to get away from it all and stepped up to the prow of the ship. The wind felt refreshing and cold. Out in the distance, a lightning strike flashed through the sky, but above me, the sky was clear.

I glanced down into the water. A blueish light was collecting around the bottom of the ship, making it glow. I leaned down a bit more to see it closely.

The blue light began to move up the side of the ship. I stepped back, my heart pumping.

"It's okay, lass. It's only St. Elmo's fire." Gibbet Hayes was also looking down at the light. "It won't hurt ya'."

I glanced over at him.

He continued, "It's good luck. It means St. Elmo is looking after us. It often comes after a storm."

I went back to the edge of the ship and watched as the blue light climbed up the ship, but gasped as it suddenly enveloped me. I walked to the middle of the ship, the light touching my skin but leaving no heat. There was a crackling sound, but nothing else.

It gathered on my hand and I tried to flick it away. It flew into the sky. I blew out a breath and was glad I hadn't been harmed by the blue fire.

The next morning, the man in the crow's nest announced, "Land ho," and as the men ate breakfast, I heard the steersman tell everyone that when I had pointed my hand into the sky and the blue light had left me, he had followed that light. That I had been the reason we had found land.

I smiled and shook my head. Such superstition these tough men had.

But magic or not, we made port in Savannah, Georgia. A colony! Looking over the port, there wasn't much to see. But there was a town and a port where I could catch a ship home.

I didn't have any women's clothes and although long hair didn't automatically make one a woman, my long, straight black and blue hair made me stand out like a sore thumb.

I grabbed my things, made sure my hair was hidden in my father's hat and tucked the coins away. I walked down the plank with the rest of the crew who were taking leave.

Once I was standing on solid ground, tears filled my eyes as the sun warmed my skin. I was off the ship and in a new town. It felt freeing.

Walking into the closest inn, I wasn't sure what I would do if they didn't let me stay. I put some coins on the counter. They didn't say a word but to give me my key.

I sat down at a table with the largest pile of food I had ever seen. And, I hadn't had to make any of it! I bit into the best bread I had ever tasted, with a layer of fresh butter.

I rolled my eyes when Billy Bones and Captain Flint walked in, already well drunk and stumbling. They sat down at a nearby table. Captain Flint called out to the barkeeper. "Darby M'Graw - fetch aft the rum...." Then Flint fell off his chair and landed silently on the floor. Billy laughed and reached down to Flint.

I drank deeply of the clean, cold water.

Billy stepped back and cried out, "Captain Flint's dead!"

The room stopped. All eyes were on the body. A few people stood and quickly walked out. I heard someone whisper near me, "A notorious pirate!"

Billy sat back down in his chair and shook his head.

I felt a little shock go through me but I grabbed the rest of my food and went to my room. I was not going to let pirates ruin this moment. Besides, I shouldn't be concerned about Flint being dead. He deserved it.

The next morning, as I sat down with a pile of scrambled eggs on my plate, I was surprised to see two of my former shipmates—Dirk and Gibbet— enter the inn, smile at seeing me, and come straight to my table.

"The Sapphire Siren!" Dirk said as they both sat down. "Billy Bones wants to take off soon, so you'll need to come back shortly."

I nodded, not intending to tell them of my plans, but feeling a lift whenever anyone called me by that new name.

"But we have a favor, too."

"A favor? From me?"

He nodded. "We're trying to talk Billy into taking us back to the island, to show us the map and share the loot with us. We've tried. The men think that maybe you can talk him into it."

It was my turn to smile. "Me?"

"You're a bit o' magic, Sapphire," said Gibbet. "We could all go get that money and split it. It would be quite a haul!" He handed me a small black bag. "Me and the, um, rest of the men wanted you to have this."

I dumped the contents into my hand and gasped. I brushed my hand over the small compass and the richly engraved gilt brass perimeter. Then I realized that just inside the brass, the silver ring lifted up. It was also a sundial! But the compass's background was deep blue with silver markings.

"We don't know much about navigation and Dirk here said that you was learning all of that."

"It's beautiful." I couldn't help noticing that he blushed. These pirates were always a mystery to me. I carefully tucked away the compass and considered their request.

They were right, with Flint dead, there was nothing between us and all that money but one Billy Bones. The man who seemed to hate me. But maybe I could talk him into it?

"You said you and the rest of the men, that isn't everyone, is it?"

He shook his head. "There are a few who voted against it, but there were more for than against."

"I'll talk to him," I said.

They smiled and walked out.

As I ate, I considered my options. I had no intention of leaving on the ship unless we were getting that treasure. That would be the only reason it would be worth it.

I would take what few things I had with me to the ship. The room was paid for a while, so I could always come back. I finished my breakfast and gathered my things.

Walking back onto the ship, I realized how much had changed since the last time I had walked up that plank. The ship was moving slightly with the waves but I walked a perfect straight line. I did feel a little nervous. How would I talk Billy Bones into sharing an enormous fortune with the men and me?

A NEW PLAN

Dirk met me on the deck and led me to the captain's quarters. Sitting at the captain's desk was Billy Bones. He was giving me a look as if he'd rather stab me in the heart, but he was nodding.

Billy pointed at the chair. "The boys tell me they wan me to have a talk with ya. They wouldn't have it any other way. I'm not sure what a cook has to say about anything, but you go 'head."

I opened my mouth but realized I didn't know exactly what to say. How would I talk him into sharing treasure? But Dirk started for me.

"She agrees with the rest of us. We deserve more payment for the work that we've done."

"Yes," I agreed. "There was a lot of money that Captain Flint set on Grimwood Isle and he did say that he intended to sign an agreement and split it. Certainly, you'd want to uphold his plans and give everyone their fair share."

"What cha saying, Little Miss, sounds about right. The money that Flint and I hid is a plenty to share. I reckon, since you're here in lieu of the crew that you're their leader?"

The words Little Miss sent a shiver down my spine and reminded me of Rage Reg. Someone who didn't respect me. Was he the same?

I stood up and nodded.

"Fine," he said. "Tomorrow we'll sail back to the island."

I wasn't sure I could believe him, but if he meant it, the money in my dream was going to be partly mine.

Dirk and I walked out and he announced to the crew, "We go back to the island for our treasure!"

There were some jubilant echoes and then the men started a chant, "Sapphire Siren for captain!"

I laughed, me a captain. I knew they didn't mean it, but it was nice nonetheless. I'd stay on until we had the whole treasure in our hands and then move on.

I felt a lightness in my heart that I had never known.

Dirk woke me the next morning. "Captain, he's gone!"

"Huh?"

"Billy Bones, he's gone. Took off 'n the night like the scourge of the seven seas that he is."

"What?" I walked out of the galley onto the deck. The men's faces were grim and they were looking at me.

"What do we do, Captain?" Dirk looked at me.

"Wait, you were serious about me being your captain?"

They all nodded. "It's a democracy here. We pick the person that will make the best decisions for ship and crew!"

"Oh," I said. Surprised at my own happiness at this touch of power that I suddenly had. But there wasn't much else to do.

"Well, there's only one thing for it. We find him. He's probably found a way out of Georgia already, whether by land or sea. We go our separate ways and search the world for Billy Bones. When one of you finds him, send word to the rest of us. Some of us should start here in Savannah. I know I'm staying for now."

Pew immediately stood forward. "Then we take a new vote for captain."

I went back to the galley and grabbed my things. For now, that treasure was clearly out of my hands.

I glanced back at the men as I walked off the ship, for good this time. They were discussing their plan.

Back at the inn, I considered my next steps. I had thought to just book passage home, but after the feeling of being captain, I wanted that again, with a crew I could really trust.

The bag of gold Flint had given me for the capture of the Spanish ship was a lot. Was it enough to buy a ship? I'd have to find out. The idea sent a thrill through my bones.

Just in case, I did ask around about Billy Bones, but other than the day that Captain Flint had died, no one had seen him in town. He was indeed long gone.

HOPELESS DREAM

I found a dressmaker in town and had him make a flowing dress in the same color as my captain's jacket. As directed, he added several hidden pockets.

I felt a whole new future beckoning as I proudly wore my red dress to the local shipmaker to buy my own ship.

I stepped into the office and admired the tiny toy-sized ships set around the room. "Are these your ship types? I'm interested in buying a ship."

The merchant shook his head at me. "Run along, Little Miss, even if women could own property, I'd not sell to the likes of you."

"What?" That didn't make sense.

"I've heard of ya, coming from the pirate ship." His

lip curled as he continued, "The Sapphire Siren with her black and blue hair."

The tiny ship near my hand wobbled a bit on its own, as if it were sailing on the seas. It stopped as quickly as it had started. I focused back on the ship builder, his white wig was pristine but his teeth were almost as dark as his eyes, his wrinkled face had two steely grey eyes that squinted at me with disdain.

I tried to process his words. Women couldn't own property? I had never tried to own property and my mother had certainly never told me this. "I..." I didn't know what to say, but he wasn't interested in hearing me anyway.

"Get out and don't come back, vermin." He stepped from around the table and spat on the floor near my feet.

I reached for my knife and imagined Captain Flint cutting this man in half and taking the ship he wanted.

"Get out!" He stepped closer.

It occurred to me that killing him would lead to more trouble than not. I needed to think. I stepped out and walked away, feeling angry and uncomfortable with the man's eyes on my back until I had walked through the gates and back into town.

By the time I reached the inn, I felt a weight on my shoulders. No way to get a ship, no crew. Had I traveled all the way here, braved the pirate world, only to end up a passenger to make my way home? And what would happen to me then?

I sat inside the inn as the owner's wife walked by, and I asked her for a moment of her time.

"Mrs. McGraw, I need to understand this thing about women not owning things."

She sat down in the chair next to me with a heavy thump. "Darlin', if you want something of your own, your best bet is to do what I did. I married the most pliable man I could find and then had him use my money to buy this establishment."

We both looked over to her husband behind the bar. His white wig was slightly askew, exposing his bald head underneath. His nose was more akin to a beak and his eyes squinted at everything. When he looked up and saw his wife, he smiled at her.

She nodded and whispered, "Yeah, he might not look like much, but he's my way to make a living."

Marriage? That didn't sound like something I'd want to do. "Maybe it's better in England?" I said with hope.

She laughed. "Darlin', the rules here in the colonies are the same as England. Take my advice. Your other option is to dress like a man to make it in this world." She stood to go, but put a hand on my shoulder. "You're young, that's true. And I'm sorry you're finding that the world isn't so kind to us women. Good luck."

Mrs. McGraw walked away and I felt even less hope

than before she had sat down. I had money and means. I could see a new ship under my feet, but it was all being taken away from me.

But then, now I understood why we had always lived in apartments. Even if my mother could have afforded a home, she wouldn't have been allowed to buy one on her own.

I walked outside and kicked a water trough. Where my kick landed, the trough split into two, water spilling down onto my feet and continuing down the road. Luckily, there was no one nearby to see my destruction. Obviously, it was old anyway.

I walked back into the inn and to my room to think. My options were limited.

I couldn't steal a ship on my own, and a crew would never sign on to a pirate ship without a ship. Or would they? An idea had sprouted.

MIDNIGHT SEARCH

At midnight, in my dad's clothes, I went for a stroll to the shipyards. It was easy enough to slip over the fence. There were, however, a couple of guards. They sat around an oil lamp chatting about their wives.

Keeping myself in the shadows, I ran quietly around the ships in various stages of building. Some of the ships were just ribs of wood. The ones I was most interested in were the three ships closest to the water. They were almost seaworthy, and plenty of details were still yet to be finished.

The timing would have to be perfect. For that, I needed more information. I needed to know dates.

I made my way to the office; the door made a slight noise as I tried to open it, so I went to a window that was already open and slipped inside. I lit a lamp and set it on the floor to keep the light from being seen.

Luckily, dates and ship designs were easy to decipher. After poring over many bundles of papers, I finally found the one I wanted. It was certainly the same design as one of the three I had seen almost finished, and the completion date was only three days away. This ship would be fast and just big enough for a small pirate crew.

I grabbed a piece of paper and a quill and carefully drew the words as they were written on the design. I didn't know what it said; I'd have to have someone else tell me.

Black Heart

Underneath was another set of words, and I copied them as well.

Cody Dimitri

Now, I'd have to work fast.

I put the papers back together and set them on the shelf. In my excitement, I had carried the lamp with me to the shelf.

"Hey, what's that light?" I heard one of the guards yell.

I rolled my eyes as I blew out the candle and hid under the desk as they walked in.

"Where did you see a light?" The other man sounded doubtful.

"It was clear as day right in here." He lifted the lamp high and moved further into the room.

My heart leapt into my throat as they stepped closer to the desk, their dirty boots scrapping along the wood floor.

When they had moved past the desk, I rolled out the other side and made my way quietly to the exit.

As I closed the door, I noticed that they were still looking the other way. A thrill went through me as I slammed the door hard behind me, then I jumped underneath the porch, scooting myself into the tiniest position I could manage.

The door opened with a slow groan.

"Ghost?" one of them asked.

The other whispered as he dashed down the stairs. "I don't know, but this place is getting creepy."

"Are we going to tell him about the light?"

"Sure. That and about the slamming door with no one there? And us scared out of our wits?"

"Oh," came the reply.

"Exactly. I don't think so. Besides, it's not like anyone would actually steal anything."

They went back to sitting around the oil lamp and kept glancing around. I felt some small satisfaction at seeing I had them worried.

I slipped away into the dark, climbed over the fence, and brushed off the dirt. "Just you wait, boys, the Sapphire Siren will steal something."

A CREW

I had a problem. I needed to hire a crew, but did I dress as a man? Or should I lean into my legacy as the Sapphire Siren? I'd have to have enough people to run the ship, fifteen at least. Any less and this would never work.

But my name was already out there - spat out by an old man. Maybe others were intrigued?

I decided to test things out under my new name. I walked into the barbershop and announced, "The Sapphire Siren is looking for a crew. I'll be in the Fat Pig Inn at noon."

The barbers shrugged nonchalantly, and the men in their seats peered over at me. I repeated this in the general store, where a woman grasped her throat like I was about to murder everyone. I rolled my eyes at her.

"If you ever want to be free and sail on the high seas, I also take women on my crew."

I moved on to the saloon, where the bartender attempted to shoo me out for not being a man. I wasn't having it, not today.

I took out my knife and held it up high. "I won't be chased out." I leaned in and gave them my best threatening glare.

They looked back at me, their brown eyes looking friendly and certainly not intimidated. "What? You're not going to stab the bar with your knife?" They asked me sarcastically.

Apparently, I'd need to work on my glare.

"I'm not dulling my knife with such a stupid move. Now, bring me a drink!"

They laughed and walked away. I assumed to completely ignore me. The other men in the bar were watching, silently. The bartender picked up a dark bottle, and dust lifted into the air around it. Then they poured a drink, setting it in front of me.

The liquid was dark. It worried me, but I dumped the contents down my throat like I meant it. I was braced for the heat of alcohol and was surprised when, instead, I was hit with a sweet taste.

The bartender, their white wig looking a little worse for wear, leaned towards me. "Listen, the owner comes in every day, and he's going to pick you up and physically throw you out of here. I'll give you one more shot, and I suggest you leave."

"What is this?" I whispered back.

"Orgeat. The owner insists on having it around but no one ever orders it. Made from barley and oranges, apparently." They poured me another, and I threw it back again and slammed the glass on the bar.

"And don't insult me again!" I stalked out, hoping that someone would show up at the inn.

In my room, I primped my hair, straightened out my red coat, and stared into the wavy old mirror. The drawings of my father, the captain, and Ben looked back at me from the wall nearby. Would my ancestors, my long-lost friends and family, watch over me? And, would I find the people I needed to make my dream come true?

I took a deep breath and walked downstairs. There were crowds of people around the tables eating their lunch, but even more were just standing around. As if they were here for me.

Had the sound of conversations dimmed as I entered? It seemed so.

I sat at an empty table and pulled my coat tail out behind me.

I recognized the bartender from earlier as they sat down across from me. The rest of those gathered around me, I didn't recognize.

"Is there a contract?" the bartender asked.

"Contract?" I hadn't thought of that. "Of course, there are contracts. I wanted to talk to my potential crew members first."

A dark man stood next to the bartender, spouting words at me that didn't make sense.

The bartender translated, "He wants to know how much it pays."

This was a question I was ready for.

"I have one piece of gold for every crew member. And you get your food and board on the ship. After that, you earn what we take."

It was a big group, and none of them looked to have much experience, much less a life well lived. That had me worried.

"Does anyone here have experience on a ship?"

One lone person had raised his hand. He stood out with a beard, but it was so grey that it looked strange with his white wig.

I asked him, "You. Do you know how to navigate?"

A smile spread across his face, and he pulled from his pocket something I had seen the captain use for navigating, a sextant.

The tension in my shoulders eased a bit. "And do you know how to use it?"

He nodded.

"What's your name?"

He set down a piece of worn paper with the word 'John' on it.

"John, you're hired."

He grabbed up the paper.

"Give me some room and I'll talk to each of you in turn. I'll start with you, bartender."

"Ty, the name's Ty."

After interviewing all twenty members of the group, I whittled the crew down to fifteen. I was looking for people willing to work, and hopefully very smart, because I was about to challenge them with the hardest experience of their lives.

There was one man who kept a hood over his face—William Cathay, or Will— who I was sure was a slave. I caught a glimpse of very dark brown skin between his sleeves and his gloves. He seemed whip-smart, and I was glad to have him on the crew.

I paid for everyone to have a late lunch, and when the inn was empty, save for the crew, I gave them the plan.

John had a grin bigger than his face.

Many of them looked shocked, and Ty shook their head.

Meg, who told me she was the sister of the woman I had scared at the general store, nodded. "I'm willing. Whatever it takes."

THE SNUB

Everyone had left, and I twirled and danced in my room, then leapt onto the bed. I had done it! I had hatched a plan, and people had listened to my crazy idea. Some of them weren't completely convinced it would work, but they would all meet me tonight.

I'm sure it didn't hurt that I had a gold coin to pay them with, but they'd get no payment from me until we had pulled this off.

I jumped and landed in a seated position on the bed. It would be hours before our next step. What was I going to do in the meantime?

I stepped outside and walked along the road, glancing at the different buildings. The scent of ginger stopped me in my tracks. Mother and I had only had ginger on rare occasions. I followed the scent down an alley to an unmarked door.

It opened just as I was going to knock. A Chinese man stepped out, no wig on his head.

I stood in shock. My mother and I were an enigma in England. What were Chinese people doing here in the colonies?

His dark eyebrows shot up, and he spoke to me in rapid-fire Chinese.

"Huh?" Was all I could find to say.

Suddenly, it was like a veil covered his face. He looked down at my feet in their normal, everyday shoes. He took a breath and addressed me again, "You're standing in my way. This place is only for real Chinese. How did you find this place?"

I could see behind him a woman and two men, all Chinese, sitting at a table, eating.

"I followed the scent of ginger. My mother cooked with it when I was a child. I didn't think I'd see any other Chinese here."

The woman with silver hair motioned for me to enter. The man at the door spoke quickly to her, obviously warning that something was amiss with me.

She still motioned for me to enter.

As I stepped forward, I was shoved from behind. I knocked into the man in front of me, and we both tumbled to the ground inside the door.

I flipped over, took out my knife, and stood in a

single second. Was the shipbuilder here? Was he trying to put an end to me?

There was a tall man that I didn't recognize, his white wig well powdered. He carried a wooden board in his hand, and he held it high as a threat. "Once again, I can smell your disgusting food from my stables."

The people at the table stood up and stepped back. The woman was being supported by one of the men. I realized she must have her feet bound like a "normal" Chinese woman. She pushed the men away and turned to give the invader a withering look.

I didn't like bullies, and this situation reminded me of stories my father had told me. I moved between the attacker and the others and made sure I had the attacker's attention. "I'm surprised you can smell anything since you reek of horse manure."

He advanced, ready to hit me with his board. As it swung down toward me, I danced under his arm and grabbed him from behind, with my knife at his throat. "Drop your weapon."

He hesitated, and I pushed the blade just enough to leave a cut. I whispered in his ear. "Do as I say or the Sapphire Siren will cut off your head."

He dropped the board.

I pushed him hard. He flew out of the door and landed on the dirt alley. "If you ever come back, I will have one of my Youxia come after you."

I realized he probably didn't know the Chinese

word for ancient warrior or the stories my father had once told me. But maybe it didn't matter.

The man stood and looked not at me, but at the foot of the stairs in horror.

I stepped forward and saw that there were at least twenty snakes, all facing the invader. I had never seen so many snakes.

He jumped up, brushed himself off, and dashed away. The men behind me were arguing and couldn't see the snakes. The man had obviously feared them, but I was more curious.

I stepped down to the last step. The closest snake, its head a beautiful red color and its body a reddish-brown, looked at me, then I swear it nodded. It turned away and slithered after the other snakes. It was so weird to watch how quickly they all disappeared in different directions.

I walked back up the steps, leaving that mystery behind me for now.

"Youxia?" the snobby Chinese man said as he got up from the floor. "You don't know Chinese, but you know that word."

My blood was still boiling, and my knife was in my hand. "Is that a question?"

He opened his mouth to answer, but I didn't want to hear any of it.

"Never mind." I reached for a bowl of food from the table, but the old woman put her hand on mine. She had a kind look on her face, she said something in Chinese, and pointed at a different bowl.

I grabbed it and headed to the door. "Consider this payment." I walked out and slammed the door behind me.

I held my feelings in until I reached my room at the inn. Then I sat on the floor and cried. To have finally met my own people and be so hated.

Much later, I finally picked up the bowl of food. I sniffed the beige parcels. They were a bit slimy and cold. Had I even picked up food? I bit into it and a burst of flavor hit my tongue. Ginger, seasoned meat, and other things that I had never tasted.

I cried some more and finally was able to eat the rest of the morsels. I would probably never taste anything like this again. My own people would despise me.

But I would get money and a place for my mother, and we'd hire a cook who would make us Chinese food all the time. I would make my mother so happy for saving my feet and giving me my life.

I also realized that was the second time I had been caught unaware from behind. One way or another, I'd make sure that didn't happen again.

GHOSTS

I pulled on my darkest clothes as the late hour approached and headed out to our meeting spot.

One by one, they appeared from the streets until we were all assembled.

The few men who had worn wigs earlier were without them now, save one. "John, we need to move with stealth. Your white wig shines in the moonlight like a beacon."

He nodded and took it off. And his shiny, bald head was only slightly less like a beacon.

"Wow," Ty said as they looked at John's brightness.

I shrugged. There was nothing for it, for I needed John most of all.

"Follow me." I led them to the fence at the ship-yards. I knew most of them would not be able to climb as easily as me, so I had come prepared. I threw over a rope ladder, climbed the fence and then secured it on the other side.

Cuddy was the first one to join me on the other side of the fence, and I was glad to see him help Zophar down from the top. And then came the rest— Ty, Owens, Prosperity, Micajah, Meg, Will, Will D, Quill, Fate, Levi, Alexander, and lastly John, who deftly jumped down from the fence and pulled the rope ladder with him.

I waved for everyone to follow me.

We wove through the ships at different stages, staying well away from the guards at their standard post. And then we came to the ship. It was dark out, but it almost seemed to be glowing.

"*Black Heart,*" said Ty.

I realized they were reading the ship's name. I pulled the piece of paper out of my pocket.

"Is that what this says?"

Ty nodded. "It also says Cody Dimitri. Who is that?"

"Must be the owner, I think."

Black Heart. The ship was one of the most beautiful things I had ever seen.

As expected, it wasn't in the water yet.

Luckily, the scaffolding made it easy for everyone to climb in.

The last to make it up to the ship was Zophar. As he stepped away from the scaffolding, one of the upright boards wobbled and fell with a clack to the ground.

"Get down!" I said and the compliment lay down on the deck.

I hurried down the side of the boat and made it to another ship as the guards appeared, running and out of breath.

"Who's here?" they yelled together.

From the other ship, I opened my mouth wide and howled in a way that I hoped sounded like a ghost. But then a fly flew down my throat, and it ended in a weird, strangled sound. I wished I could spit out the fly, but I couldn't.

The guards were silent and stock still. I moved so I could see their faces. Their eyes were wide open and one had grasped the other's arm. They backed up the way they had come until they were a few feet back and then turned and ran.

I laughed and followed them to see what they would do.

I wiped happy tears from my eyes as I spied the guards back at their usual location. One of them set the lantern down.

"That's it. No more going after sounds or light or whatever. We stay right here where nothing outlandish ever happens."

The other nodded. "Yeah, we're definitely not telling the boss about that. I don't know what that was, and I don't want to know."

Perfect. I returned to the *Black Heart.* Everyone was still lying low on the deck.

I spoke in a whisper that bounced around the ship. "Let's start."

They all got up and came close.

"I'm going to teach you everything about this ship, from the stem to the stern." I pointed to the front and back of the ship.

I talked the group through each section of the ship and the work that would be done there. There were a lot of attentive eyes on me.

As dawn approached, we quietly made our way out of the shipyard and as we stood outside the fence, I felt a sense of pride.

These people not only accepted me, but they also listened to me, and they looked up to me.

"Listen, tomorrow night I'll have the contracts for you to sign. And we'll get back on the ship to practice working with the sails. We have only three more days to learn everything about sailing. Once you sign the contract, you will forever be a warrior and pirate of the Sapphire Siren. I am proud of all of you."

Of course, I'd ask Ty to help me write the articles if they could.

There were smiles and nods. They walked back into the streets and disappeared into their homes.

ON OUR WAY

For two more nights, we went through the most important steps - how we would sail the ship out of the harbor. John stood at the helm and pointed a direction, and the crew would rush to their stations and pretend to set everything accordingly.

Ty had taken to the quartermaster roll, steering. And, Meg was turning out to be a perfect boatswain, ensuring the sails and rigging were correct and putting the others in the crew to work.

So far, though, the one person who hadn't found a good role among the many jobs was Zophar. Even as I thought about what he might do, he tripped over his own feet and landed in the middle of the deck. Will D had been running across and accidentally tripped over Zophar.

I looked to my right to see John surveying the scene and shaking his head.

"I know," I said to John. "I think Zophar might do well in the galley."

John nodded.

I pulled Zophar and Will D aside. "I have a special project for you both."

Zophar's brown hair was matted with sweat, and his brown eyes looked around nervously.

"Nothing to be worried about. I need a team to get our supplies to last us for our trip to England. I'll get you the money and a list. You'll need to have all of the supplies here by nightfall, and the crew will help get them to the ship."

Zophar shook his head, his voice high in anxiety. "Everything I do, I just mess up. Maybe I should stay behind."

"Zophar," I noticed he cringed at his own name. "I think it's time you received your pirate name."

His eyes lit up. "A pirate name?"

"I name you Caitiff Caldron."

"A villain?" he asked.

I nodded. "We're all villains now, in a way. But you'll be a villain and a cook."

He smiled and nodded.

I gave them the long list of items we would need, as well as a great deal of money. "I trust you both to bring the goods back."

They nodded.

In the last couple of days, we had devised a quiet system of communication. I snapped my fingers. The two pirates closest to me stepped to the nearest person and repeated it. Within a moment, it had been broadcast around the ship, and as the snap requested, everyone came and gathered around me.

"Good job today, everyone." I could see the smiles on all their faces. "Tomorrow night is the big night. The ship is being moved to the edge of the water. We'll be able to launch her. Now, let's go and get some rest."

On our way out, I overheard a few of the crew talking.

"I don't know if I want to leave Georgia," Cuddy said.

"Why did you sign up?" Meg asked him.

He was silent for a moment. "There aren't enough opportunities to make money. I don't want to live in my father's cabin for the rest of my life."

"Ha," Meg responded. "Well, at least you don't have to get married in order to have money. How would you feel if your only choice in life was to marry or join the ladies in the brothel under the whip of yet another man? Piracy sounds much better to me."

Fate grumbled, his deep voice cutting through the night. "None of it matters. We're here, we signed a contract. To get as far from here as possible has always been my goal. See you tomorrow, Captain." And he turned and disappeared into the night.

They were all looking for something more, something that piracy could give them, except for maybe John. I had a feeling that he wanted to get back to the sea. At least they all seemed to get along, and no one had the backstabber mentality as far as I could see. But when treasure was on the line, how would they react?

They had all signed the contract, some with an educated hand, most with an X. How much could I trust each and every one of them? Only time would tell.

STUMBLING

I could feel the energy in the air as I packed up my things from the inn. Before I folded the images of my friends and father, I asked of them, "Please, let this go smoothly. I know teaching them on land wasn't the best idea, but it was the only one I had. So many things could go wrong." I stopped there. I didn't want to think about any of those things, so I focused on carefully packing the drawings.

Downstairs, Mrs. McGraw had a pile of white sheets ready for me tied up in a bundle. "There they are, dear. All washed and worth every penny you paid."

"Thank you, Mrs. McGraw."

She put her hand on my shoulder. "Be well, young lady. I hope to hear about all your exploits someday."

I couldn't stop myself from hugging her. "Thank you." I took a step back and a deep breath. I was no longer a little girl, I had to be strong for my crew and myself.

"But," she continued, "let things cool here before you return. There are some men who are kicking up trouble in town. It won't be safe much longer, even here. My husband and I have kept them out until now."

"Thank you, Mrs. McGraw."

The front door swung open, and it was the Chinese man from the restaurant, only he was wearing a white wig, blending in a bit with the locals. He still had his unhappy expression on his face. "It wasn't too hard to find you, girl. My great-great-grandmother wanted to see you."

He pulled the door open wider, and behind him was the old woman. She shambled in, much like my mother, and for a moment, I missed my mother's face more than anything.

The old woman walked up to me and gently grasped my hand. She spoke in Chinese.

When she was done, I shook my head. "I'm sorry, I don't understand."

The man handed me a package. He leaned in, a sneer across his face. "Don't squander what she's giving you. It should belong to me. And don't come looking for us. We must keep moving."

The woman said something biting in Chinese.

He turned back to the door.

"What did she say?" I asked him. He ignored me, and the two of them left.

There was no time to look inside the package. I added it to my stash of things, grabbed up the bundle of sheets, and headed out the door. Will D and Caitiff were waiting outside as I had instructed.

"Were you able to get everything on the list?" They nodded.

I handed them the sheets. "Good. Let's get to the meeting place."

As we approached our usual meeting spot, John and Cuddy were standing in front of everyone, and I could see they were anxious to talk to me. Cuddy had taken to being John's voice, since John didn't have one of his own.

Cuddy ran up to the wagon as soon as we stopped. "There's a problem."

"What?"

Cuddy shook his head. "I don't understand John's hand signals enough yet."

I turned to the rest of the crew. "Quill, thank you for taking apart the fence. While I find out what's going on, the rest of you unload this wagon and get everything inside the fence. Then put the wagon and fence back."

They got to work as we walked away.

Had the buyer come and taken the ship? Was it gone?

Even worse. It was still sitting on land, surrounded

by scaffolding. It had been slated to be in the water as of this morning.

"Damn it."

John nodded.

We walked around the outside of the ship. "What do you think, John? It looks seaworthy."

He nodded as he inspected the hull.

The ship was facing its back to the ocean drop-off and surrounded by scaffolding. All of which would make this so much harder. At least it was on a ramp, but even then, we'd need a way to pull it into the ocean.

I couldn't go back to the inn. I had already created problems. And who knew when the owner would come for it? Possibly tomorrow and we'd have to wait for another ship..

This had to happen tonight, while the tide was high and everyone was ready.

The crew showed up then, silently carrying the supplies.

Caitiff whispered, "Captain, some of the supplies are heavy. Is it safe to take them up the ramp? I'm worried they might break them."

"An excellent question, Caitiff. You're a villain and a pirate. Make some decisions. If you have to get a rope and have them pulled up the side, do it and get everyone to help. And tell Ty to get someone to help them with that special project."

He nodded and stood a little taller.

At the same time, I hoped we could get this ship out of here, or all this work would be for nothing.

John tapped my shoulder and motioned for me to follow him.

He pointed up to the back of the ship. Several anchors were hanging from their keel holes.

"Anchors?"

John nodded and grimaced. He was trying to tell me something.

John waved at me to follow him. He went to a small boat sitting by the ramp. He pointed up at the anchors, motioned as if he were pulling one with him, dropping it into the boat, rowing out to the ocean, then dropping the anchor.

Then he motioned toward the ship and then leaned forward with his arms straight out as if he was pushing something. But what?

Cuddy walked up and John grabbed him by the arm and set him up in the same stance - arms straight out, leaning forward, then he gently pulled Cuddy forward and motioned him to walk in a circle. Then John got behind Cuddy in the same way. As if they were lined up pushing the capstan!

"Okay, so you're saying," I started, and John looked at me expectantly. "We put an anchor out, and then the crew uses the capstan to pull on the anchor, and it pulls the ship forward into the ocean?"

He nodded and put a hand out to stop Cuddy from walking in circles.

It sounded like it would work. For all I knew, it was what the shipbuilders did.

"Let's do one more check of the ship."

John nodded and we went off in different directions.

I went inside the ship and inspected everything. If anything wasn't seaworthy, I didn't see it.

I couldn't help envisioning us sinking only a few feet offshore. It would be a sight to see, and the Sapphire Siren would be a laughing stock.

NIGHT SKY

Another check on the guards, and they were at their favorite spot, hovering over their fire for heat.

Back at the ship, I could see a flaw in my plans. I wanted everyone to think that the ship had been spirited away magically. If we cut away the scaffolding, that would look too real.

As I examined the scaffolding, John was having someone lower one of the anchors to him.

A smile spread across my face as I came up with a brilliant idea.

I walked up to John, watching for the anchor to reach the ground. "John, are you taking out the boat with the anchor?"

He nodded.

"When you're done placing the anchor, wait in the

boat nearby. I'll need you to pick up three of our crew after the ship is launched."

He nodded, grasped the anchor as it came within range of him, and started walking it toward the boat.

I stepped in to help him. The anchor was flat and not as heavy as other anchors I had seen.

"Is this anchor made for this kind of maneuver?"

He nodded.

That made me feel less nervous about using this idea.

We placed it in the boat that John had already set at the edge of the water. I helped him put it into the bay and watched him row away with the expertise of someone familiar with rowing.

I turned back to the ship. In the scaffolding, she looked like a caged animal. I walked around to the bow of the ship and climbed up the scaffolding until I reached the figurehead. She was wearing a dress, and one arm was reaching out to the ocean.

I set my hand on her shoulder. "Lady, I hope you'll allow me and my gang to set you into the sea, and maybe you could help this go smoothly."

I wasn't expecting an answer and she didn't give me one, so I climbed up the rest of the scaffolding and into the ship.

Two crew members were at the capstan, giving more line from the anchor for John. All the equipment and food were tucked away. Ty and their team had finished with the project.

Three crew members were standing around. "Prosperity, Micajah, Fate." They came running. "Come with me."

They followed me to the stern of the boat.

"We're going to cut the ropes on this side of the scaffolding. Open it up like a door, and then you'll close it back up once we've pulled the ship out. Tie as many of the ropes back as you can to make it look like it never opened. John will pick you up in the boat. And, when we start pulling the ship out, you'll be keeping an eye on the guards. If they start to come look, distract them. But make sure they don't see you."

They nodded.

I hoped it would make it look like the ship had become a spirit. It would certainly make the shipbuilder scratch his head.

The crew climbed over scaffolding and cut the ropes within minutes. They peeled it back just as I saw John throw the anchor down into the water.

We were ready.

I signaled Cuddy, and within minutes, the rest of the crew was with me on the deck, waiting.

I pointed to the capstan. "Now, the future of the ship and all of us rests with pulling it out of this slip. You'll be pulling on the anchor that John just placed in the bay. Line up two by two on each capstan bar and push."

The crew rushed to the capstan and began to push. Some crew members stood by as there wasn't enough room for everyone.

I went to the stern to watch. The crew was grunting and pushing with all their might, and finally, the ship began to move toward the ocean.

The back end of the ship slowly touched the water, and I could feel my stomach unknot.

William was watching too and ran to the capstan. "Keep going! The ship is touching water." He tapped Zophar and took his place, and the capstan moved a little faster.

Soon enough, the ship was fully in the water.

John was waiting in the boat for Prosperity, Micajah, and Fate. I didn't have time to see if they were able to put the scaffolding back together.

As the ship turned around the anchor to set the stern toward the sea, there was a flurry of activity. Everyone was doing their job, unfurling the sails, using the winds to move the ship away from the coast and the dangerous rocks nearby.

I went to the bow and made sure no one was looking when I set my hand on the figurehead and whispered, "Thank you."

Meanwhile, I appreciated Ty's handiwork. They had placed strips of cut sheets to make the sails appear as if they were torn, and larger sections to appear as if ghosts stood upon the deck. One in particular was placed between the wheel and the coast to hide anyone standing at the post.

Then I noticed there was something sitting on the railings next to me. It was barely visible in the dim moonlight.

The little stowaway screeched. "Wock."

I put out my hand and it hopped onto my wrist.

"Wock. Rock the boat." it said.

"Hello. What's your name?"

"No stupid questions," came its answer.

I smiled. The parrot was well-trained. Where had it come from? "Well, then I'll call you Yīngwǔ, another of the words I know in Chinese. It means parrot."

"Wock. No stupid questions," it repeated.

"Captain, John and crew are aboard and we're well away. Do we have a destination?' asked Cuddy.

The parrot answered as it climbed up my arm to my shoulder. "To the King!"

I laughed. "Well, you're not wrong. Cuddy, we're heading to England, with all haste."

The parrot followed me to the captain's quarters and landed on a bird perch. The owner must have left his bird here, expecting to collect it soon. "I hope you don't mind being stuck with me?"

"No stupid questions," it answered.

We sailed off smoothly. However, three crew members quickly developed severe seasickness.

I had Cuddy repaint the ship, and we christened her *Night Sky*. Someone carved a star from wood and secured it into the hands of our figurehead. Two days later, I turned seventeen. I didn't want to tell anyone how young I was, so I made my own cake and celebrated in my cabin.

PART TWO

ANDY

I sat on a rock by the water's edge. Beyond me was the cove; green hills on either side reached around in a choking hug that almost closed off the ocean, yet allowed just enough room for a small boat to enter, if they dared the rough waves.

I had often imagined taking a boat through those cold waves and out into the ocean or getting a horse from the village and riding across the country, feeling the cool English air rush past me.

But my dreams felt very far away.

My father called from the back door of the inn, "Andy, get in here and help your mother in the kitchen."

Ignoring my father, I tossed a rock into the water. I knew he'd give me a little time before he yelled at me again, and then I'd be forced to spend the evening inside our family's inn.

I grabbed up a stick and pretended to be a princess, fighting pirates to save my kingdom. I had never met a pirate, but I had heard enough about them to know they were dangerous and deserved to be cut down, especially if I was keeping my kingdom safe.

But then I glanced down into the water and saw my distorted reflection. Men's clothes and my brown hair cut short by my father. The dream fell apart.

I stamped into the rocks and water, erasing the fake me. Before we had moved here, I had worn my hair long. Now my father insisted I dress as a boy. It had taken me a while to figure it out, but from the whispers of the locals, I figured out that I was illegitimate.

For some upside-down reasoning, it was much more appropriate to have an illegitimate boy than a girl. I assumed that's why we lived out here, away from the village. But would I ever be able to be me and stop paying for someone else's sins?

I threw the stick away and gave in to the inevitable. I headed back to the inn.

That's when I saw him. A dark figure in dark clothes walking along the coast. The closer he got, the more I realized that this man might be a pirate.

He was dark, tall, and heavy. He appeared to be strong, plodding along with a wheelbarrow. A large, tattered sea chest sitting in the wheelbarrow looked as if it had come right off a pirate ship.

His long blue coat was frayed and dirty, certainly

not something a gentleman would wear. He had no gentleman's wig. Instead, his hair was tied into a tail.

He had a bright scar across one cheek and a short beard. His hands were ragged and scarred, with black, broken nails.

"Lad!" His voice was low and scratchy.

It took me a second to realize he was addressing me.

"Get your mangy self over here and help me." He stepped back and pointed to the wheelbarrow.

I picked up the handles and pushed. It was heavy, but not so heavy that I couldn't move it faster than he had done. He kept up with me, though, almost right by the side of the chest, as if afraid it would disappear.

He didn't make a move to open the door, so I opened it. It tried closing on me. I shoved the wheelbarrow in, causing the front door to swing back, smack the wall, and then swing forward, knocking the wheelbarrow over.

"Ya blasted land lubber!" The pirate was next to the chest in a flash, setting it back in the wheelbarrow. He turned to me and stepped toward me, and for a second, I could feel death hovering near me.

"He didn't mean to do it," my father's calming voice echoed in the room.

I felt like I could breathe again.

The pirate ignored my father, took one more close look at me, and then turned to look around the quiet cove behind him. He put one hand on his precious cargo and softly broke out into a sea-song.

"Fifteen men on the dead man's chest
Yo-ho-ho, and a bottle of rum."

For a moment, I could picture him on a ship in rough seas. His brown eyes reflected the fire from another ship, and he was holding a sword with the blood of innocent people.

The pirate stopped his singing and then sat at one of the tables and knocked on the surface. He finally turned to my father. "I'll have a glass of rum."

As my father procured his rum, he continued, "I've cast me anchor at six different inns across the seven seas, searchin' for the finest establishment a sailor could hope to find. I had asked of inns along the coast back at the Royal George and heard yours well spoken of. This is a handy cove," he said, "and a pleasant sitty-ated location. Much company, mate?"

My mother walked through the room and started a fire in the fireplace. The pirate's eyes followed her, and it sent an eerie shiver down my spine.

My father shook his head. "Not as much as I'd like. We get traffic from the road, for those who are set to travel through the quiet countryside. And neighboring villagers will come for dinner." My father was too nice to tell the pirate to move on.

"Well, then," the old man said, "this is the berth for me."

He wanted to stay here? This could not be good.

The pirate continued, "I'm a plain man; rum and bacon and eggs is what I want, and that rock out there to watch ships go by. You can call me captain. Here you, matey," and he threw down four gold pieces on the table. "You can tell me when I've worked through that."

My father's eye grew wide at the gold. He turned to me and motioned me to take the chest. "Andy, take that to the room around the corner."

I nodded, but as I approached the chest, the Captain held up his hand. "Lad, I expect ye to take it straight in and leave it be." He leaned forward and growled.

Keeping it upright was also insinuated.

I parked the wheelbarrow in the room, took one long look at the sea chest and its rough wood, and shut the door behind me, all the while wondering what might be in the chest that he had brought with him all the way from the Royal George to this isolated cove.

A DARK CAPTAIN

The next morning, I could hear the Captain snoring as I worked at cleaning the inn. Then he was up, dashing into the dining room as if he were late for something.

"I'll take that bacon and eggs!" he roared to no one in particular. Our other visitors looked horrified by his stern bark.

My father delivered his food to him, and a long, quiet conversation followed between the two. I bent over the railing from the second floor to hear, but went back to work when my father glanced up and gave me a look.

Finally, my father shared some of the news. "The Captain wants his lunch delivered to him while he's out on the end of the cove. Neither your mother nor I are in good health to go for that walk, so you'll have to do it."

I certainly didn't like the Captain, but I smiled anyway. I was never allowed to go to the end of the cove, those green arms that closed off the view of the ocean.

My father leaned in. "I want you to be careful."

I nodded. I rushed through my morning chores so that I could enjoy my precious time beyond my tiny cove.

After my mother handed me the Captain's lunch, she rested her hands on her wide hips. "Now, I know you, Andy. You'll spend as much time as you can out there. Just don't do anything dangerous. You'll give your father a heart attack."

I would have hugged her if I hadn't had a tray in my hands.

As I walked out of the inn, I could see my friend Ron walking up the road from the village, his dark brown hair being blown in the wind. Although I liked his company, and he was one of only two people who knew the real me, I didn't want to wait for him. I didn't want to share this moment with anyone.

I walked quickly around the beach and then stepped up to the rocks that had been my prison walls. There wasn't much to see from here, so I kept going until I reached the end of the green expanse. The view opened up. The open ocean was the most beautiful thing I had ever seen. And, two ships were passing out in the distance. It made me feel not so alone.

"Where's my lunch!"

I jumped a little, not realizing the Captain was sitting on a high rock. He held a brass telescope in his hand and stared at me.

"Sorry!" I said and climbed up the rocks with one hand while holding the tray in the other.

He took his lunch with a yank.

"My mother says to wait for the tray." Not that she had said that, but it was a good excuse, and I didn't see him caring enough to bring it back.

"How old are you, lad?"

"I'm fifteen."

"When I was fifteen, I were sailing the seas."

"Sounds harsh, being on your own at fifteen."

He grunted. "Best life anyone can ever have."

I climbed up to a higher rock and stared out to the ocean, watching the ships glide by. Where were they all going? What wonders were out there to see? Would I ever venture beyond the English coast?

As soon as he was done with his lunch, the Captain set the tray near him and went back to staring through his telescope.

As I picked up the tray, I asked him, "What are you watching for?"

He set the telescope in his lap.

"Tell you what, lad, I'll give you a silver fourpenny on the first of every month if you would keep your eyes open for a seafaring Chinese woman, and let me know the moment she appears."

"Woman?" I asked, surprised that he would feel such alarm about a woman. I thought that she might be his wife, but he continued.

"She's a sly dog, that pirate. And she's got a magic about her that I best keep far away from. There are other sea dogs I'm watching out for, but that one be the worst of the lot." He handed me the fourpenny.

I stowed the precious money in my pocket and climbed down the rocks.

Was that what he was doing here? Watching for a Chinese pirate? A woman? I glanced back at the ocean, wondering what sort of ship she sailed. What did a Chinese pirate ship even look like? I'd heard of China— one of my books called it a land of mysteries, its people rarely seen beyond their own shores. Surely a Chinese pirate would stand out anywhere.

And what did a woman pirate wear? Men's clothes? Women's clothes? And what was it like to be a woman pirate?

I had so many questions as I headed back to the inn.

EVIL SPIRITS

Ron was waiting for me at the inn.

I told him all that had happened and how I felt with the Captain around.

His dark brown eyes reflected his need to ask questions of everything, but he let me finish.

"I worry about the danger he's brought to the inn."

"Danger?" Ron asked.

I nodded. "Don't you feel it in the air?"

He shook his head. "How much trouble can one man be?" he asked with certainty.

"You should come by this evening at dinner and see him. Then I think you'll change your mind."

An agreement was made, and Ron headed back home.

Later that night, I was sure that he must have invited the whole of his village to come and dine with us. The dining room was full to the brim of locals, and every seat at the bar was taken.

The Captain sat in the corner of the parlor, drinking rum, seemingly oblivious to the crowd.

Ron and I stopped in our tracks when a villager asked the Captain. "Sir, what ship did you sail?"

He grunted and pushed his hat back on his head. Seeing the sea of people in front of him, he cleared his throat.

"I'm no sir. I'm a Captain!" The last was yelled across the room and made everyone jump.

He continued, "I've sailed many ships, including with Captain Flint himself."

There was a collective gasp in the room, but I didn't understand the reference.

Ron whispered in my ear, "A known pirate! I heard he died in the colonies."

The Captain continued. "Flint and I went way back. Our first job as wet behind-the-ears sailors came on a moonless night, black as the devil's heart it was. Our captain of the time, Captain Leatherboots, had been sent by the pirate king to retrieve the ancient gold sunk by the gods of the sea."

"The other pirates warned us that the gold was guarded by spirits, but that the gold and diamonds littered the sunken ship like pebbles. We both spit at the word spirits. No such thing."

He paused for a moment, looking around at his attentive crowd.

"The promise of riches certainly lured us in, as it would any man of the sea."

"Our cap'n, hell-bent on provin' his mettle to the pirate king, drove us hard to see it done. We dropped anchor in waters what lay still as death—unnatural-like. We dragged out them diving bells, hats of metal, our cap'n had surely plundered from some poor merchant vessel. Locked inside that iron cage, I could scarce see further than this."

He put his weathered hands in front of his face and then took a large swig of rum.

I couldn't imagine what kind of hat, hard or otherwise, would allow a man to go underwater, but it sounded fascinating.

"The Captain said to us five, 'Tread carefully, lads! Find what treasures you can and bring it back fast.'"

"Wait," Ron said to the Captain, "If it was black as pitch, how could you go underwater?"

Our guest leaned forward. "Ah, that's the part no one believes, but we had a luminary, a rare gift from the pirate king."

No one reacted to his words. He smacked his hand on the table. "A luminary is a magical creature that gives off light. Anyways, the five of us and our luminary were lowered down in our boat, then we stepped over the side into the cold, dark waters. As we sunk to the bottom, the luminary's light was enough to see a few feet, but that was it."

"Andy, come help your mother." My father's words were barely a whisper as he was listening intently.

I walked backwards, not wanting to miss a word.

"We went a short distance and the shine of the gold practically blinded us. As we approached the gold, a woman appeared, walking towards us. Walking as if she were on land with plenty of air to breathe. She was wearing a heavy gold necklace round her neck and a white garment. Her black hair was pulled up on her head." He lifted his hands to his head, as if to demonstrate her hair.

"All I could do was gape like a landed fish. She come up to me bold as brass and threw open the porthole of me diving bell. The sea came rushin' in."

There was another gasp from the crowd.

"I had to act fast. I pushed the hat off me shoulders and used the pipe to pull meself up to the waiting boat. Thank the gods that I had a good breath of air in me lungs and that there was light long enough for to see where the pipe was."

"After I grabbed hold and started pulling meself up, the light died. We never did find that luminary."

He leaned back and took another drink.

"What happened to the rest of the men?" I asked.

His shoulders slumped a bit. "Flint and I were the

only ones t- survive." With that, he grabbed his bottle of rum and headed for his room.

Ron and I conferred over the bar.

Ron rubbed his chin, like his father often did. "What do you think of this luminary? Could something really glow?"

I nodded. "I've heard stories from travelers before. Magical beings, lights in the sky without thunder, strange sightings. It sounds plausible."

Ron shook his head. "But a woman walking at the bottom of the ocean? A vengeful spirit?"

That did sound a bit far-fetched, but the way the pirate had described her, I could see her so clearly.

Ultimately, we decided that he must have been hallucinating or just trying to keep his audience's attention.

FULL HOUSE

First thing in the morning, I found my father sitting in the dining room, looking pale, and lamenting to my mother. "The inn will be ruined! No one wants to hear stories that will have them shivering in their beds."

Ruined. A thrill went through me at the thought. That would mean we would leave this desolate and cold place. I could make friends, have a life outside of cleaning an inn.

The Captain came out just as he had yesterday, in a hurry as if he was late for an appointment, and yelled for his breakfast. Father went to his bed, so mother served the pirate.

I watched from the bar as she set down his plate. He looked at her as if she were his breakfast, leering at her as she walked away. My stomach turned, and I appreciated being dressed as a boy.

Feeling bold in my disguise, when it came time for lunch, I left the inn full of questions that I wanted to ask the pirate.

When I did find him, as I handed him the tray, I asked, "Have you ever tried to go back for the ancient gold?"

He looked surprised, and then he shook his head. "I ain't got no head for navigation on the open sea. The pirate king knows where she lies, and only he. Mayhaps me old cap'n knew, but he's gone to Davy Jones long since. Besides, I've had me fill of sorcery and spirits." He spat out the last word, and then he scooped his dish off the tray and handed the empty back to me.

My hopes that the Inn would be ruined by having a pirate stay were crushed when night fell. Once again, our dining room was full—this time full of those from the next village over and some from the night before. Obviously, word of our visitor was spreading, and these villagers weren't afraid of a harrowing story.

Ron had come by as well and started to help me, but ended up sitting at a table with some friends. I gave him a dirty look to let him know I was mad at that, but he ignored me.

Our pirate was very glum at first, drinking his rum and looking down at his table. Outside, the weather had turned. A late fall wind and rain were whipping against the windows, and the fire was crackling. At least my mother's fresh bread filled the room with the smell of comfort.

With the Captain quiet, it gave me time to rush around and help my mother, since my father was still in his sick bed.

Finally, Ron ventured to ask the pirate a question, "Captain, is there anything that scares a pirate?"

The pirate glared up at him.

"Not you, of course. But other pirates?"

The pirate slammed his bottle onto the table and looked up at the crowd. "The black spot." Then he leaned back and nodded. "Aye, the black spot."

He was staring up at the wall, thinking perhaps.

I wiped a mug at the bar for the fifth time, waiting with the rest of the room to see if he'd continue.

He nodded suddenly, as if he just remembered what he was going to say, "The last thing a pirate wants to be handed is the black spot. You're nothing without your mates, and once you've lost faith, you can be voted down."

"Five year ago, the crew 'n I gave Butcher Cross a black spot. We gave him a day to make his peace with his god or give him a chance to jump over the side."

Ron asked the question I was thinking, "What did he do to be given a black spot?"

The pirate slammed his fist on the table. "He were

hoarding food on a long voyage. We discovered all sorts of stores hidden in his bed."

If no one understood the importance, he leaned forward.

"Every scrap of victuals aboard ship is to be divvied up fair and square amongst the crew, so's every man keeps his strength. It's in the Code, it is."

"We gave him a good bleed and knocked him over into shark-infested waters."

I swallowed hard, my eyes wide.

"Andy!" My mother called from the kitchen.

In frustration, I slammed the mug onto the floor, smashing it into pieces. Then, just as quickly, regretted breaking it.

Ron came up behind the bar, just as my mother appeared.

"Andy, what happened? We can't afford to lose any dishes."

Ron put his hand on my mother's arm. "I'm sorry, Mrs. Hawkins. It was my fault. I can pay you back by working some hours."

Mother's eyebrows stayed knitted together, but she nodded and went back to the kitchen.

Ron helped me clean up.

"Thanks, Ron." If ever I needed help or a friend, he was the one I could count on.

The pirate didn't spill any more stories that night, but I still had to shoo everyone out so I could close.

Ron finished cleaning all the tables, save the Captains', as he was still there, and headed home.

Once the place was empty, the pirate stood shakily from his table. As he walked by, he grabbed my shoulder. "You haven't seen any pirates, have you, lad?"

"None but you, Captain," I answered.

He nodded and stumbled off to his bed.

My mother came out of the kitchen and handed me a grilled slice of her bread with a valuable layer of cinnamon, my favorite thing to eat in the whole world.

As I ate, I felt even more guilty for hating this place. She seemed to love it here in her kitchen.

In my room, I considered reading from one of my books, but the candle blew out in a draft. I wrapped myself in my blanket and stared out at the stormy cove.

The rain had stopped, and through the ripply glass, I thought I saw a flash of light from a boat, perhaps, but I couldn't tell if it was from the tiny slice of ocean or the cove. I wished anyone out there luck and curled up in bed.

THE WOMAN PIRATE

The next day, when I gave the Captain his lunch, I asked him, "Will you tell me about the female pirate?"

He said in a surly voice, "Which one?"

The question caught me by surprise. "What?"

"Lad, the fairer sex makes up a large portion of the pirate world. Be specific."

My mouth fell open. I would have argued the point, thinking that couldn't be true, but the pirate glared at me. "The Chinese pirate, the one you have me looking out for."

His lip curled at the mention, but he nodded. "I'll consider it."

I could tell he wasn't going to share the story now, so I went back to the inn.

There was a lot of work to do with Father in his bed.

He was crying about pirates and that the Inn would come to ruin, not realizing that we were busier than ever.

When the pirate came back in the evening, I was behind the bar serving drinks while Ron helped my mother in the kitchen. The Captain asked me if I had seen any seafaring men, and especially that Chinese pirate.

I shook my head. We had a few new patrons who had gotten rooms, but no one who appeared to be a pirate, Chinese, or otherwise.

Even so, the Captain seemed in bad spirits. He stalked in between the tables to his favorite spot in the corner, and villagers and patrons alike moved out of his way.

I could feel the anger coming off of him in waves, glad that he wasn't carrying his saber with him, as that would truly be dangerous in his generally rummy condition.

He had his captive audience before him as he slapped his hand on the table. His audience obliged with silence all round.

Meanwhile, what truly annoyed me was that in the other far corner, there was a growing number of young men who acted as if they admired him. Ron would occasionally step out of the kitchen and sit down with them, which made me even more mad.

They clapped at his stories and sometimes even

bought him some rum, as if he needed more. And although I wanted to hear his stories, he was not someone to be admired. He was a cold, stone killer.

Tonight, the group had grown to ten. The rest of the room was also packed, and the bar was lined up with patrons.

Right now, the young men were leaning forward, waiting for the Captain to start his story for the evening.

I saw my father peek his nose out of his room and grow wide-eyed at the crowd. I figured he'd go back to bed, but he came out of his room a few minutes later. His face was pale, and he walked slowly. The easiest job in the Inn was standing behind the bar, so I wasn't surprised he brought a chair and shooed me out.

I made my way toward the kitchen, but stopped in my tracks when I heard the Captain say, "I'll tell you of the woman pirate on Captain Flint's crew."

One man in the audience laughed as if the old seaman was making a joke.

The Captain turned to him and sneered. "Think it funny? She started as a doxy, but she slit enough men's throats to earn her keep as a pirate."

I pulled out a rag from my pocket and pretended to clean the front desk. All the while, my mind was spinning. A prostitute turned pirate, I had never heard of such a thing.

"When she first joined the crew, the captain gave

her a chance to prove her salt. She was nimble, that one. We were going to attack a merchant ship the next morning. It had anchored near our favorite hiding place. We planned to attack in the morning."

"Now you see, that Chinese gal told us instead, to give her a boat and she'd signal us when it was time to come over. "Just you wait," said she."

"She took that boat, as quiet as a church mouse, she crept across the waters to the merchant ship. We watched her from the spyglass as she crawled up the anchor rope like a monkey."

"Not an hour later, a light shone across the water. We sailed out to the boat, expectin' a fight. Instead, we found a host of men dead, their throats cut." He motioned his hand across his neck, then lifted his mug towards me, the sign for more rum.

The audience was quiet the whole time that I gave him a full glass. He drank back his rum and then slammed down his glass.

"There are some people that have a magic about them, a way with the world." He was glaring at me when he said that, and I wondered if he was talking directly to me. Then he glanced away and continued, "That Chinese gal is one of them." He leaned forward and shook his dirty index finger at us all. "So, you might think I'm trouble, but watch out. A female pirate is even more cutthroat than the likes of me."

He stood with a flourish and made his way to his

room. As the curtain closed behind him, the voices of the other visitors rose in conversation.

Pirates were indeed dangerous, I thought. Now my image of the Chinese woman had a cutlass in one hand and a knife in the other.

My father shook his head. "He's bringing in the bar business, but your mother said that louse has yet to renew his payment for his room. Will you talk to him? You seem to get along."

I didn't know about that, but I knew my father was just not feeling well enough to have it out with the Captain. I nodded. I'd see what I could do tomorrow when he was more sober.

That night I dreamed of a stormy night. The wind was shaking the four corners of the Inn, and the surf roared along the cove and up the cliffs.

Standing on the top of the rocks was a woman with long black hair, flying about her like a dark villain's cape as she drew a cutlass. I could see the Captain walking up behind her with his own cutlass drawn. I tried to warn her, to scream out, "Turn around!" But the words wouldn't come out.

At the last second, just before his blade reached her back, she turned and met his blade with her own. She kicked him in the stomach and knocked him back. Her own blade raised high, ready to cut him in half.

The sound of the real wind battering against my window woke me from my sleep. Dangerous, these pirates were dangerous and all I could think of as I fell asleep again was that having one here might bring others. In fact, the Captain seemed certain that at least one might find him. And what would that mean for my family and me?

DR. DAWE

The next morning at breakfast, I thought about how I'd ask the Captain for what my father was owed. It was obvious he hadn't spent much money since coming here.

All the time he lived with us, the Captain made no change whatever in his dress but to buy some stockings from a hawker. One of the feathers of his hat having fallen down, he let it hang from that day forth, though it was weird when the wind blew, to see it flapping.

His coat had obvious patches that looked like he had done himself. And although I had never seen the inside of the sea chest, it couldn't contain clothes unless he was holding on to them for a special occasion.

I decided I'd wait until lunch.

"Andy," my mother called when lunch was ready.

"Take this out to the Captain. And keep an eye out for the doctor. I asked Ron to send him word that he needs to look at your father. He's back in his bed again."

I nodded, glad to hear that Mother had called for the doctor. I took the tray for the Captain and rehearsed words in my head. But when I reached his lookout, the words left me.

He took his tray and snarled, "Why are you staring, you scrawny landlubber?"

I suddenly felt angry. "This scrawny landlubber has been delivering your lunch every day." I put my hands on my hips as I had seen my mother do. I could see why — it made me feel bigger. "You owe us for your drinks, your room, and your food."

He snarled, crooked his head towards me, and refused to move an inch. "Remind me when I come in for dinner." And he went back to eating.

I jumped from one rock to another, a weight lifted off my shoulders for now.

He seemed especially in a dark mood when he came in from the sea, but I asked him for the funds immediately. He stomped into his room and came out with four gold pieces. He slapped them in my hand with a grunt and stomped over to his corner. "Get me my rum."

I sighed with relief, delivered his rum, and let my father know that we had the next payment, hoping that would make him feel better. He merely nodded and closed his eyes again. That worried me. Money had always made father brighten.

Soon after, Dr. Dawe arrived. He was the only person, save my parents and Ron, who knew I was a girl. He visited with my father, took a bite of dinner from my mother, and went into the parlor to smoke a pipe until his horse could be brought down from the village, for we had no stabling.

I followed him in and observed the contrast in the neat, bright doctor, with his powdered wig as white as snow, his clean-shaven face, and his bright, brown eyes and pleasant manners. On the other side of the room was that dirty scarecrow of a pirate of ours, sitting, far gone in rum, with his arms on the table.

Suddenly, he—the Captain, that is — slapped his hand upon the table before him in a way we all knew to mean— silence. The crowd of voices stopped at once, all but Dr Dawe's; he went on as before, speaking clear and kind, and drawing briskly at his pipe between every word or two.

The Captain glared at him for a while, slapped his hand again, glared still harder, and at last broke out, "Silence, there, bilge rat!"

"Were you addressing me, sir?" said the doctor, not even turning to face our pirate.

"You know it to be true."

"I have only one thing to say to you, sir," replied the

doctor, "that if you keep on drinking rum, the world will soon be rid of a very dirty scoundrel!"

The Captain sprang to his feet, drew and opened a clasp-knife that I didn't even know he was carrying, and balanced it open on the palm of his hand. "I'll pin you to the wall, you mangy, no-good..." He didn't complete the sentence but stood threateningly.

I dearly loved the doctor. I considered running to the kitchen to grab my own knife so I could protect him, but I was frozen in place.

The doctor never so much as moved. He spoke to the Captain, as before. Over his shoulder, and in the same tone of voice, rather loud, so that all the room might hear, but perfectly calm and steady: "If you do not put that knife this instant in your pocket, I promise, upon my honor, you shall hang at the next possible tribunal."

The Captain stood for a moment and then soon knuckled under, put up his weapon, and resumed his seat, grumbling.

"And now, sir," continued the doctor, "what is your name?"

The Captain sat resolutely and didn't answer.

"I've heard word that there's someone here who claims to be a pirate. An offense punishable by hanging. If I find you're truly a pirate, I'll see to it that you hang. Since I now know there's such a fellow in my district, I'll have an eye upon you day and night. I'm not only a doctor; I'm a magistrate, and if I catch a breath of complaint against you, if it's only for a piece of incivility like tonight's, I'll have you hunted down and routed out of this place. Let that suffice."

Soon after Dr. Dawe's horse was brought to the door, and he rode away, but the Captain held his peace the rest of that evening.

BLACK DOG

That next morning, fall had been swept away ahead of a very cold, windy gale.

My mother was looking pale. I assumed that Dr. Dawe had delivered bad news, and she didn't want to tell me.

It was plain from my father's face when I stopped in to see him, that he might not see the next summer. That worried me. Even though I wanted to escape, I certainly didn't want to lose my father.

It was all this stress with the pirate that was wearing him down, I supposed.

The Captain arose earlier than usual and, without eating breakfast, headed for the door. He made a loud snort of indignation as he opened the door to a gust of wind. I assumed he'd come back inside.

Instead, he set out down the beach, this time with

his cutlass swinging under the broad skirts of the old blue coat. His brass telescope was under one arm and his hat under the other, as the wind whipped at everything.

The rest of the Inn was empty of visitors, and dinner guests wouldn't be arriving for many hours.

Mother was upstairs with father, and I was laying the breakfast table for the Captain in case he returned, when the front door opened, and a man stepped in who set my blood to ice.

He was a sickly pale man in a black coat. He had no wig, no gentleman's airs, but he also didn't seem like a sailor. His hair wasn't tarred, and he had no scars, but he had a way about him that suggested danger.

"Hello," I said in my most masculine voice. "How may I help you?"

He made his way to the Captain's table that I had just set and sat down. "I'll take rum."

I turned to grab it from the bar.

"Before you get that, come here, lad."

I took a few steps forward, leaving space between us. I noticed he was missing two fingers on his left hand.

"Come here, sonny," he said. "Come nearer here."

My heart thumped loudly as I stepped as near as I dared, but although he didn't appear to be a pirate, I could see he had a knife at his belt, and his expression was angry.

"Is this here table for my mate, Billy Bones?" he asked.

It was obvious that this was someone looking for our Captain. Should I out him? I answered honestly. "We don't have anyone here named Billy Bones."

"Well," said he, "my mate Bill has a cut on one cheek, and a mighty pleasant way with him, particularly in drink, has my mate, Bill. Now, is my mate Bill in this here house?" He touched his knife at his belt.

This man could cut me here if he found I lied; it wasn't like the Captain could hide the jagged cut on his face. "I don't know if the Captain is your man. He does have a scar on his face. He's out walking."

"Which way, sonny? Which way is he gone?"

I pointed out the rock and told him how likely the Captain was to return and how soon.

"Ah," said he, "this will be a good place to wait for my friend, Bill."

As I grabbed the rum, I wondered if there was anything I could do. Rousing my mother or father would likely only cause more trouble.

After I got him some rum, the stranger stood with his glass and kept hanging inside the inn door, peering round the corner like a cat waiting for a mouse.

I felt guilty for outing the Captain and considered trying to warn him. I tried quietly stepping out into the road, but the scary man immediately called me back, and, as I did not obey quickly enough for him, a most horrible change came over his tallowy face, and he ordered me in, with an oath that made me jump.

"I'm going to go visit my friend Ron," I told him. But, he shook his head.

As soon as I was back inside, he returned to his former manner, half-fawning, half-sneering, patting me on the shoulder when I walked near, telling me I was a good lad.

"I have a son of my own," he said, "as like you as two blocks, and he's all the pride of my ' art. But the great thing for boys is discipline, sonny—discipline. Now, if you had sailed along with Bill, you wouldn't have stood there waiting for me to repeat myself—not you. That was never Bill's way, nor the way of such that 'as sailed with him."

I pitied the child of this mad individual. Were all pirates so desperate and mean?

His eyes grew wide as he looked out to the distant beach. "And here, sure enough, is my mate Bill, with a spy-glass under his arm, bless his old ' art, to be sure."

"You and me'll just go back into the parlor, sonny, and get behind the door, and we'll give Bill a little surprise— bless his ' art."

The stranger backed along with me into the parlor and put me behind him in the corner, so that we were both hidden by the open door, and I'd have no opportunity to warn the Captain. Was this man going to cut him down?

I was very uneasy as the stranger put his hand on his knife, and all the time we were waiting, he kept swallowing as if he felt a lump in his throat.

At last, in strode the Captain, slamming the door behind him, without looking to the right or left, and marched straight across the room to his table.

BILLY BONES

"Billy Bones," said the stranger.

The Captain spun round on his heels; his face turned ashen. He took a step back, and I almost felt sorry for him, seeing him look so old and sick.

"Come, Billy Bones, you know me; you know an old shipmate, Bill, surely," said the stranger.

The Captain gasped, "Black Dog!"

"And who else?" replied the other, getting more at ease. "Black Dog as ever was, come to see his old ship-mate Billy. Ah, Bill, Bill, we have seen a sight of times, us two, since I lost them two talons," holding up his mutilated hand.

"Now, look here," said the Captain, "you've run me down; here I am. We go aways back, Black Dog."

The Captain, whom I now knew was Billy Bones,

took hold of my arm and pulled me away from Black Dog. "Lad, go get me something to drink with my breakfast. Well, then, Black Dog, speak up: what is it?"

"All right, Bill," returned Black Dog, "you're in the right of it, Billy. Lad, I'll have a glass of rum too and we'll sit down, if you please, and talk square, like old shipmates."

When I returned with the rum, they were already seated on either side of the Billy Bones' breakfast table —Black Dog sitting sideways, with one eye on his old shipmate, and one on the front door.

Back in the kitchen, I took several deep breaths. I was glad that I was in one piece, and better yet, there was no blood spilled.

I brought Billy Bones his breakfast and went to stand behind the bar to listen.

Billy Bones waved his hand at me. "Leave the room, Lad."

I went up to the second floor and sat down right above where the two were seated.

It sounded as if Black Dog were trying to convince Billy Bones of something. I could hear Black Dog's voice drone on for a while, and then Billy would make some sort of agreement. But then, as the conversation went on, Billy said no to each of Black Dog's demands.

At last, the voices began to grow louder, and I could pick up a word or two, mostly oaths, from the Captain.

"No, no , no, no; and that's an end of it!" Billy Bones yelled.

Then, there was a tremendous explosion of oaths— the chair and table went over in a lump, a clash of steel followed, and then a cry of pain.

I dashed downstairs to see Black Dog opening the front door, and Billy Bones hotly pursuing, both with drawn cutlasses, and the former streaming blood from his left shoulder.

Just outside the door, the Captain swung hard at Black Dog, which would certainly have split him to the chin had it not been intercepted by our big signboard.

Billy Bones pulled his sword out of our sign, taking a huge notch out of it, and swore.

That blow was the last of the battle. Once out upon the road, Black Dog, holding onto his shoulder, ran swiftly on his heels and disappeared over the edge of the hill in half a minute.

The captain, for his part, stood staring at the signboard like a bewildered man. Then he passed his hand over his eyes several times, and at last turned back into the Inn.

"Andy," he said, "rum," and as he spoke, he reeled a little and caught himself with one hand against the wall.

"Are you hurt?"

"Rum," he repeated. "I must get away from here. Rum! Rum!"

I ran to fetch it, but I was quite unsteady from all that had just happened. Never had I seen a man draw blood in the heat of a fight. I dropped the first glass I grabbed, the pieces splaying in different directions. While I was still getting in my own way, I heard a loud fall in the parlor. Running in, I found the Captain lying full length upon the floor.

My mother came running in. I told my mother what had happened, and she shook her head.

Between the two of us, we set his head on a pillow. He was breathing very loudly and hard, but his eyes were closed, and his face had a look of great pain. We thought that perhaps he had been injured in the fight, but could find no wound.

"Dear, deary me," cried my mother, "And your poor father sick!"

It was a happy relief when the door opened, and Doctor Dawe came in on his visit to my father.

"Doctor! He fell after a fight. We're not sure where he's wounded," I said.

The doctor leaned down and examined the pirate. "Wounded? He's no more wounded than you or I. The man has had a stroke, as I warned him. Now, Mrs. Hawkins, keep an eye on your husband, and tell him nothing about this. Andy, help me get him to his bed."

Between us, we managed to hoist him to his room and lay him on his bed. Most of the way, whenever I could, I held my breath, for it was obvious that the captain never bathed.

The doctor shook his head. "For my part, I must do my best to save this fellow's worthless life; and Andy, you get me a basin."

When I got back with the basin, the doctor had already ripped up the captain's sleeve and exposed his great sinewy arm. I was surprised to see tattoos, although it made perfect sense.

"Billy Bones", an anchor, and a sketch of a gallows and a man hanging from it. It was quite impressive in its design.

"Prophetic," said the doctor, touching the picture with his finger. "And now, Master Billy Bones, if that be your name, we'll have a look at the color of your blood. Andy," he said, "are you afraid of blood?"

"No, sir," I answered. As long as it wasn't drawn at the end of a cutlass.

"Well, then," said he, "you hold the basin," and with that he took his lancet and made a small opening in the captain's vein. He bled him out for a good while, then stopped the bleeding and bandaged the wound. A few minutes later, the captain opened his eyes and looked mistily about him.

First, he recognized the doctor with an unmistakable frown; then his glance fell upon me, and he looked relieved. But suddenly his color greyed, and he tried to raise himself, crying, "Where's Black Dog?"

"There is no Black Dog here," said the doctor. "You, sir, have been drinking rum, and you have had a stroke, precisely as I told you; and I have just, very much against my own will, dragged you headforemost out of the grave. Now, Billy Bones—"

"Don't call me that," he interrupted.

"Just calling you by your tattoo, though much I care," returned the doctor. "It's certainly the name of a buccaneer; and I call you by it for the sake of shortness, and what I have to say to you is this: one glass of rum won't kill you, but if you take one you'll take another and another, and I stake my wig if you don't break off the drink, you'll die—do you understand that? —die."

Billy's eyes grew wide.

"Now, mind you," said the doctor, "My conscience is clear for I have named your death 'rum' and it's up to you to change it." And with that, he took me by the arm and led me outside the Captain's room.

"This is nothing," he said as soon as he had closed the door. "I have drawn blood enough to keep him quiet a while; he should lie for a week where he is— that is the best thing for him and you; but another stroke would kill him."

He had done it on purpose! Would it keep the Captain out of our hair for a while?

"But there was a man here named Black Dog, I'm sure Billy and Black Dog are pirates. What if he comes back?"

The doctor nodded. "This is serious business. I'll see if I can send one of my stewards to keep an eye on the place. The last thing we need is more like him." He pointed at the Captain's door.

I nodded. The thought of more pirates crawling around the Inn left me with a hollow and terrified feeling.

FAMILY SECRETS

It felt strange to be back in London. I wasn't happy that it had taken me and the crew of the *Night Sky* so long to get back after so many side trips and delays along the way.

As I walked along the London streets, my sea legs almost itched to be back on the ship, but that could be because I was nervous.

My heart raced as I climbed up the pipe outside my mother's apartment building and leaned over to the window. The room was empty, but my mother's things were there; she should be home from work soon.

I climbed through the window and looked around the apartment. There was food in the pantry, of which I was thankful.

She walked in, and my heart soared to see her. After seeing me standing there, she shuffled her way to the one chair in the room and sat with an audible sigh. I bowed my head so I wouldn't have to look her in the eyes and see disappointment.

She started, "When you disappeared, I thought the worst. Had someone kidnapped you? But then I found some of your father's things gone."

"I'm sorry, Mother. I didn't want to clean houses. I wanted to make us money so we could live in luxury."

I took her hand and put the gold coins in her palm, enough to keep her in food for a year.

She was silent for so long that I finally looked up at her.

"Did you become a courtesan?" She asked with dismay. "That's the only thing I can think of when I see money like this."

I shook my head and opened my mouth to tell her. But how would she take it? I forced the words out, "I'm a pirate."

Her facial expression went from disappointment to disbelief, so I added. "But I try to be a good pirate."

She sighed again and slapped her hands on the armrests. "Of all things. You know we came here to keep you safe?"

I nodded, "From the foot binding."

She shook her head. "No."

It was my turn to be in disbelief.

She nodded at me. "There was more to it than just the foot binding. Your father always wanted to tell you, but I wanted to wait until you were older. Sit, and listen."

I sat cross-legged before her.

"Have you heard of the Youxia?"

"Yes." I nodded. "Father told me stories of the Youxia."

"Of course, you remember those." She looked off into the distance, perhaps thinking of father. "What do you remember?"

I could recite some of the stories from heart. "There once was a wandering band of Youxia. they would go town to town, righting wrongs. One such dashing Youxia was young Haitao."

"One day, the band came upon a traveling caravan that was stopped by a military general. The general was attempting to steal a young girl from the caravan. The girl's father was trying to stop him. The general drew his sword and was about to cut the father down."

"Haitao drew his sword and flew across the field to defend the father, slamming his sword into the general's just in time to save the man and telling the general he must leave, giving him a chance to survive and walk away."

"The general said that it was his right to take anyone he wanted and started the fight by swiping his sword towards the farmer again. Haitao easily bested the general and the ten men who traveled with him. Haitao then escorted the caravan to their destination."

My mother continued the story, although I had never heard this part before. "The general lay on the battlefield, feigning a fatal injury, until the caravan left. He was injured but had hidden among his soldiers to escape death."

"Later, through his spies, he learned that Haitao's wife was about to have their first child. The general decided he would have that child, no matter what. That the child would be his slave forever to pay for its father's ways."

"The general sent spy after spy to snatch the baby, but" she rolled up her right sleeve to reveal a deep slashing scar on her shoulder, "the baby's parents put up such a fight, he was never able to acquire the child."

"The parents wanted their child to be safe, so they paid a sailor handsomely to take them away."

I gently set my hand on my mother's arm, The sword that had made that scar had gone deep. No wonder she was always favoring that arm.

We sat in silence while I tried to reconcile the story. The story that I had heard all my life. I had pictured the dashing Haitao defending the farmer and his daughter, never putting my father's face on the hero.

And me! I was part of the story. A pawn in an evil man's plan, sent beyond his reach. I thumbed the knife in my pocket and wondered if I'd ever come across him in the future.

My mother finally continued, "It makes sense that

you would wish to wander. Your father was much the same. I just wish he had lived to teach you his ways."

She got up and hobbled over to our chest that held our few precious family things.

"As for a good pirate, perhaps you could be even better. Not just a good pirate, but a seafaring Youxia."

It sounded like an interesting idea, but pirates needed to make money.

DISCOVERED

Mother leaned over the chest and pulled up the wood that lined the bottom.

Curious, I stepped forward.

Lying on a black cloth was the most beautiful sword I had ever seen. It had a rounded ebony hilt tipped in ornate silver. Centered above the crossguard was a gold gem.

My mother handed it to me.

It was lightweight. I danced around the room as I had with that mop more than a year ago.

"Your father would have wanted you to have that." My mother bent back down over the chest and pulled a bag out, then slowly straightened up her back. "Let's go see your ship."

I stood for a moment, open-mouthed.

"You do have a ship, don't you?"

I laughed. "Yes, mother. I'm just surprised you want to see it."

"Of course, I want to see where my daughter is living."

I helped her down the stairs and outside. I wanted to run in circles around her, like I had done the last time we had walked together, but I was a ship's captain now. That wasn't something I wanted anyone to see.

So, I walked slowly by her side.

As we entered the harbor walkway, all I could see was my glorious ship. I wasn't watching my mother when she suddenly stumbled. I couldn't move fast enough to catch her. She landed on the wood on her hands and knees, and the package in her hands flew a few feet away.

"Mother!"

She waved her hand at me as if she was fine, but the worry and pain that showed through her eyes told me something different. "Get the package, I don't want anyone trampling on it."

I grabbed the bundle and then helped her up. "Can you walk?"

She nodded. "Take me to your ship."

I sighed. She was just as stubborn as ever.

We approached the ship, and the members of the watch, William and Meg, came down the gangway to meet us.

"William or Meg, can one of you help my mother up the gangway. She wants to see the ship."

Meg nodded, picking up my mother and taking her up the gangway so quickly she didn't have time to decline. Of that I was very thankful.

On the ship, my mother was wide-eyed and nodding. She ran her hand along the railing. "It looks like a good ship."

"I've named her *Night Sky*."

She nodded, then handed me the bundle. "Your grandmother made this for your father. She said it was to warn all huàirén that they were to watch out. Wait to open it. You must be Youxia first."

"Huàirén?" I asked her.

My mother looked at me quizzically at first, not realizing I didn't know the word, or maybe she couldn't remember the translation. Finally, she said, "Oh, yes. It means evil doers."

I took the bundle, my concern for my mother growing. The harsh life of a domestic servant wasn't something she should do at her age. "I will put it somewhere safe, Mother. Which reminds me, I have something else. A woman in the colonies-"

"You've been to the colonies?" My mother asked, her eyes wide. "That's amazing."

I smiled at her surprise. It had certainly been a surprise to me. "Let me go get it. I need you to translate it for me."

I ran to my cabin, placed the bundle in my wooden chest, and retrieved the package.

When I came back out, William had found a stool for my mother and she was talking to him about eating better. He nodded and thanked her as I walked up.

"Here's the letter that came with the items. She saw me once and then showed up right before I left." I didn't mention how rude everyone else had been to me or the strange actions of the snakes.

She took the note and began to read:

"Dear child,

I feel, within you, resides the spirit of the snake. I was also born of the snake, long, long ago.

I give you what I no longer need.

May love soften your heart and hone your steel."

Mother gasped and read the name.

"Bai Suzhen"

"The White Snake?" My mother asked herself softly, and I realized she was crying.

"Mother?"

She shook her head. "I'm fine, I'm fine. What did she give you?"

I showed her what was in the package. "They seem strange gifts, a package of mushrooms and a small umbrella."

My mother gently took the items in her hands as if they were precious.

I continued, "I know I was born in the year of the snake. Is that what she means?"

Mother nodded. "But I think it's more than that. First, let me tell you of the legend of the White Snake. She was a demon."

I laughed, thinking of the old lady I met could be anything but a woman.

Mother gave me a withering look so I stopped laughing.

"She was a demon, a white snake, who changed into a beautiful woman to lure young men to their death."

THE WHITE SNAKE

Mother continued, "One rainy day, a kind-hearted man, Xu Xian, offered her his oil-paper umbrella to her and her servant, Xiao Qing." Mother lifted the umbrella. "This protected them and it was a link for him to find her again."

"She fell in love with this kind and generous man and decided she should stay human. She began doing good things with her powers and married Xu Xian. But there was a monk who only knew her for her evil ways."

"The monk tricked her into drinking a poison that exposed her as the White Snake. Xu Xian was so jolted at the sight that he died of shock.

"Bai Suzhen was devastated. She quickly traveled to the mountain of the gods, intent on retrieving the immortal herb that would save her husband. She fought the guards bravely but lost against them."

"It was the Old Man of the South Pole who took pity on her and gave her the herb that much resembled a mushroom."

I looked at the wooden box with mushrooms that looked innocent enough. Certainly, all of this was just a story. I thought back to the woman and tried to picture her face, but it was only a blur now. "But she was an old woman. She wasn't immortal."

Mother nodded. "A demon can live forever, but she chose never to become the snake again. As a human, she has a limited number of years, though certainly more than a normal human." Mother shook her head. "She lived on the mountain of the gods, but then disappeared when she was hunted by monks. It was said that she traveled far away. If only I could have been there when you met her. I have so many questions for her. "

"What do you mean?"

It was her turn to laugh. It was so rare that I didn't interrupt.

She continued, "I've been so worried about you, but she's given you things to protect you." She turned toward me. "There were whispers that our family was related to the White Snake. It was something we were to never reveal to anyone as we might be seen as demons ourselves. I would have liked to ask her if that was true."

Related to a demon? I sat down on the deck. Today

was a prodigious day. What would that mean for me, if it were true?

I looked at the mushrooms and wished that it was true. "Mother, if these are indeed the same mushrooms, they might heal you." I felt silly even saying it out loud. Mushrooms didn't make one immortal. My father's stories of magic and a fighting style that included flying through the air had been flights of fancy for a young child.

Mother shook her head. "No, these are not for me. But, when you face an evil spirit, make sure to have this."

She handed the umbrella back to me.

"Yes, Mother." I didn't think a flimsy umbrella would help, but I took both the items back to my cabin and put them with her package. I grabbed a few more coins.

Back outside, I put them in my mother's hand. "Mother, I don't want you to work anymore. Here's money to pay the rent for several months. I'll get what I can to you as soon as possible."

Mother smiled and shrugged her shoulders. "What will I do with my time?"

"I don't know, but I don't think you want to clean that rich man's house, do you?"

"Cook always sneaks a bread roll to me, even two once in a while, since you disappeared. She felt sorry for me."

"Someday I'll get you enough money that you can buy all the warm bread rolls you want."

"I will think about it, Chen."

I blew out a sigh. That was at least a small victory. She had a choice for now.

"William, can you take my mother down and get her a hackney?" I handed him some coins.

"Mother, I have to go and find some new members to join the crew. I had two people quit. The pirate life wasn't for them."

Mother grabbed my hand. "My daughter, while you were tucked away in London, where no Chinese have come yet, you've been safe. But beware of General Fukang'an. He is a powerful member of the Fuca clan. They may well have spies out among the sea. And consider more about being Youxia. The power of good."

"I will, Mother." I kissed her on the cheek and watched William carry her down the gangway.

Maybe the real gift from the old woman was the words in her letter. My love for my mother would harden my steel to get what was needed. I got an empty sheet of paper and drew the old woman's face as best I could remember, not that there was much. I knew her brown eyes had been kind, and her silver hair had been piled on her head. I set the picture with the others.

As for the general, it seemed so unlikely that I would ever meet up with him.

RUMORS

On my way to the tavern to meet Cuddy and John, I window shopped. A woman's clothing shop displayed the latest in elaborate contraptions meant to slow women down as well as choke them with tight corsets, but at least sleeves were growing shorter.

It was the newest shop that stopped me in my tracks. The window displayed the most beautiful pies with glossy fruit in delicate rows and rolls of bread that looked very flaky.

I wasn't the only one glued to the window; a group of children of all ages were staring in at the delicacies. There were even a few from the girls' school in their fancy uniforms.

I walked into the store, and the scent of fresh bread and sugar was a delight.

"Madam." A man, obviously French from his accent, was kneading bread dough. "Welcome."

"How much for the pies in the window?"

He shook his head. "I'm sorry, but these are all for a party for the Fourth Earl of Chesterfield."

I set two gold pieces in front of him.

He raised an eyebrow at the gold and then looked back at me, waiting.

The French, I thought to myself. I placed one more gold piece on the table, and he nodded.

I bowed to the man who was making such wonderful things; it was too bad I couldn't get a chef like this on the ship. I opened the door and spoke to the children. "Avast, ye mates. Come inside and get one pie each from the window."

The rush was immediate, some of the children pushing shoulder to shoulder to get inside.

The Frenchman stepped forward, "They cannot be in here!"

I whipped out the dagger in my pocket and held it to his throat, not looking away as the children picked a pie with delight and rushed out, even the school girls.

Once they were all gone, I put away my dagger, grabbed up two pies of my own, and gladly ate them while I headed to the tavern.

In the tavern, I spotted Cuddy and John. They waved me over to their table.

"Did you find me anyone good to replace Fate and Levi?"

"Well," Cuddy replied, "we found men to replace them." Their expressions looked less than disappointed. "If we had a little more time-"

I shook my head. "We were a skeleton crew as it was, and I want to ship out before the pirate hunters come sniffing." Word was that the King was striking out at pirates across the sea to make traveling safer. "We have to have two more, at least."

I was personally worried that a rumor about a Chinese woman serving as a pirate captain would spread quickly and lead the hunters to me. I was keeping the name, Sapphire Siren, quiet for now.

John nodded toward a table across the room. One robust man and one very skinny man sat drinking, looking glum.

"Slim Jim and Buck are their names," Cuddy said. "They have plenty of ship experience. John and I made sure of that."

John nodded.

"So what's the problem?" I asked.

"They belonged to Ned Low's ship."

I leaned back in my chair. I wasn't up on all the pirate lore, but even I knew there was only one pirate more feared than Blackbeard, and that was Ned Low. He was cruel and often used torture on not only hostages but also his own men. It could mean that these men followed the same beliefs.

As I stood, Cuddy said in a whisper, "There's something else."

I sat back down and leaned in.

He continued, "Someone's asking around for a ship called the *Black Heart*."

My jaw dropped. "How could word have spread so fast?

Cuddy shrugged. "Some fella named Crazy Eye Dimitri."

Dimitri, the name sounded familiar, and then it struck me. The purchaser of the ship was Cody Dimitri. "We'll get out of here soon, and he won't even know we were here."

At least I hoped so as I headed for the other table. The two seemed surprised when I sat down.

"I hear you two are looking for work."

They nodded.

"If you want a job, find the *Night Sky* at the harbor before midnight."

"I want to know more about this job," Slim Jim said as he set down his mug.

"Yeah, what could a little man like you offer us?" The wide man asked.

It took a second for me to realize that, because I was wearing men's clothes and a men's-style red coat, they assumed I was a man. It also worked for me that they weren't aware of who I was; the safer my crew would be until the pirate hunters knew more about me.

"You either come aboard and sign on to find out, or don't show. We leave without you if you're not there." I stood, hoping they would show, but not wanting them to know they had any leverage.

They nodded, and I could hear them start to whisper together as I walked out of the tavern.

As I headed for the ship, the name Crazy Eye Dimitri bothered me. That sounded like a pirate. I had assumed the ship had been bought by some tradesmen, not a pirate. This did not bode well, but at least we had renamed her and changed up the figurehead; it wouldn't be easy to spot.

BUCK AND SLIM JIM

Buck and Slim Jim, the two men from the tavern, introduced themselves as they were welcomed aboard. Ty talked them through the contract.

I watched as they listened to the stipulations.

No killing hostages.

No torturing hostages or fellow crew.

No raping women.

No stealing from fellow crew.

etc.

"This is a pirate ship?" Slim Jim asked.

"You got that right. We take what we want, but you must also follow the rules," I answered.

"No torture?" Buck asked.

Ty nodded.

Buck and Slim Jim stepped away for a moment to confer, then came back to sign the contract with an X.

They seemed to take the contract in stride, and if they didn't follow the rules, the penalty was to lose their heads.

Ty took them below decks.

I waved over to Meg. "Let's make ready to sail."

"Aye, Captain."

There was a yell, and Buck came running up to the deck with a young man held above his head. "Captain Chen, what do we do with this stowaway? He was hiding behind a barrel."

The boy was clinging to Buck's shirt.

I walked up to Buck. "Set him on the deck."

Buck looked twice at me before he finally plopped the boy down like a sack of potatoes.

I asked the unfortunate, "Boy, why are you on my ship?"

The first captain who had ever given me a break had told me his rules. Never kill anyone unless it was during a battle or they were in your way. This boy wasn't in my way,

The boy looked up with wide eyes, backing away from Buck a few steps. "I'm tryin' ta get across the way. I heard about the Golden Sun. I wanted ta see if I could find my way ta it and have my hand at treasure. I thought ya would be a good ship until I realized-"

"Until you realized we be flying the Jolly Roger." Slim Jim stepped up to the deck and leaned in toward the boy. "And you realized that we wouldn't take kindly to a stowaway. The story of the Golden Sun is a myth anyway, ya land lubber."

"You have a choice, boy. You can join the crew as our cabin boy, or you can get off now, before we pull that gangway. If you stay, you'll start by holding watch in the crow's nest." I pointed up at the mast.

He looked up and fell backwards from the effort. He stood back up, shaking his head. I followed him to the gangway and watched him disappear into the night.

Ty stood next to me. "I thought we didn't torture hostages?"

I smiled, "If he was too scared to go up into the crow's nest, then this isn't the life for him."

I turned to Slim Jim. "Jim, what's the Golden Sun?"

He laughed. "It's an old myth, Captain. The myth goes that Mayan gold was stolen by the Spanish. The Spanish ship never reached its destination. There's all sorts of rumors that it was cursed, but it's also the golden crown for any pirate. If a pirate were to ever capture that treasure, they'd be set for life. Part of the treasure is said to be a golden sun worth millions. But it's all rumors and no one's been able to locate where the ship went down."

Treasure! Money to set my mother and me for life, money to share with my crew.

To my surprise, the boy came back up the gangway. "I change my mind. I'll be a cabin boy." He started to climb the ropes to the crow's nest.

I put my hand on his shoulder. "Never mind, boy. Ty will show you to your bunk space, and you'll get started tomorrow. What's your name?"

"Gregory."

"Gregory?" Buck retreated and pealed with laughter.

Gregory wouldn't be tortured, but he certainly was going to have a hard time of it.

"Captain Chen!" The call came from the pier below.

I was surprised to see an old familiar face. It was Dirk, and behind him a few of the others from Captain Flint's crew. I leaned down in anticipation.

"Captain, we've found him."

He didn't have to tell me who. Every member of Flint's crew had been looking for Billy Bones. He was the only one who knew the location of Captain Flint's treasure. Treasure we had every right to take now that Captain Flint was dead. The treasure we had worked hard for. The treasure we deserved. Much closer at hand than some mythical gold.

"Where?"

"He's in a small Inn at Kit's Cove. Everyone is heading for Bristol."

I nodded and welcomed the men on board. We had a new destination, and treasure hunting was afoot!

I went to my cabin and walked up to the parrot's cage. He was preening his bright feathers as I told him, "Yīngwǔ, we're seeking treasure."

"Treasure!" Yīngwǔ yelled, as if he understood, and sometimes I think he did. He was certainly smarter than many people.

He trilled, "Find the Golden Sun. Find the Golden Sun."

I did a double-take. I wondered what this parrot knew of myths. Maybe he knew something of the Mayan treasure. But for now, I was after a treasure that belonged to Captain Flint's crew and me.

After we were on our way, I picked up my mother's package. I knew she wanted me to wait until I felt ready to be an avenger of wrongs, but I was too curious at what it held. She had said it was a flag made for my father by my grandmother, a woman I had never met.

It made me sad to know I'd never know her.

I unwrapped the black flag, laying it out on my bed to admire the amazing work. It was a snake! The scales looked almost metallic. I brushed my hand over the image and realized it was all stitching.

Yīngwǔ landed on my shoulder and said, "Whoa," in a long, drawn-out whisper.

"I agree," I whispered back.

The snake's scales were deep blue and gold. It had a set of gold horns, shorter gold spikes poking out behind its head, and a gold tongue. I wondered whether such snakes existed in China or if this was just a creative idea. Either way, it was beautiful.

I had assumed that I was related to the White Snake

through my mother's side, but what if it was my father? Was that why he had been such a strong warrior? Now I had an urge to turn the ship around and ask my mother more questions.

But of course, there was only one thing I could do for now, and that was sail for Captain Flint's gold.

I carefully packed the flag away and wondered how Billy Bones would react when he saw his old shipmates.

THE BLACK SPOT

The cold Bristol wind blew hard from the ocean, whining against the windows and reminding me of how secluded we were at the inn.

I took my father's breakfast to him. He was lying in his bed, his face was pale and his breath was labored. He sat up as I set the plate near him.

He smiled a weak smile. "How is everything, Andy? Are you and your mother able to keep up with the work?"

"Everything is fine, Father."

He nodded. "I'll be back on my feet soon."

"Good." The words calmed my fears for my father, but I was still worried about pirates. I hadn't heard from the doctor and so far he hadn't sent anyone to watch the inn.

I headed back downstairs and took the pirate's breakfast, whom I now knew to be Billy Bones.

He was lying very much as the doctor and I had left him. He was weak, but his eyes grew wide when he saw me.

"Andy," he said, "you're the only one here that's worth anything; and you know I've been always good to ya."

I forced myself not to roll my eyes at that comment.

He continued, "And now you see, mate, I'm pretty low, and deserted by all; and Andy, you'll bring me one noggin of rum, now, won't you, matey?"

I shook my head. "The doctor-," I began.

But he broke in, cursing the doctor, in a feeble voice. "Doctors is all swabs," he said; "and that doctor there, why, what do he know about seafaring men?"

"I been in places hot as pitch, and mates dropping round with Yellow Fever, and the blessed land a-heaving like the sea with earthquakes—what do the doctor know of lands like that?—and I lived on rum, I tell you. It's helped me survive all these years; and if I'm not to have my rum now, I'm a poor old hulk on a lee shore, my blood'll be on you, Andy, and that doctor swab."

He held up his hands so I could see them tremble. "Look, Andy, how my fingers shake," he continued in a pleading tone. "I can't keep 'em still, not I. That doctor's a fool, I tell you. If I don't have a drain o' rum, Andy, I'll have the horrors; I seen some already."

"I seen old Captain Flint in the corner there, behind you; as plain as print. I seen him; and if I get the horrors, I'm a man that has lived rough, and I'll raise Cain. Your doctor hisself said one glass wouldn't hurt me. I'll give you a golden guinea for a noggin, Andy."

I glanced in the corner, just in case there was a ghost standing there. Luckily, it was empty. I weighed my options. Compared to my father, he looked a practical picture of health. Certainly, a glass would keep him quiet. "I'll get you one glass, and no more."

When I brought it to him, he seized it greedily and drank it down.

"Ay, ay," said he, "that's some better, sure enough. And now, matey, did that doctor say how long I was to lie here in this old berth?"

"A week at least," I said.

He sat up with a start but then lay back down. "Thunder!" he cried. "A week! I can't do that. The others have found me and will have the black spot on me by then."

He stared into the corner, where he had sworn that Captain Flint had been sitting. "What do you think?"

I was sure he wasn't talking to me, so I stayed silent.

He nodded toward the corner as if someone had responded.

"True enough. He had to've been by himself or he

wouldn't have scurried away like a lubber. But they'll be back. Besides, I'm not afraid on 'em. I'll shake out another reef, matey, and daddle 'em again."

He slowly sat back up in bed. He paused when he had gotten into a sitting position on the edge.

"That doctor's done me," he murmured. "My ears is singing. Lay me back."

Before I could do much to help him, he had fallen back again to his former place, where he lay silent.

"Andy," he said, at length, "you saw that seafaring man?"

"Black Dog?" I asked.

The captain nodded. "Ah ! Black Dog. He's a bad ' un; but there's worse that put him on. Now, if I can't get away nohow, and they tip me the black spot, mind you, it's my old sea-chest they're after; you get on a horse — you can, can't you?"

I nodded.

"Well, then, you get on a horse and go to—well, yes — to that infernal Doctor swab, and tell him pipe all hands — magistrates and such — and he'll catch 'em — all old Flint's crew, man and woman and boy, all of 'em that's left."

"I was first mate, I was, old Flint's first mate, and I'm the on'y one as knows the place where we stashed our treasure. But don't you worry unless they get the black spot on me, or unless you see that Black Dog again, or a seafaring Chinese woman — her above all."

"But what is the black spot, Captain?" I asked.

"That's a summons, mate. I'll tell you if I get that. But you keep your eye open, Andy, and I'll share with you equals, upon my honor."

He lay back down again, his voice growing softer. He fell at last into a heavy, swoon-like sleep, in which I left him.

He wanted to share a treasure with me? Was it a real treasure? It was hard to tell if he was telling the truth or just delirious. But why else would he be hiding from other pirates?

And if he expected the whole of a pirate crew to show up, riding out to the magistrate was exactly what I needed to do.

FUNERAL

I walked around the inn, thinking about how we could protect ourselves from the pirates. My father's old gun was stored in the cellar. I grabbed it and set it behind the counter, checking to ensure that it was loaded.

Then I picked out one of the sharpest blades out of the kitchen knives and tucked it into a bit of leather and into my pocket. I was determined not to let my family fall victim to any of these pirates.

I let my mother know that I was riding out to the magistrate, then went to check on father.

He looked so peaceful that I didn't want to wake him, but then I realized there was no sound of his labored breathing. I grabbed his hand and just as quickly released it. It was growing cold.

I ran to my room and looked out at the bay. A book

lay on the windowsill, one that my father had bought me last Christmas. The tears started, and I couldn't stop.

What felt like hours later, my mother opened my door. Her eyes were red with tears, too. We sat together on my bed and mourned my father.

Mother finally spoke. "This couldn't be happening. I don't know what will come of us. We're penniless now."

"What?" I asked. "But we have the inn."

She shook her head. "He owned the Inn. A widow owns nothing. It's possible that no one will try to take it, but it's not something certain for us."

I was worried, but also intrigued. Somehow, we would find a way out of this, but perhaps somewhere else.

I walked to the village to spread the word of my father's passing.

Ron expressed his condolences. "Is there anything I can do?"

"Thank you, Ron. There is, actually."

"Ask it."

"Billy Bones, our pirate, is sure that a crew of pirates is on their way. I need someone to go tell the magistrate and send some men to protect the inn. I would borrow a horse, but I can't leave my mother alone."

"Certainly, Andy! I'll do it right away. Please, be careful."

I arranged for my father's funeral with the local clergy. They would send a cart the next day to pick up the body. The body that had once been my father.

Back at the inn, I dropped off some soup and water for the pirate.

He looked with disdain at the food and snarled, "I want some rum!"

"Get it yourself."

My response left him wide-eyed.

"My father is dead. I have more important things to take care of right now."

For once, he looked thoughtful and nodded as I shut the door on him.

Ron dropped by that night, and he didn't have good news. "There's a blacksmith in the next town who's taken ill. The doctor is there at the moment. His men are busy but said they'd drop by occasionally."

That was not at all comforting.

Ron continued, "Andy, if Captain Flint's crew is coming to the Inn, maybe you and your mother should leave. You don't need to stay here."

I looked around the Inn, my prison. "But what would we do?"

"Your mother could remarry."

"Very funny." I rolled my eyes.

"No, I'm serious. That's what I've seen other widows do."

He was serious, but the idea sounded horrible. A

new father, a new place to be stuck in. But right now, we have no clear place to go. "Tomorrow is Father's funeral. After that, I'll talk with my mother, let her know what's going on. I don't want to trouble her yet."

The captain stepped out into the dining room that night for dinner. He ate only a few bites and then walked himself to the bar and grabbed a bottle of rum. It was easier to let him drink. He took it with him to his room, disappointing the few people who waited for his next story. The dinner crowd was growing smaller each night as word spread of the threat of pirates.

We heard him in his room, drunk as ever, singing his old sea-song.

The next morning, I dropped off his breakfast, dressed in my black funeral attire. The captain wasn't in his room. Instead, he was wandering the inn. He went from the parlor to the bar and back again, and sometimes put his nose out of doors to smell the sea, holding on to the walls as he went for support, and breathing hard and fast like a man on a steep mountain.

His eyes scanned over my black clothes, but otherwise, he ignored me.

I took the bottles of rum from the bar and locked them in the kitchen, then walked with my mother to the village. We arrived in time to hear the church bells calling everyone to the funeral, and I said goodbye to my father one last time.

DEATH

The next night, as the captain sat drinking, he set his cutlass on the table. There were only two others dining. The village was willing to face one pirate, but not more than that.

Suddenly, to my surprise, the captain began singing a kind of country love song that he must have learned in his youth before he had begun to follow the sea. I tried to imagine him younger, hearing that song for the first time, but the image of his scarred face kept blocking my imagination.

He finished the song, grabbed his cutlass from the table, and stumbled to his room.

THE NEXT DAY, at three o'clock on a bitter, foggy, frosty afternoon, I was standing at the door when I noticed a blind man walking up the road.

He walked with a cane and used it to tap in front of him. He wore a black hat that was pulled low over his eyes, and he was hunched, as if with age or weakness, and wore a huge old tattered cloak with a hood, which made him appear positively deformed.

He stopped a little from the inn, and, raising his voice in an odd sing-song, addressed the air in front of him.

"Will any kind friend inform a poor blind man, who has lost the precious sight of his eyes in the gracious defense of his native country, England, and God bless King George! —where or in what part of this country he may now be?"

I was leery of anyone coming up to the inn. He could have been pretending to be blind, but when he looked up, his eyes were filmy and sent a shiver down my spine. I walked down the steps but kept my distance. "You are at the Admiral Benbow Inn,' Kitt Cove."

"Ah, just the place I was looking for. Young voice. Will you give me your hand, my kind, young friend, and lead me in out of the cold?"

"Sir, I will keep my distance. You are welcome to follow my voice into the inn."

A look passed over his face, something akin to

anger, or hatred and I knew I had made a good choice to stay away. I dashed to the front desk and brought out the rifle.

When I reached the front door, I was surprised to find him already stepping into the building.

"I have a rifle pointed at your chest. Turn around and leave, now."

He kept walking, the tapping of his cane sounding like time ticking down.

I moved up behind him and pushed the gun into his back. "I told you to leave."

In a flash, he yanked the gun from my hands and had my arm twisted behind my back. I tried to pull away, but he twisted harder.

"Now, young woman," he said, "take me in to the captain."

My heart skipped a beat for several reasons. "You mean, boy, sir, and the captain isn't taking visitors."

He sneered. "I don't care if you're a bilge rat. Take me in straight, or I'll break your arm."

He twisted hard at my arm, and I was afraid he could do as he said, so I obeyed him, but at each step I wondered if there was a way to knock him down and keep him out of the inn. But his arms were strong for someone who looked so frail.

He clung close to me, holding me in one iron fist, and leaning a great deal of his weight on me, restricting my movement. He whispered in my ear, and the smell of his breath almost made me retch.

"Boy, lead me straight up to him, and when I'm in view, cry out, 'Here's a friend for you, Bill.' If you don't, I'll do this," and with that, he twisted my arm hard again behind my back.

"Oh!" I cried out in pain. He released my arm from the twist but still hung on tight.

I opened the front door, and we walked in together.

There was the captain, having talked me into giving him a bottle, sitting at a table, none the wiser.

I said with a tremble in my voice. "Here's a friend for you, Bill."

The poor captain raised his eyes, and at one look the rum went out of him, and left him staring sober and quite ashen looking.

The captain made a movement to rise, but he didn't seem to have enough force left in his body.

"Now, Bill, sit where you are," said the beggar, as if he could see. "Hold out your left hand, Bill. Boy, take his left hand by the wrist, and bring it near to my right."

We both obeyed him to the letter, and I saw the blind man pass something from the hollow of the hand that held his stick into the palm of the captain's, which closed upon it instantly.

"And now that's done, with a witness," said the blind man; and at the words, he suddenly let go of me, and, with incredible accuracy and nimbleness, skipped out of the parlor and into the road, where, as I still stood motionless, I could hear his stick go tap-tap-tapping into the distance.

The captain looked at what was left in his palm. "Ten o'clock! " he cried. "Six hours. We'll do them yet," and he sprang to his feet. Even as he did so, he reeled, put his hand to his throat, stood swaying for a moment, and then, with a peculiar sound, fell from his whole height face-first to the floor.

A PLEA

I ran to him, calling out to my mother. But my haste was all in vain. The captain had been struck dead by a thundering apoplexy.

It is a curious thing to understand, for I had certainly never liked the man, though of late I had begun to pity him, but as soon as I saw that he was dead, I burst into a flood of tears. It was the second death I had known, and the sorrow of the first was still fresh in my heart.

My mother came running and stood in shock at the captain's body. I immediately told my mother all that I knew of the pirates, and perhaps I should have told her long before.

Mother sat down on the closest chair.

My heart was racing. "Mother, we can't stay here."

She shook her head. "This inn is all we have. What if we leave and they burn it to the ground? We'll have nothing to live on! Someone has to be here to protect it."

All around us, the cove seemed haunted by approaching footsteps. Between the dead body of the captain on the parlor floor and the thought of that detestable, blind beggar hovering near at hand and ready to return, I felt a chill settle on me.

I would have considered the captain's order to mount at once and ride for Doctor Dawe's, only there was no one at the inn tonight except for the two of us. It would have left mother alone and unprotected.

But at the moment, one of his shipmates could appear again. Indeed, it seemed impossible for either of us to remain much longer in the house. The coals in the fireplace collapsed, making me jump. The ticking of the clock reminded me that time was of the essence.

I thought of Ron and the other villagers. "We can go together to the village for help. It's not far."

She nodded. "Certainly, we can quickly bring back some men to help us protect what is ours."

We ran out at once into the gathering evening and the frosty fog. Luckily, the village was in the opposite direction from where the blind man had dashed.

It was already candlelit when we reached the hamlet, and I was cheered to see the yellow light in the doors and windows. We went straight to the church and rang the bell that sat along the church's fence. We didn't have to wait long before our neighbors began to appear.

"We need your help!" I said. "We have pirates that are coming to the inn, members of Captain Flint's crew. We need to protect it."

The silence that met us was overwhelming. Some turned back to their houses and disappeared into their candlelit homes. Others began whispering to each other. "Did he say Flint? The pirate?"

Ron and his father were among those standing quietly.

"Ron, please!"

Ron's father grabbed him by the shirt. "I don't need to lose my best farm hand to pirates."

The two of them walked away, and Ron didn't fight it. His father let go of his shirt, and the two of them continued to walk together. Ron didn't even look back.

I would have thought the men would have been ashamed of themselves — no soul would consent to return with us to the inn. The name of Captain Flint, though it was strange to me, was well enough known to some here and carried a great weight of terror. The more we told our troubles, the more — man, woman, and child—stepped backward and walked away.

A few men stayed.

One stepped forward, and I hoped.

"I was out on the road today when I saw strangers on the road. They looked like smugglers. It must be those pirates. They looked pretty formidable. Anyone would be crazy to go against pirates. But, I can ride to Dr. Dawe's and see if he can send some men."

Another man nodded. "I was fishing and saw a boat tied up in Kitt's Hole. That's where they must have come ashore."

While we could get several who were willing enough to ride to Dr. Dawe's, not one would help us defend the inn.

And it hit me most right then. If I ever revealed to the world that I was a girl and with so few avenues open to me, I would be expected to marry one of these cowards. The idea did not sit well with me.

My mother gave them a speech. She would not, she declared, lose money that belonged to her fatherless child; "If none of the rest of the rest of you dare," she said, "Andy and I dare. Back we will go, the way we came to collect what we can from our inn, and small thanks to you big, hulking, chicken-hearted men."

Of course, I couldn't let my mother go back alone.

But even then, no one would go along with us. One of them gave me a loaded pistol, in case we were attacked, and they promised to have horses ready saddled, in case we were pursued on our return; while one lad was to ride forward to the doctor's in search of armed assistance.

I felt exhausted from the past two days and devastated by Ron's capitulation to his father, but as we rode back toward the inn, I felt a bit of excitement, too. I brushed my hand over the pistol, ready to use it to protect my mother and me, but not necessarily the inn.

THE CHEST

A full moon was rising and the fog cleared, making everything as bright as day. If anyone was watching or looking for us, we'd be easy to spot. We could see our breath in the air and I wished we had brought our coats when we left.

Outside the Inn, I kept the pistol at the ready as we quietly walked along the hedges. We didn't hear or see anything to suggest that anyone was waiting inside.

We dashed inside, and to our relief, we soon closed the door of the inn behind us.

I slipped the bolt on the door, and we stood gasping for air in the dark, alone in the house with the dead captain's body. Then my mother lit the candle, and we looked at the captain.

He lay as we had left him, on his back, with his eyes open, and one arm stretched out.

"Draw down the blinds, Andy," whispered my mother; "they might come and watch from outside. And now," she said, when I had done so, "if there is any money in his chest, we should get it now, and collect anything else we need."

She went into the pirate's room while I lit more candles around the inn. She came out and stared back at the body. "The chest is locked. I'm sure the key is on his body, but I don't want to do it."

I went down on my knees at once and tried to close his eyes, but they stayed open, staring at the ceiling. On the floor close to his hand, there was a little round piece of paper, blackened on one side. I knew that this was the black spot, and picking it up, I found written on the other side in clear handwriting: "You have till ten tonight."

"He had until ten, mother," I said, and just as I said it, our old clock began striking the hour one by one.

I held my breath while I counted the strikes. The news was good. It was only eight PM.

"Now, Andy," she said, "that key."

I felt in his pockets, one after another. A few small coins, a thimble, a piece of pigtail tobacco bitten away at the end, his gully knife, a pocket compass, and a tinder box were all they contained, and I began to despair.

"Perhaps it's round his neck," suggested my mother.

Overcoming a strong repugnance, I opened up his shirt at the neck, and sure enough, there was a string. I cut it with his knife.

Pulling it away, I found a key. At this, I was filled with hope, and hurried to the little room where he had slept so long, and where his box had stood since the day I had brought it in.

Though the lock was stiff, I was able to unlock it and throw back the lid.

A strong smell of tobacco and tar rose from the interior, but nothing was to be seen on the top except a suit of very good clothes, carefully brushed and folded. They had never been worn. So I had been wrong about him owning any other clothes, but there was nothing for them now except to use them for his burial.

Mother sat next to me, and I handed her the items. She stacked them neatly, almost as if she expected the captain to need them.

Underneath the clothes was a quadrant, a rope, several sticks of tobacco, two braces of very handsome pistols that I set next to me, a piece of bar silver that my mother put in her bag, an old Spanish watch and some other trinkets of little value and mostly of foreign make, a pair of compasses mounted with brass, and five curious seashells. It seemed strange that a tough pirate would carry shells with him in his wandering, guilty, and hunted life.

Next, there was an old boat-cloak, whitened with

sea-salt on many a harbor. My mother pulled it up and set it on the pile, and there lay before us, the last things in the chest, a bundle tied up in oilcloth, and a canvas bag.

I lifted up the bag, and we both gasped when it made a sound like a jingle of gold. I was so excited, I poured out the contents to see what was inside.

The coins were from all countries and of all sizes — doubloons, and Louis d'ors, and guineas, and pieces of eight, and I know not what besides, all collected together at random.

We stared at them for a while. Not a fortune, but certainly enough for some kind of a start. We picked them up and were putting them back in the bag when I put my hand on Mother's arm, for I had heard in the silent, frosty air, a sound that brought my heart into my mouth—the tap-tapping of the blind man's stick upon the frozen road.

It drew nearer and nearer. Mother sat next to me, and I drew out the pistol given to me in the hamlet, as that was the only one I knew was loaded.

GOODBYES

We sat holding our breath while the blind man struck his stick sharply against the inn door, and then we heard the handle turn and the bolt rattle as he tried to enter.

Then there was a long time of silence. He was surely listening for any sound.

We didn't move, and I was worried even about the sound of my breath. How much could he hear through that door?

At last, the tapping on the road recommenced and, to our indescribable joy and gratitude, died slowly away again until it ceased to be heard.

I felt like I could breathe again.

"Let's go, Mother. I'm sure that the bolted door has made the blind man angry. It doesn't appear as if they are waiting until ten." But I was also very thankful that I had bolted it.

"We'll take what there is," she said, putting all of the coins in her bag and jumping to her feet.

I added the oilskin to my own sack. "I have to grab something." I ran upstairs and grabbed a few of my books, my coat, and then met her downstairs.

One moment, we left the candle by the empty chest, and the next, we had opened the door and were in full retreat.

We had not started a moment too soon. As we moved away from the inn, we could hear a loud whistle in the distance.

"Mother, this way." I led her to a low wall near the bridge on the road. It was our only way of hiding with the full moon shining so bright.

From here, we could hear the sound of footsteps running, and as we looked back in the direction of the Inn, a light tossing to and fro and still rapidly advancing, showed that one of the newcomers carried a lantern.

"My dear," said my mother, panting, "take the money and run on. I can't keep up this pace."

"Mother, I won't leave you."

I wished I had the sword of the princess I dreamed about, so I could go out and defend us if needed. But even if I had one, I wouldn't know how to use it. I held the pistol close. It would have only one shot. One shot against what looked like five or six men gathering around the inn.

If we survived, I would make sure that all the county knew of the village's cowardice and I sorely wished Ron would appear and come to our aid. My mother leaned against me.

There was a mist forming above the cove. I hoped it would spread to cover our escape.

Now that the men were closer, I could see them running. There were about eight of them, running hard, their feet beating out of time along the road, and up in front of the group was a man with a lantern.

Three men ran together, hand in hand, and I assumed that the middle man of this trio was the blind beggar, bent over in his grotesque form. The next moment, his voice proved to me that I was right.

"Knock down the door!" he yelled.

"Ay, ay, sir!" answered several at once, and they rushed to the inn's door. The lantern-bearer followed, and then I could see them pause, and hear speeches passed in a lower key, as if they were surprised to find the door open.

But the pause was brief, for the blind man again issued his commands. His voice sounded louder and higher, as if he were afire with eagerness and rage.

In, in, in!" he shouted, and cursed them for their delay.

Four or five of them obeyed at once, two remaining

on the road with the formidable beggar. There was a pause, and I could see the lantern moving around the inside of the Inn.

One of the men came to the door; his voice was that of Black Dog. "Bill's dead!"

"What? How'd he die? Did someone strike him down? Did they steal what we came for?"

"No. He looks to have gone just like Captain Flint."

"Damn him. Search him, some of you shirking lubbers, and the rest of you find his room and get the chest," the blind man cried.

I could hear their feet running through our house. Promptly afterwards, the window of the captain's room was thrown open with a slam, and a jingle of broken glass, and a man leaned out into the moonlight, head and shoulders, and addressed the blind beggar.

"Pew," he cried,"Someone's turned the chest out, and there's nothin' here for us."

"You mean it's gone?" roared Pew.

"We don't see it here, no how," returned the man.

"Here, you in the parlor, is it on Bill?" cried the blind man again.

At that, another fellow, probably the one who had remained to search the captain's body, came to the door of the inn. "Bill's been overhauled a'ready," said he,"nothin' left."

Pew's voice turned even colder. "It's these people of the inn— it's that young person, I'm sure of it."

I slinked back a little, knowing that they'd be looking for me in particular.

"I wish I had put his eyes out!" cried the blind man, Pew. "They were here not long ago— they had the door bolted when I tried it. Scatter lads, and find 'em. They can't be far."

"Sure enough, Pew. The candle they left is still lit," said the fellow from the window.

"Scatter and find 'em! Rout the house out and make sure they haven't hid it in the walls!" reiterated Pew, striking with his stick upon the road.

Then there followed a great to-do throughout our old inn, heavy feet pounding to and fro, furniture thrown over, doors kicked in, and the sound of walls being split.

Every destructive sound made my mother shake.

An Unfitting End

Finally, the men came out again, one after another, on the road, and declared that neither we nor the item they were searching for were to be found.

And just then, the same whistle that had concerned us on our way out of the inn rang through the area again. This time it was repeated twice.

"It's Novak giving us a warning," said one. "We have to leave, mates."

"Leave, Israel? You skulk," cried Pew. "Novak was a fool and a coward from the first— you shouldn't mind him. The inn folks must be close by; they can't be far. Scatter and look for them, dogs! And someone set fire to the inn. If they are hiding in there, the flames will get them moving."

"No," my mother said softly. "Everything I have of

your fathers is there." My mother started quietly sobbing.

I felt for my mother, but I also lamented my books! My precious books.

Pew was still appealing to his men to look for us. Two of his men were looking around the outside of the inn, but half-heartedly, I thought. They kept looking up the hill towards the village. The rest of the men stood irresolute on the road. Meanwhile, flames began appearing in the windows of the Inn.

"You could have your hands on thousands of coins, you fools, and you hang a leg! Israel, Nails! You'd be as rich as kings if you could find it, and you know it's here, and you both stand there skulking."

One man broke from the pack and started looking around the landscape in earnest, coming closer to us with every step.

"There wasn't one of you who dared face Bill, and I did it—a blind man! And I'm to lose my chance because of you! I'm to be a poor, crawling beggar, sponging for rum, when I might be rolling in a coach! If you had the pluck of a weevil in a biscuit, you would catch them still."

"Hang it, Pew, we'll get the gallows if we get caught!" grumbled Black Dog.

Pew began striking out with his stick, left and right, his stick making contact with a few of the men.

These, in their turn, cursed back at the blind

miscreant, threatened him in horrid terms, and tried in vain to catch the stick and take it from him.

Another sound came from the top of the hill on the side of the hamlet— the thundering of horses galloping. I thought maybe, at first, that Ron had finally found his courage.

A shot rang out, and the buccaneers turned at once and ran, separating in every direction, one seaward along the cove, one slant across the hill, and so on, so that in half a minute not a sign of them remained but Pew.

Him they had deserted, whether in sheer panic or out of revenge for his blows. Finally, he took a wrong turn and ran a few steps towards the village, crying: "Iron Tom, Black Dog, Novak," and other names, "you won't leave old Pew, mates— not old Pew!"

Just then, the noise of the horses topped the rise, and four or five riders came in sight in the moonlight and swept at full gallop down the slope. From their shadows, I could tell it was Dr. Dawe's men, not Ron.

At this Pew, turned with a scream, and ran straight for a ditch, into which he rolled. But he was on his feet again in a second, and made another dash, now utterly bewildered, right under the nearest of the coming horses.

The rider cried out and tried to turn his horse, but it was too late. Down went Pew with a cry that rang high into the night, and the four hoofs trampled and spurned him and passed by. He fell on his side, then gently collapsed upon his face, and moved no more.

I leaped to my feet and hailed the riders. One, tailing out behind the rest, was the young man from the village who had left to inform Dr. Dawe; the rest were indeed revenue officers.

"The pirates have scattered! You might find a few that way!" I pointed in the direction that most of them had gone and the revenue officers took off.

I helped my mother to her feet and we stared at the inn, now engulfed in flames. I had what I wanted, a way out of this life. But I still had tears in my eyes. I had no idea what mother and I would do now.

Not far behind the revenue officers was Doctor Dawe, leading two horses. He leaped off and ran up to us.

"My god! Ladies, are you alright?"

I glanced around to make sure there was no one around to hear him refer to me as a lady.

He repeated. "Are you all right?"

My mother shook her head and pointed at the inn as a wall collapsed.

I responded, "The pirates. They came for the captain and something that he had in his possession."

I wanted to tell him more, but the doctor grabbed a blanket, covered my mother's shoulders, and led her to a horse. "I know. I'm sure we'll figure things out. In the meantime, you'll come with me. Andy, get on the other horse and let's get your mother somewhere she can have some tea and put her feet up."

I got on the horse, took the reins of my mother's horse, and followed the Doctor along the road. I took one last look at the inn, my home of fifteen years. Would I ever return? I hoped not.

Hunted

As we sailed into Bristol at sunrise, I climbed up to the crow's nest and joined Dirk. "Do you see them?"

He lowered his spyglass. "Not today, Chen."

I looked out to the sea. Four days in a row, our lookouts had spotted a ship following us from London. I hoped we had lost them; I didn't have time for anything else right now.

We made dock in Bristol, and I sent Dirk to buy a ride to get to Kitt's Cove. He returned with horses and bad news.

"Captain Chen, I've heard that Pew and some of the others from the crew have already made their way to the cove. They could have delivered the black spot by now."

The last thing we needed was Pew getting involved.

I didn't trust him not to do something stupid. "We'll have to get there fast. If there's anything to find or anything left of Billy Bones, it will be our only link to the treasure."

I took Dirk, the few members of the old crew, and a few of my current men that I trusted, and told Ty that they were to wait for us. Someone I trusted needed to be on the ship.

I had never ridden a horse, but it was the fastest way to get across the countryside.

"Dirk, do you know the way?"

He nodded.

It took us a few minutes to get all the horses pointed in the right direction, but once we figured it out, we began galloping behind Dirk and his horse along the dusty road. The cold wind pushed at us as we rode, and I was glad of my warm coat.

We stopped a few times to rest our horses and have a bite of food.

The sun dipped down below the horizon as we rode, and the moon was light enough to see the dirt road even as a light fog rolled in.

I knew we were too late when I could see fire in the distance. I didn't need Dirk to lead me anymore, and I let my horse take the lead, but there was nothing to save.

Some people were riding away, but none looked like Billy. Meanwhile, the flames licked at the walls of a building, and the heat was too great to even approach.

There was nothing to find here, and a group of pirates hanging around would definitely attract attention.

"Damn it, Pew. He's left this place in shambles. Gregory!" I yelled for my cabin boy. He rode his horse up next to me. "I want you to go into town, pretend to be an orphan who needs help. Get me some information about what happened and if there's anything left of Bones or the map. I'll send Dirk or one of the others to meet you at this spot in two days. Understood?"

Gregory nodded and turned his horse toward the local town.

I handed my reins to Dirk and walked around the building, the remains of an inn from the sign, just in case there was anything to find. Pew's body was lying in the road. I had never liked Pew, but this was no way to leave a pirate.

"Dirk, get some men over here, and we'll take Pew's body back with us. Give him the burial at sea he deserves."

Dirk walked over and spat on the ground. "Damn, Pew." But did as I asked.

I walked down to the edge of the cove. The fire behind me echoed in the water. I leaped back when a dark blue tentacle reached out of the water.

Dirk called to me, "Captain Chen."

I backed away from the water and turned to address Dirk. when I glanced back, the tentacle was gone.

"Yes?"

"The body is secure."

"Fine, let's go."

I took one last look back, but there was no sign of whatever that had been. I got on my horse and led the way back, hoping that Gregory would find the news I wanted. That treasure was meant to be mine and the crew's. If there was any lead, I wanted it.

SPLENDER

As we left our inn burning to the ground behind us, I kept looking to the shadows. Was there a pirate hiding along our way? But after a few miles, I felt we had left all of them behind.

Mother was still sobbing, and my heart hurt for her. At least I was less concerned about the inn, but father's death was too fresh. I wasn't even sure she knew she was on a horse. All I could do for her was hold onto the reins of her horse and keep an eye out that she didn't fall off.

After we passed the village, I wished it were daylight so I could see the countryside. I had never been this far.

We eventually came to a set of open gates and up a long, leafless, moonlit avenue. There were expansive gardens on both sides of us, and beyond those were two long white buildings.

"Dr. Dawe, is this your property?" I asked, incredulous that anyone could own so much land.

"No. I don't think my house is large enough to accommodate both of you for any length of time. Squire Trelawney is the estate owner. He's a good man."

I nodded, though I knew the doctor couldn't see me. Meanwhile, my hands clenched the reins a little harder. The doctor I had known all my life. This squire I had only heard of. It was easy enough for some people to say someone was a good man, but could we really trust him not to be a brute to my mother or me?

The doctor assisted my mother down from her horse. She wiped her eyes and stood up straight as we approached the door. A servant opened the door almost immediately upon the doctor's knock and let us in.

The servant led us down a long hallway, his white wig bouncing with his walk, while we all walked in dog-tired steps. The worn but thick carpet swallowed the sound of our foot falls.

We walked into a great library, all lined with bookcases, books, and busts. I stopped in my tracks and turned a full circle to see so many books. But what kind of books would a squire have? Someone who ran an estate probably read a lot of boring things. Still, I longed to wander every shelf. It would take days to look through all of these books, and I would love every minute of it, if we were indeed to stay here for a time.

The servant led us up to an enormous fireplace where a man sat with his feet up on a cushioned stool. He stood as we approached. He was a tall man, over six feet high, and broad in proportion.

He had taken off his white wig, and it sat on the table beside him, probably thinking his day was done and no one would come visiting. His hair was dark and matted, his face was reddened and lined, and his eyebrows were very black and bushy.

His eyebrows suggested he was angry to see visitors so late at night. But he shook hands with the Doctor and smiled. His voice boomed across the room, echoing. "My friend, good evening to you. What good wind brings you here?" Although he did glance at us with a question in his eyes.

"Not so good, I'm afraid. Mrs. Hawkins and her da son have just lost their Inn to a set of Pirates. The thieves were searching for a pirate staying there and set the place on fire."

"What?" The squire looked affronted.

The doctor nodded. "I feel responsible. As soon as I knew of that rogue staying at the inn, I should have arrested him or at the very least routed him out. I'm sure he was nothing but trouble and now this." The doctor looked back at us.

The squire turned his eyes to us and waved at the

chairs around us. "Please, take a seat and tell me what happened." He turned to his servant. "Jenson, get us some hot tea with a little extra."

My mother sank back into one of the deep chairs and gave me a weak smile. I could see her exhaustion and could feel it in my own bones.

The doctor turned to me. I sank into my own chair, and told the tale of the captain, the squire leaned forward to listen, his great eyebrows dancing on his face from surprise to dismay. I told of the captain's arrival, his actions while he was a tenant, his falling over dead after receiving the black spot, my mother and I going to the locals for assistance, and then our returning to the inn. I ended with, "We thought we could do something to protect the inn, but in the end, there were just too many of them, and they had murder in their hearts."

The doctor nodded. "I'm glad that you were smart enough to hide when the pirates came. And, as for the captain, the world is a better place without him, I'm sure. I knew he couldn't resist the urge for rum, but to die at the moment that he should have left the inn. What terrible timing."

"There's more to the story," I added and touched the parcel inside my bag that I had taken from the Captain's sea chest. But before I could continue, the servant entered with the tea and one of the revenue officers.

"Mr. Taylor," the doctor greeted him.

Meanwhile, Jenson served us tea. I realized that the 'extra' was the addition of brandy, which sent welcome heat down my throat and the heat from the cup into my cold hands.

Mr. Taylor stood straight and stiff and started with the grim death. "One of the pirates ran right in front of my horse. There was no way to avoid him, and I have to report that he is dead. We then attempted to follow the fellows, sir. However, they had gone in different directions. After our attempts, we came back together. I had heard rumors of a lugger in Kitt's Hole, a few miles from the inn."

"We rode as fast as we could to Kitt's Hole. If you've never been there, well, it's a dark and wooded cove with a narrow cliff trail that leads down to the water. We left our horses tied up and hoped that the pirates weren't behind us. We crept down in darkness, groping along the wet stone wall to find the trail, looking out for ambushes all along the way." Here, Mr. Taylor used his hands as if he were back on the trail, and we all leaned forward a bit more.

I wanted so badly to know that they had caught them.

THE ESCAPE

"We could see a lugger in the water, moving toward the cove opening. I hailed the boat, and a voice replied. 'Step out into the moonlight so we can see you better.' I ignored the request; of course, I wasn't about to be in their sights in case they had a gun ready at hand. Good that I did, as a bullet whistled close by my arm. The lugger doubled its speed and disappeared. There was no way we could catch up to them."

We all leaned back in our chairs. I was disappointed that none of them would have to answer for their destruction.

He put his hands in the air, "I am sorry sir that we could do nothing more."

"Mr. Taylor," said the squire, "you are a very noble

fellow. And as for riding down that atrocious miscreant, I regard it as an act of virtue, sir, like stamping on a cockroach. Jenson, forget giving him tea, give him a draft of rum."

Mr. Taylor shook his head. "It's been a late night, squire. My men and I need to ride on to home."

"Sure enough."

Mr. Taylor nodded and turned to go, never once acknowledging mother or me, just the doctor and the squire. Was it not our inn that had been burned to the ground?

My mother got up and moved to be in front of the fire. Her tears had dried, and she was back to herself. "Sirs, I appreciate your help, but I'm sure my son is as exhausted as I am. Could we have a room to rest?"

The squire nodded. "Certainly, Jenson, show them to some rooms in the West wing."

The unknown package would have to wait until tomorrow. I would bring it up now, but between the late night and the alcohol in my tea, I could feel exhaustion seeping into every layer of my being.

We followed Jenson with a candle in his hand along the hallway and up a set of wide stairs. He finally indicated a door. I started to follow my mother in, but he held up his hand. "No, young sir. Your room is here." He pointed across the hallway.

Our own rooms. It made sense as this house was so

big, but it felt opulent to be offered my own room as a visitor to someone else's home.

I nodded to my mother and walked into my own room, closing the door behind me. There was a single candle sitting on a dresser. It reflected in the mirror, making the room glow.

I tossed my hat onto a chair and washed my face in the water basin. Peering at my reflection, I could easily see my feminine details: soft cheekbones and my breasts pushing out at my boyish clothes. I would have to bind them in the future if I continued to dress like a boy.

A thrill went through me. With my father no longer here to enforce that rule, I could be whatever I wanted to be. Hide as a boy or show myself for who I really am?

I took the candle with me to the bed, blew it out, and lay down on top of a cloud of goose down blankets and mattresses.

I drifted off to sleep in seconds, dreaming of pirates and princesses with long gowns, and a creature that glowed in the dark of the ocean.

The next morning, I woke to find myself still lying on top of the bed, my hand still holding onto the candle base, and my clothes still on. All of which was good as Jenson opened the door.

"Young sir, breakfast is served in the dining room." He dropped some clothes on a chair. "These might fit you, sir. I've done my best to estimate your size."

Behind him, a woman walked in and filled the wash-basin with steaming water. The two of them walked out and closed the door behind them.

I sat up and looked around the room, but instantly felt the soreness in my legs from horse riding. I moved stiffly off the bed and dipped my hands in the water. It felt good. The squire was rich indeed to send up hot water and clothes for me.

I stripped out of my clothes, washed up as best I could, and threw on the clean clothes. For now, I'd pretend to be a boy until I didn't have to anymore.

They were a little too big, which was much better than being too small and possibly showing off more of my girlish figure.

I put my bag over my shoulder. I didn't know what was in the package I had taken, but I wasn't going to leave it anywhere until I knew what it was and if it was worth all the trouble the pirates had put us up to.

I knocked on my mother's door.

"One moment," she replied.

When she opened the door, I didn't recognize her. She had put her hair up and was in the fanciest dress I had ever seen. I suddenly felt an urge to match her. Oh, to wear a fancy dress!

"Isn't it beautiful?" she asked. "I've never seen anything like it." She turned in a circle to show it to me. Shades of blue, and the skirt was puffed into a bell shape. "When the maid was doing my hair, she told me that this is what all the fashionable women are wearing and that the squire keeps a whole room of clothes for visitors." Her face glowed with pride and it was the happiest I had ever seen her.

It also worried me. We were so spoiled here, but what would become of us next?

THE MYSTERY

My stomach growled, and my mother laughed.

"Come on, Andy. Let's go eat."

We followed the scent of food to an expansive dining room. A table twenty feet long was in the middle of the room, and a sideboard along the wall was covered with dishes of food.

The doctor, the squire, and a young boy whom I had never met were already dining. I stepped up to a plate and started to pick it up when one of the servants stopped my hand.

"No, sir. You can sit, and I'll bring you your food."

I nodded, feeling a little guilty that someone else would be doing the work, but sat next to the doctor.

The boy sitting next to the squire was eating his

breakfast as if he had never eaten before. The squire noticed my stare.

"We have young Gregory here. He's been orphaned, and one of the village women brought him up this morning. Asked me to see him to the city and the orphanage there."

Mother sat next to the boy. "Squire Trelawney, I can't thank you enough for your hospitality."

Servants set plates of food in front of us at the same time. The squire was eating with gusto and was too busy to notice our looks of surprise and delight. "Oh, you both are quite welcome. This place is too quiet by myself. I welcome visitors, and you both are welcome to stay here as long as you must until you figure out your future."

I felt a small weight lift off my shoulders.

"How do you feel this morning, Andy?" the doctor asked.

"A bit fatigued, sir." And indeed, every muscle was aching from the night's adventure.

I focused on my food for a while, as did the others. On my plate was a piece of chocolate, two muffins, dollops of butter and jam, a large piece of ham and two slices of bacon. Then a bowl of porridge was set down next to that, and a cup of tea.

It only took a short while for me to clean my plate, bowl, and cup.

Jenson stood next to me. "Would you like more, young sir?"

I shook my head and let him take my plates. "I couldn't eat anymore. My compliments to the cook."

He smiled and nodded.

Mr. Trelawney was leaning back, a fresh cup of tea in his hand. His white wig was now on, and his black eyebrows looked even more out of place.

Last night I had dreamed of pirates, but also of that imaginary creature, I had to ask. "Mr. Trelawney, I'm wondering if you know anything of mysterious creatures of the sea? The pirate spoke of one called a luminary, something that could glow even under water."

Gregory finally looked up from his now second plate of food, as if he was going to say something, but went back to eating.

The squire nodded. "Well, young Andy, I'm a world-traveled man, and I have indeed seen many a creature. I can't name any of them, though. However, there are a few books in the library - journals from seagoing men. Do you know how to read?"

From the way he spoke, I had a feeling that he had never seen a sea creature. I nodded.

"Good man. Reading is the key to knowledge."

Gregory nodded, "I can read a little too, sir."

The squire patted the boy's head. "Good for you, lad. Well, while you are here, feel free to check the library. There aren't many sea-faring books, mind you. Many a man that goes to sea doesn't know how to read or write. But the few that I've been able to find are in my library." He sat up straighter. "You are welcome to peruse the selection while you are here, but do make sure to have clean hands. I wish my library to last for ages and to bequeath it to the world."

I nodded, my fingers tingling with the idea of touching all those books! I took a deep breath and moved on to the next important subject. "Thank you. I look forward to that."

"There is something else. The pirates weren't just looking for Billy Bones. They were looking for something the captain had, and I think that I have it in my possession." I removed the oilskin package from my bag and set it on the table.

All eyes turned to the space on the table with the mysterious package.

THE MAP

As I started to open the package, Mr. Trelawney stopped me. "First, tell me more about the pirate."

"He said he'd been a member of Captain Flint's crew," I responded.

The squire's bushy eyebrows raised high on his forehead.

The Doctor nodded and looked at the squire. "You have heard of this Flint, I suppose?"

"Heard of him, you say!" exclaimed the squire, standing up from his chair. "He was the bloodthirstiest buccaneer that sailed. Blackbeard was a child to Flint. The Spaniards were so prodigiously afraid of him that I was sometimes proud he was an Englishman. I've seen his top-sails myself, off Trinidad, and the cowardly son of a rum-puncheon that I sailed with put his back - his back, sir, to the pirates and ran."

"I've heard of him myself, in London," said the doctor, lighting his pipe. "But the point is, did he have money?"

"Money?" replied the squire. "Have you heard the stories of him and his vast hidden treasure? Besides, what were these villains after but money? What do they care for but money? For what would they risk their rascal carcasses but for money?"

"That we shall soon know," replied the doctor. "What I want to know is this: Supposing that Andy has some clue to where Flint buried his treasure, will that treasure amount to much?"

"Amount, sir!" Cried the squire. "It will amount to this: if we have the clue you talk about, I'll fit out a ship in Bristol dock, and take you and Andy here along, and we'll have that treasure if I search a year."

My heart skipped a happy beat. An adventure on a ship!

"Very well," said the doctor. "Now, then, if Andy is agreeable, we'll open the packet."

I nodded and stood. Mother, the squire, and the doctor came over to watch over my shoulder. Gregory continued eating, but I could tell he was listening intently. I mean, who wouldn't?

I tried to unroll the bundle, but realized it was sewn together.

"Jenson," I asked, "do you have a sharp knife?"

Jenson quickly delivered a knife, and I cut the stitches and rolled it out. It contained two things - a book and a sealed paper.

"May I?" The doctor asked as he reached for the book. I nodded.

The book's cover was dark brown with spots that could have been water stains. The papers inside were crisp and crinkled loudly as the doctor turned the pages.

He set it on the table so we could all see. On the first page, there were only some scraps of writing, such as a man with a pen in his hand might make for idleness or practice.

The next ten or twelve pages were filled with a series of entries that included numbers. On the twelfth of June, 1745, for instance, a sum of seventy pounds had plainly become due to someone, and there was nothing but six crosses to explain the cause. In a few cases, to be sure, the name of a place would be added, as "Offe Jamaica"; or a mere entry of latitude and longitude as "62° 17' 20", 19° 2' 40."

The record lasted nearly twenty years, the amount of the separate entries growing larger as time went on, and at the end, a total was made out after five or six wrong additions, and these words were appended, "Bones, his pile."

"A total of his hoard of money?" asked Dr. Dawe.

"Certainly," cried the squire, taking the book from the doctor. "This is the black-hearted hound's account-book. These crosses stand for the names of the ships or towns that they sank or plundered. The sums are the scoundrel's share, and where he feared an ambiguity, you see, he added something clearer. 'Offe Jamaica,' now; you see, here was some unhappy vessel boarded off that coast. God help the poor souls that manned her."

"Right!" said the doctor. "See what it is to be a traveller."

There was little else but a few bearings of places noted in the blank leaves toward the end, and a table for reducing French, English, and Spanish moneys to a standard value.

"Thrifty man," said the doctor. "He wasn't the one to be cheated."

Thrifty, I thought, more like miserly.

"And look at that total!" The squire looked on. "It's more money than I've ever had. We could split it a hundred times and still be very well off."

I could feel the energy in the room turn to excitement.

I rolled out the paper on the table. It had been sealed in several places with wax and a thimble; the very thimble, perhaps, that I had found in the captain's pocket. I opened the seals with great care, and there came out the map of an island.

The title on the top said *Grimwood Isle*, and it included latitude and longitude, soundings, names of hills, bays, and inlets, and every particular that would be needed to bring a ship to a safe anchorage upon its shores.

It was marked as nine miles long and five across, shaped like a fat dragon standing up, with two harbors and a hill in the centre part marked "The Spyglass." There was a drawing of a sea creature with giant teeth, which I spent some time examining, and there was a square labeled "old fort"; but, above all, two crosses of black ink—both were close together with a note - "*10 paces 'tween the two. Bulk of treasure here.*"

On the back, the same hand had written this further information:

"*Grimwood Isle is found E.S.E. and by E. of Skeleton Island.*
Approach from the other island if you know what's good for ye.
Commence at the tall tree atop the Spy-Glass shoulder.
From the wood, take the South-East course, but mark this well: once you descend into the canyon, the black sand is the only honest ground.
Come at last to a black crag, with a face wore into it by wind and years. It keeps watch o'er the pass.

*From the gate, proceed ten strides hence. There lies
the first cache.
The silver bars lie another ten fathoms beyond.
J.F."*

That was all, but brief as it was, it sent a chill down my back at the idea of the money we could find.

"Dawe," said the squire, "you will give up your medical practice at once. Tomorrow I start for Bristol. In three weeks - three weeks! We'll have the best ship, sir, and the choicest crew in England. Andy shall come as cabin-boy. You'll make a famous cabin-boy, Andy."

He continued, stomping around the room as he spoke. "You, Dawe, are the ship's doctor; I am the admiral. We'll take Cooper, Joyce, and Hunter. We'll have favorable winds, a quick passage, and not the least difficulty in finding the spot, and money to eat — to roll in—to play duck and drake with ever after."

"Trelawney," said the doctor, "I'll go with you. As for Andy, I'm not sure this is a venture for him to take." The doctor was trying to protect me because of my sex, but I didn't want this.

I stepped forward, visions of adventure flashing in my mind. "I'll go, and indeed be the best cabin boy. Don't worry about me, Doctor. I'm as tough as the rest of you."

My mother put a hand on my shoulder and whispered only to me, "We'll talk about this later."

"Indeed!" answered the squire. "You had the mettle to go back to your Inn, full well knowing the pirates were coming. You'll do."

"There's only one problem," said the doctor.

We all stopped and looked uncertainly at him.

The doctor continued, "There's one man I'm afraid of."

"And who's that?" Asked the squire. "Name the dog, sir!"

"You," replied the doctor, and let the squire stand for a moment in silence. All of us were wondering what he meant. "You cannot hold your tongue, and we are not the only men who know of this treasure. These fellows who attacked the inn last night —bold, desperate blades, for sure— and the rest who stayed aboard that lugger, and more, I dare say, not far off, are one and all, through thick and thin, bound that they'll get that money."

The doctor leaned forward. "We must none of us go alone till we get to sea. Andy and I shall stick together in the meantime, and perhaps I can spend some time teaching him to use a sword or knife. You, squire, will take Joyce and Hunter when you ride to Bristol, and, from first to last, not one of us must breathe a word of what we've found."

"Dawe," returned the squire, "you are always in the right of it. I'll be as silent as the grave."

PIRATE'S PLAN

I grabbed an apple from the galley and headed to my favorite place on the ship. Climbing up into the crow's nest always gave me the feeling of freedom, like when I used to climb out the window of my mother's apartment. That felt like it was ages ago, but it was only a few months ago that I had relived my favorite pastime.

The sun was setting and I preferred this harbor to Bristol. It was always noisy in Bristol, but here in a quiet bay, we could stay here and wait for Gregory without prying eyes. Hopefully, Dirk would have Gregory with him tonight and maybe some news.

I sat on the edge of the nest and looked out over the waves. There was no mysterious ship following us, for now.

Below, I could see a different kind of tagalong. I had

spotted it the last two days that we had been anchored here. A large, dark octopus. It hovered near the aft of the ship. I was sure it was of the same tentacles that I had seen back at the cove, but what had brought it miles away to here? And what had it been doing at the inn during the fire?

So far, I had seen a mermaid, even a glowing squid, but this was my first octopus. It, however, never came out of the water. It hovered just underneath the surface, and I swore it was watching me.

I waved at it, but it didn't respond. I finally lowered my hand, feeling a bit foolish.

I sighed as I heard one of the many arguments among the men start again. My new hires were trustworthy and had signed an agreement stating that no one would be killed unless absolutely necessary. But bringing some of Flint's old crew on board had created a conflict. I owed something to Flint's men, but the two didn't mix. Flint's crew was of a different breed. Murder was in their blood.

I could hear Buck, his voice going high as he got more upset. "Just because you're a visitor on this ship doesn't mean that you get out of work. You can swab the deck same as anyone else."

I knew without hearing the voice that he had to be talking to the laziest of Flint's crew, Black Dog.

Then came Dog's voice, clear as day. "Swab the deck? That's work for the cabin boy."

Buck replied, "The cabin boy is out doing more work than you'll do in your whole bloody life."

I climbed down from the crow's nest. "Black Dog, if you want a share of the treasure, you'll listen to Buck."

Black Dog's eyes narrowed and his lips curled into distaste. He turned away, I assumed to start cleaning.

"You know he'll just pretend to swab, right?" I said to Buck.

Buck nodded. "I know, Captain. The lazy-good-for-nothing. But I can't fathom letting him lie in his bunk while the rest of us are getting the ship ready."

I nodded.

He touched me on the shoulder, then stepped back. "I don't think you should take any of these black-hearted men with you, Captain. I don't think they can be trusted."

"I know what you mean, Buck. But I owe these men. Not all of them are black-hearted. Besides, there's no way I'd be able to go after the treasure without them; they'd cut out my heart and feed it to the fish. I'll keep my eye on them. The absolute worst of the lot I wouldn't allow on this ship, so ...

"You have a luck about you, Captain. I hope it keeps you safe."

Speaking of black hearts, Israel Hands came running. "Captain, Dirk is approaching. He's got someone with him."

I went to the railings, and in fact, there was Dirk,

riding along the beach on a horse, with Gregory sitting behind him.

"Buck, send the boat over."

Buck and a few of the men lowered the boat into the water and rowed over to pick up Dirk. I went to my cabin to wait to hear what Gregory had to say - not wanting everyone to be in on the conversation.

While I waited, I sharpened my father's sword.

Yīngwǔ came and sat on my shoulder. "Walk the Plank! Walk the Plank!" he crooned in my ear.

Gregory and Dirk came straight to my cabin, and they closed the door on a crowd of pirates who were hoping to hear more.

"Gregory, any word?" I asked.

He nodded. "Aye, Captain. Billy Bones is dead, his body left in the burning inn. They have a map and a book from Billy Bones. They plan to go to Bristol and get ready a ship." Gregory had a bag over one shoulder, and I wondered if he had plundered on his way back.

"What's in the bag?"

He pulled out a cooked chicken, golden and dripping with juice. "I have three of them!" He said it like it was incredulous that anyone would cook three chickens at a time. "They cooked them for lunch. I thought it might be enough for everyone."

I laughed. "Gregory, you have good instincts. Take them to the galley and we'll add them in for dinner. Who are these people going after our treasure?"

"The innkeeper's son, a squire, and a doctor."

It sent my blood boiling. How could these people think the treasure was for them? I had worked for that loot. My mother had worked hard all her life and I wanted to set her up in style. They didn't deserve any of it. My shipmates and I did.

"Plans, Captain?" Dirk asked.

"Trying to get the map and book now would be difficult. Instead, we'll sail for Bristol and see how many of us we can get on board their ship. At some point, we can take it over, and everything will be ours."

"Weigh anchor!" Yīngwǔ said.

"You heard the parrot," I said. "Dirk, tell them to weigh anchor. We head for Bristol again."

CHANGE

That afternoon, the squire had already left for Bristol, so it left fewer of us to sit at the lunch table.

Jenkins came to find me. "Andy, sir, a young man, Ron, is at the door and would like to see you."

I was surprised Ron had come all the way out here. "Please, tell him I'm not interested in a visit."

Jenkins nodded and went back to the door.

The doctor was busy smoking his pipe and reading his paper.

My mother shook her head. "I know you're mad at him, but he is your friend."

"Mad? Mother, I'm more than mad. He deserted us when we needed him."

"But would one young man have made a difference?"

"His courage might have encouraged others. Or at least with his help, we might have been able to leave the inn sooner and had been far out of the reach of the pirates."

The cook came out and wrung her hands. "I'm so sorry, but the cooked chickens have gone astray."

"Astray?" my mother asked.

The cook shrugged, "I roasted a right group of chickens, but the oven is empty now. I don't understand who would have taken them."

My mother stood. "I'll come with you and see what we can pull together."

The cook let off a loud sigh and led her to the kitchen.

I asked the doctor, "Have you seen Gregory?"

He grimaced. "I was to take him with me to London, but I couldn't find him anywhere. And yes, if you're thinking he might have absconded with the food, you're probably right."

I hoped the orphan was okay.

The doctor stood. "There's no need for me to wait. I'll check the house one more time for Gregory. I have to find a physician to take over my practice. I know the squire would suggest I scrap it, but there are people here who need a doctor, and who knows if we'll come away with any treasure. I need to know there's still a practice to come back to."

"Cooper, the squire's gamekeeper, will take charge of the house. See that you mind him."

Seemingly realizing that he could talk freely since we were alone, he added, "I support you going on this trip, Andy. But be aware that there will be considerable danger. Don't trust anyone with your secret, and while you have the time, take advantage of anything in this house to learn to protect yourself." He whirled out of the room and suddenly it felt very quiet, and I felt more alone.

Mother came back, wiping her hands on a towel. "We'll have a stew out soon. Where's the doctor and the orphan?"

"Gone, the both of them."

"Ah, well." She sat down across from me, and I knew it was coming. "We just lost your father. Why would you think you could leave on a ship without asking me first? I don't want to lose you, too."

"If I don't go, and they find the treasure, who's to say they'll give any to us, even though we found the map?"

Mother looked off in the distance. "Any money would be a help. But what are you going to do about protecting yourself?"

I had been thinking about this. "I have the pistols."

"But pistols have to be reloaded, Andy. You need something more practical and, well, deadly. It's a shame we couldn't have saved the captain's sabre from the fire."

I shook my head. "The sabre would have been too heavy."

The cook entered with a tureen of stew, and we ended our conversation.

But I kept thinking about that as I ate. I'd come up with something, I just didn't know how long I had before the squire called for me to join him in Bristol.

WOOD CUTTING

After lunch, I went to the library and pulled everything that had to do with the sea and piled it up on a table. I was reading a journal from a sailor, I felt I was with the sailor sitting up in the crow's nest seeing pirates in the distance, when Cooper entered the room.

In his thick Irish accent, he said, "There ya' are. Ya won't learn much from a book, lad. Come with me."

I set the book down and followed him out of the house. We walked down a rough path to a shack hidden by trees. I didn't want to tell him I was cold, so I followed on. Next to the shack was a pile of logs.

"The woodsman is sick, taken to his bed with a fever. I need someone to chop wood, and you're just the lad."

"What? I don't know how."

Cooper elbowed me in my shoulder, almost knocking me over. "Lad, you're as frail as a spider's skein. Cutting firewood will put meat on your bones, and you'll need it if you're going to be on the seas."

He turned and walked away.

"Can you show me how?"

"Sorry, lad. There have been some poachers on the property. I've got to do muh occupation."

"How much should I do?"

"All of it!" He called over his shoulder.

I looked at the wood, piled higher than me. I hoped he was joking. It would take me months to do all that.

Father had usually done any wood chopping for the inn, and in the last two years, he had hired some young men from the village. I had seen them cut the wood small enough to fit into the fireplace and then split it into chunks. They'd swing out the axe, slam it into the wood, then take a few more swings to break it up.

I picked a log that wouldn't require me to cut; I just had to split it, but when I went to pick it up, it was too heavy for me. I dragged it with all my strength closer to where several implements were lying.

There was a type of flat cutting tool with a pick on the opposite side. That seemed too dangerous. I picked up the axe and whacked at the piece. The axe bounced off and flew out of my hands, towards the woodpile.

This was going to take a while.

I tried again, and this time the axe ended up buried in the dirt.

I moved my log to a wide tree stump to serve as a work area, then switched to the heavier axe.

It took a few more logs to realize that hammering the axe, once lodged in the log, was the best method of splitting. At least this warmed me up.

By the time I went in for dinner, my arms and hands were so tired and blistered I could barely pick up my fork, but that didn't stop me from eating almost a complete chicken and everything else my mother put on my plate.

I retrieved the sailor's journal from the library, dragged myself to my room, washed up in the clean, hot water in the basin, and lay in bed. I found I couldn't hold the book up, so I gave up and blew out the candle.

POACHERS

The first week, I spent every waking moment either chopping firewood or memorizing the map to Grimwood Isle. In the evenings, I would sit by candlelight and read about sea adventures until the candle died out, and I would fall asleep in the chair.

This morning, I could swear the pile of wood to cut was growing bigger, thinking that the gamekeeper was trying to trick me, but I wasn't sure. It certainly felt like I would be here for an eternity.

I added a new piece of wood to my working tree stump and grabbed the axe to start splitting it. I took a swing, better than my first swing, but it only cut into the wood the width of one of my fingers.

There was a laugh from the woods.

I rolled my eyes. The gamekeeper was having a laugh at me.

"Look at this kid. Thinks he's a woodsman."

The rough voice immediately made me think of the pirates. I whirled around. Had they found me here?

But no, the three men who stood on the far side of the clearing were no pirates. They wore simple breeches and shirts, and one carried a rifle. The poachers!

"You need to get off this land," I said in no uncertain terms.

There was another laugh from the group, from the man carrying the rifle. "The fancy man that lives here can do with a bit of prunin' of his animal stock. That includes his servants." He stepped toward me, and the others were right behind him.

"Stay back!" I yelled, more in the hopes that someone on the grounds would hear me. I still held the axe in my hand.

"What, are goin' ta use your axe on me? Ah, you fancy little lad, we could use you for sport, maybe you should start running." He laughed again.

My heart was pounding out of my chest. These men were just as bad as pirates. I lifted the axe over my head and used both hands to throw it as hard as I could at his head. It hit him in the chest and then fell to the ground.

He looked surprised, his hand went to his chest, and he looked at the small amount of blood that came away.

The cut wasn't enough to stop him, but just enough to make him look back at me with murder in his eyes. "Well, then. I'll make sure you die a slower death for that, lad."

A gunshot rang out, and I jumped. The rifle-carrying man fell to the ground, and the other two scattered into the woods. Cooper came running through the clearing.

"Come on, lad. Get that axe and follow muh."

I grabbed it and ran with Cooper.

"We got to get those two rascals, or they'll come back again. Take up where their ruffian friend left off."

We ran hard through the woods. I wasn't even sure if Cooper knew their trail. Then we came around a tree, and there they were. They had turned in their tracks and were ready to fight.

One ran up to Cooper and attempted to knife him, but Cooper smacked him in the head with the butt of his empty rifle. The other came running up to me, with his own knife out. I held the axe long-ways with both my hands and blocked his knife thrust. I stared at the sharp end of the knife, only inches from my eyes, while I used what muscles I could to hold it back. The young man was groaning under the strain of pushing it towards my face.

WEAPONS

The next thing I knew, Cooper was swinging his rifle down on my attacker. The young man and the knife fell to the ground, and I took a step back.

"Impressive young man, Andy" Cooper said. "You'll make a good and smart sailor yet. Now, go fetch the cart."

By the time I returned with the cart, Cooper had tied up the two men. I helped him pick up the unconscious boys and set them in the cart.

"That's enough wood cutting for today, Andy. I'll take these two to the jailhouse and have someone fetch the man's body. I'll see you at dinner tonight."

I nodded and walked back to the house. On my way, I stopped to look at the wound I had left on the dead man. The axe had left a two-inch gash on his chest. It seemed like a good weapon if I could gain strength in my arms.

I ignored Cooper's suggestion of stopping for the day. All the wood chopping was making me stronger, and if I wanted to survive a treasure hunt on the sea, I would have to be stronger for it.

I did go into dinner a little early. I asked Jenkins if I could possibly have a bath. He didn't even raise an eyebrow. I felt awful for asking, knowing that someone would have to carry hot water from the kitchen to the bathroom in the hall.

"Certainly, young sir. You are a visitor to the estate. You will have a bath."

I waited in the hallway while two servants came back and forth with the water.

"Mr. Andy," said one of them, "you can undress and get in the bath. No need to be shy. We can work around you."

"No, thank you," I assured her. "I'll wait." After the tub was full, I made sure to let them both know that there was no need to come back. I ran to my room and grabbed up all the clothes I needed as well as a dress I had found in the squire's visitor closet. It was just for trying on, but I couldn't resist.

I luxuriated in the now warm bath, feeling the week of sweat and grime fall away. I washed my hair and then sunk up to my face.

When the water was as cold as the marble, I finally

got out. I dried off and then shook out the dress. It was the most beautiful shade of periwinkle blue, and white lace at the end of the sleeves. Normally worn with a corset and a petticoat, but I had none of those. I put it on, and in the mirror, I transformed into a young woman, me. Too bad I couldn't be both strong and feminine, but maybe I'd find a way in the future to balance that out.

For now, I'd choose to be a young man.

I reluctantly took off the dress and changed into my boy's clothes. I put the dress back in the visitor's closet, hoping that when I returned from the sea adventure, perhaps the squire would let me take it when I finally shared who I really was.

At dinner, the gamekeeper recounted my deeds to my mother, whose eyes grew wide.

"Really?" she asked.

I nodded.

"It sounds like you'll do well," she said.

After dinner, Cooper asked me to follow him to the study. On the table were two axes and a garden tool that had a short, straight handle and a curved blade.

"I saw you throw that axe. If it had been sharper, it would have been able to cut off his arm. I've sharpened the one you were using, and I've had the blacksmith make one just a little lighter and even sharper. The blade is thinner, less for wood cutting and more for cutting skin and bone. It's also a slightly different shape."

I could see the difference in the two axes, and I picked up the one with the thinner blade. "I can feel the difference." The keen edge of the fighting axe was also longer.

"Right. The squire told me to get you ready for this adventure, and I expect we will be safe enough, but I want you to be ready with these, just in case. I wouldn't want it said I sent a lad out into the world without some form of protection."

"What about this?" I picked up the curved blade.

"That's a sickle. Usually it's for the farmer, but the blacksmith had this up on his wall, and I thought it perfect for you. The axe isn't going to be good for close up, the sickle is altogether different. It's light enough for you to manage."

I picked it up. It was certainly lighter than the axe and lighter than any sword would be. "Thank you, Cooper."

"Ya welcome, Lad. As soon as I have time, we're heading into town together to gather clothes and other supplies."

STORIES

Another week had gone by since the poachers and I found myself having even more unusual dreams. Sometimes I dreamt of pirates and sometimes about Grimwood Isle.

In my dreams, I had climbed a thousand times to the tall hill called spy-glass. Sometimes the island was thick with locals, chasing us. Other times it was empty save for our group and dangerous animals.

That night, I dreamt I was on a ship approaching Grimwood Isle. Before we could reach the island, a sea creature arose out of the ocean, its teeth as big as my head.

I held up my axe and sickle and yelled.

The creature laughed so hard it fell backwards into the ocean.

I woke with a start. "That was rude."

I got up, got dressed, and went out to the woodpile. It was very early morning, the moon was just beginning to dip down, and the sun was touching the other side of the sky, soon to rise. I worked until daybreak and headed in for breakfast.

I walked into the kitchen, famished. I found my mother, surrounded by the women servants, teaching them to make bread. She was known for her bread far and wide. The scent of it permeated the kitchen. I snatched up a loaf that was near at hand and hurried out, just in case anyone had an idea of making me leave it behind.

I sat at the dining table with my latest find, a book by a pirate. I took a big bite of bread and leaned closer as I read the messy handwriting. He had written a few journals about attacking ships, but this particular section was a list of sea creatures.

This here is a compilation of my knowledge of the creatures of the sea especially written for that barmaid in Bristol who said there was no such thing as a Mermaid. And thanks to my pal, Fred, whom translated my words onto paper.

- Luminary. First encountered at Jamaica. They hate being in a cage and will spend a lot of time trying to escape. They will glow for several hours after you feed them - they love fish. Baby sea serpent? Unknown.

- Selkie - Seen along the Scotts coast. They look like seals but can transform into humans if they remove their seal skin.

- Selkie? - I put forth a question here as I'm not sure what to call what I've witnessed along the English coast. Several times I've spotted a dark octopus and there's been word that it can transform into a man.

- Kraken. Rarely has anyone seen the Kraken and lived, but I was on a ship in the Indian Ocean when across the way we saw it heave out of the water and take the unlucky ship that was next to it down into the deep. We sailed as fast as we could away, but you never know where that blasted demon of the deep will appear. It had enormous tentacles like an octopus, but a mouth the size of a small island that could crunch a ship in half.

-Mermaids - Beautiful creatures with tails and the upper body of a woman. Be warned: They are as friendly as the Kraken.

-Sirens - I think that Sirens are mermaids who can sing. They look the same - a tail of shining scales like a dragon, an upper body of a woman. They sing, and men will go to their deaths if they don't fight the urge.

-Sea Serpents - Great snakes under the ocean. I've seen one from a distance that had the head of a dragon, but no wings. They can scurry along the top of the ocean and take down a boat in seconds.

-Ghosts - I speak of ghosts because even though they might exist on land, I've only ever encountered them on the sea.

I reread the list. This man was saying that these creatures truly existed. I pulled out the map again. The image of the beast around Grimwood Isle looked just like his description of the sea serpent.

The delivery of breakfast broke me out of my concern. Besides the food set in front of me, bacon, eggs, butter, and jam for the bread, and hot tea, were much more important in the here and now.

THE CALL

After breakfast, Cooper pushed back from the table. "Let's go, young Andy. Time to collect whatever we might need from the shops."

I followed him out to the carriage, excited to see the town.

"We'll stop at the tailors first."

Knowing that we were going shopping, I hoped the tailor wouldn't ask me to undress, but would measure over my clothing.

We arrived at the tailor's, and Cooper did all the talking. "Andy needs some clothing fit for a sea journey, and I want him to have a long coat."

"Sea journey? Oh. Well, young man. Let's get you up on the platform."

I stepped up to what was really a small stool, my heart pumping.

He walked up with a tape and started measuring over my clothes.

I let out a sigh of relief.

He repeated the measurements to his assistant, then to me, "I'll leave a little room in the clothes for you to grow. I wouldn't want you to outgrow your clothes on your journey. They'll be delivered in a couple of days."

We left the tailor and stopped at the chemist's and the silversmith.

When we arrived at home, Jenkins handed Cooper an envelope and said, "From the squire."

Cooper handed it to me, "Read it, Andy."

I tore it open and pulled out a sheaf of paper.

Old Anchor Inn, Bristol, March 1, 1751,

Dear Andy, Cooper, and Dr. Dawe (if you are still at the house),

As I do not know where you are, Dr. Dawe, you are at the Hall or still in London, I am sending this to both places.

On my way to Bristol, a bright young man asked about my journey. He is sharp-witted and interested in adventure, so I asked him to join us. His name is Ron Adkis, I'm sure you must know him as he's from the local village.

Even better news, the ship is bought and fitted. She lies at anchor, ready for sea. You never imagined a sweeter schooner—a child might sail her—two hundred tons; name, Hispaniola.

I got her through my old friend, Blandly, who has proved himself most helpful. The admirable fellow jumped at the chance to help, and so, I may say, did every one in Bristol, as soon as they got wind of the part we sailed for—treasure, I mean.

"Oh no." Both Cooper and I said at the same time.

I sighed, and then continued to read:

Blandly himself found the Hispaniola, and by the most admirable management got her for the merest trifle. There is a class of men in Bristol monstrously prejudiced against Blandly. They go to the length of declaring that this honest creature would do anything for money, that the Hispaniola belonged to him, and that he sold it to me absurdly high— the most transparent calumnies. None of them dare, however, to deny the merits of the ship.

So far there was not a hitch. The workpeople, to be sure —riggers and what not—were most annoyingly slow; but time cured that. It was the crew that troubled me.

I wished for a group of strong and hardy men—in case of attacks from natives, buccaneers, or the odious French— and I had the worry of the deuce itself to find so much as half a dozen, till the most remarkable stroke of fortune brought me the very person that I required.

I was standing on the dock when a Chinese woman tried to converse with me. I resisted getting caught up in her enthusiasm for ships, for we know that few women are as knowledgeable as a good seaman. But to my surprise, she actually seemed as if she knew what she was talking about. Of all things, I found she had been sailing before, knew all the sea-faring men in Bristol by way of her cooking prowess, had wanted a good berth as a cook to get to sea again. She had wandered down to the dock that morning for a scent of the sea.

I thought this the perfect opportunity. I engaged her on the spot to be ship's cook. Chen, she is called.

Well, sir. I thought I had only found a cook, but first she went about inspecting the ship and showed me some changes that could be made for sailing. A strangely impressive young woman, indeed. And it was a crew I had discovered. Between Chen and myself we got imaginable—not pretty to look at, but fellows by their faces, of the most indomitable spirit. I declare we could fight a frigate.

Chen even got rid of two out of the six or seven I had already engaged. She showed me in a moment that they were just the sort of fresh water swabs we had to fear in an adventure of importance.

I am in the most magnificent heart and spirits, eating like a bull, sleeping like a tree, yet I shall not enjoy a moment till I hear my old tarpaulins tramping round the capstan.

I paused at that last, unfamiliar to me. I looked up at Cooper, but he just shrugged. I made it my goal to read and take some of the books I hadn't read from my pile; they might explain what a capstan was.

I continued reading again:

Seaward ho! Hang the treasure! It's the glory of the sea that has turned my head. So now, Dawe, come post; do not lose an hour, if you respect me.

Let young Andy say goodbye to his mother and send him with Cooper for a guard; and both come full speed to Bristol.

Your friend,

John Trelawney

"*Postscript. — I did not tell you that Blandly, who, by the way, is to send a ship after us if we don't turn up by the end of August, and has found an admirable fellow for our captain - a stiff man, which I regret, but, in all other respects, a treasure.*

We have a very competent man for a first mate, Mr. Arrow. As well that Chen unearthed a very competent man for third mate, a man named Dirk. Also, I have a boatswain who plays the bagpipes, Dawe; so things shall go man-o-war fashion on board the good ship Hispaniola.

J.T.

COOPER SENT a message to the tailor to rush the clothing.

Meanwhile, I had all sorts of concerns about that letter. Ron was in Bristol. I hoped that didn't prove to be a problem. And, I was concerned about the Chinese woman. Could she be the Chinese pirate? But she had sold herself as a cook, and there was no way that Captain Flint's crew could have known that the squire would head to Bristol for a ship.

It seemed that there was no way she could be the woman that Billy Bones had been worried about, so I pushed the concerns aside for now.

BRISTOL

The night passed, and the next day, all of the packages were delivered to the estate. It seemed that Trelawney's name or more than likely all his money got many things done quickly.

Cooper handed me the items ordered from the silversmith. The first one was a silver flask embossed with the image of a ship. I ran my hand over it and wondered how similar the *Hispaniola* was to this design.

Cooper explained, "That's for courage. Find your favorite and load it up. You might need it on cold stormy nights."

The other was a beautiful copper flask that I knew had to be for gunpowder.

I opened the clothing items and immediately fell in

love with the coat. Long, black leather with two rows of thin rope sewn to the edges of the collar and sleeves.

There was a note from the tailor:

What says sea journey more than leather and rope? Enjoy!

As per Cooper's instructions, they had sent extra pieces of leather. Cooper had told me to sew them into the inside of the coat to hide away my weapons when I had them on me. I'd bring the leather, weapons, and sewing kit to Bristol.

I tried some "courage" - Squire Trelawney had a wall full in the study of all kinds of libations. Everything was so strong! I settled on Brandy as I knew that was what Jenkins added to tea.

I hugged my mother, and she cried a little as I walked out of the house. I missed her the moment I walked out, but adventure called louder.

We took the carriage past the old cove. The remnants of the building lay in a disarrayed pile. It felt like someplace I no longer knew. I imagined myself standing out near the cove, and I could only see myself as I had been before the pirate. Young, naive, and trapped.

The next moment, we had turned the corner, and my old home was out of sight.

We changed to the mail coach at the Royal George Inn on the Heath. I was wedged in between Cooper and a stout old gentleman, and despite the swift motion and the cold night air, I slept a great deal; for when I was awakened, at last, it was by a shake of my shoulders.

I opened my eyes to find that we were parked to the side of a city street, there was a large building next to us, and it was midday.

I stretched and found I was stiff as a board, doing my best to stand and step out of the coach.

Cooper was standing outside, stretching his neck.

"Where are we?" I asked.

"We've made it to Bristol," he said. "Now we head to the inn where Mr. Trelawney has taken up residence. It's near a dock on the far side of town, so he can be close to watching the schooner."

We walked along the quays and beside great multitudes of ships of all sizes, rigs, and nations. In one, sailors were singing at their work; in another, there were men aloft, high over my head, hanging to threads that seemed no thicker than a spider's.

Although I had lived by the shore all my life, I felt as if I had never truly been near the sea till then. The smell of tar and salt was something new. I saw the most wonderful figureheads, which had all been far over the ocean. I saw many old sailors with rings in their ears, and whiskers curled in ringlets, and tarry pigtails; and I could not have been more excited.

I was even more excited to go to sea. To sea in a schooner, with the doctor and Cooper, and pig-tailed singing seamen; to sea, bound for Grimwood Isle, and to seek buried treasure.

While I was still in this delightful dream, we came suddenly in front of a large inn, and met Squire Trelawney, dressed like an officer, in stout blue cloth, coming out of the door with a smile on his face.

"Here you are!" he cried. "The doctor came last night from London. Bravo! The ship's company is complete. Come join me and the others for our last meal on land before we ship out."

He led us into the Landoger Trow's dining room. It was all white walls, white linens, and white plates against the beautiful red carpet and brown tables. Almost as fancy as the squire's estate.

I paused at one of the fireplaces to warm my hands. Then, while I said hello to Doctor Dawe, enjoying his pipe, the others sat down, leaving the only seat next to Ron.

Ron looked over and smiled at me. I gave him my steeliest glare.

"I do have an errand for someone, if you're interested." The squire was looking at me. "But it means you will miss the meal." He genuinely looked appalled at the idea, his bushy eyebrows knitted together in worry.

"I am happy to," I said. All the better not to sit next to Ron.

"Jolly good, I knew you were up for the task." He wrote a note and handed it to me. "Chen must be notified that we sail tonight, now that everyone is here. Take this to the Rummer." He also handed me some coins. "She makes a wonderful meal; you can get your repast there before you join us to board the ship."

I took his message from him and turned without looking at Ron.

LAND LIVING

While Flint's crew and I lived in Bristol, keeping an eye out for the squire or anyone talking of sailing to Grimwood Isle, my crew of the *Night Sky* was sailing to and from London, moving cargo for pay. By not pirating, we all figured they would be safe from the pirate hunters. I was a little worried, what if when I was done, they didn't need me as captain? I hoped it was worth the risk.

Meanwhile, waiting for the squire to show up, I thought to make good use of my time. I procured a job as a cook at the Rummer to hear the sailor scuttlebutt. I stopped at a bookseller and searched for any texts about fighting techniques, the shop owner looking at me over his glasses, as if deciding whether or not I should be allowed to purchase them.

I had taken to wearing simple dresses in a more Chinese fashion. I definitely didn't fit in. But I walked out with the books nonetheless.

One book was about bare-fisted fighting, the other was a rare book from China about a form of martial art called Taijiquan. It was unfortunately in Chinese, but there were hand-drawn images of thirteen different movements that intrigued me.

But I didn't want to just work, I wanted to have fun! I went to taverns in the evening and drank beer with sailors. In the morning, I would dress as a man and head to a male-only coffeehouse where politics were debated, gossip spread, but more importantly, I could learn news of the world.

I went to theatre nights and learned how to gamble from Dirk.

On one particular night, I was sitting at a gambling table, winning at cards when a man sat next to me. He had no wig, as about half of the men here, his hair was dark brown, almost black, and his eyes were the color of a stormy sea.

What was intriguing was his facial hair. Even most sailors, pirates or not, followed the fashion of shaving daily. But his mustache and beard were very short and cleanly shaped.

I realized I had been staring, but he had also been assessing me.

"I'm sorry, I didn't mean to stare."

His smile was soft, and I could swear his eyes changed to a lighter shade of blue.

"It is of no consequence." His accent sounded a bit like Italian.

"Chen," I introduced myself and reached out for a handshake.

He took my hand and kissed it, something no one had ever done before. A thrill went through my whole body.

"Renard. It is a pleasure to meet you, Chen."

Dirk slapped his hand on the table. "Are we going to get back to the game?"

My cheeks flushed at forgetting there were other people as well as a card game.

There was small talk around the table; most of the men were sailors, some possibly pirates like Dirk or me, so no one asked what ship anyone was from or anyone's latest voyage.

Instead, talk centered around the latest pirates to be caught by the King's pirate hunters, and especially about the newest pirate hunter, Jonathan Barnett. Barnett had been a pirate himself.

"The King's plan is working," one of the men said. "Giving a pardon to a bloodthirsty pirate - he's caught over ten pirates over the last month."

Dirk and I exchanged glances. At least for now, we were safe.

Renard won the game and then stood to go. "I'm sure we will meet again, Chen," he said on his way out.

I certainly hoped so.

The next morning, I was in my men's disguise at a coffeehouse when a man stood up and yelled over the other gossiping voices of men and the haze of smoke from the cigars. "I must introduce to you all, Squire Trelawney."

Finally, this was the first time I had heard his name, and to see him in person was even better.

The voices dimmed only slightly.

The squire stood, waved his hands, his bushy eyebrows. "You will all be astonished at what I'm about to venture out to find."

Was he going to reveal to a room full of people about treasure? I stood on the table to the dismay of my other male counterparts. "Gentlemen! Laramie has discovered some interesting news about the King."

All eyes turned to Laramie, whose face went quickly from dismay to excitement to have so many listening ears.

The squire seemed to give up and sat down with his friend.

The last thing any of us needed was word getting out beyond our group.

I changed into my dress and followed the squire as he walked the docks until I had a chance to meet him and easily talk him into using my help.

A CLOSE CALL

I wiped my hands on the dish towel and stepped out into the dining room. It was my last day working at The Rummer.

All these worries about the treasure, and yet I found myself pleased to see so many people in the dining room, mostly seafaring men. When I started here, the food was mediocre and the dining room fairly empty. I felt a great deal of pride in my work.

Dirk was waiting just inside the dining room.

He asked, "Any luck?"

I shook my head. "I climbed into Squire Trelawney's room and searched high and low. Either he keeps the map on his person or someone else has it."

He shrugged, "At least we have plenty of our men on the crew. Whether we mutiny or take the treasure after it's found, it will be ours, Captain." He turned and walked away.

A young man with brown hair and green eyes walked up to me, a note in his hand. "Ms. Chen?" he asked.

"Just Chen, boy. What's this?"

"A note from Squire Trelawney."

I couldn't help but sigh at that. The man sent messages almost hourly about the simplest things. "Thank you."

One of the customers rose suddenly and made for the door. I didn't think anything of it until the boy pointed at him. "It's the pirate, Black Dog! He burned down my inn!" The boy moved to run toward him as the pirate leapt through the front door.

I grabbed the boy's jacket and held on. He was a bit shorter than I, probably a few years younger, but I had to use a lot more strength than I had thought to keep him from running out the door.

"Harry!" I yelled to one of the employees. "That sea-dog didn't pay his bill. Run and catch him." Harry took off, but I also knew that Black Dog would not be caught; he was faster than Harry. Of course, I had told Black Dog to get out of Bristol to keep from being seen —that blasted pirate.

"Boy, it's not a good idea to run after a pirate, but that was brave of you. Sit down. I'll get you some breakfast, and you can tell me how you met a pirate named Black Dog."

I went to the kitchen and pulled together a plate of food and two cups of tea. There was a chance this boy knew something of Billy Bones and where the map was hidden.

The boy looked hungrily at the food. "Thank you, Chen. I've been traveling, but Mr. Trelawney was in a hurry to get the note to you."

"Yes, it says that we sail at four. I assume you're coming on the voyage?"

The boy nodded as he dug into his food, then took a moment to stop and say, "Yes, I'll be cabin boy."

"What's your name, cabin boy?"

"Andy. I met the pirate at the inn my parents ran."

It was the young man from the inn, the one who had more than likely taken the map.

"Andy, I'm curious about this pirate and your inn. What happened?"

In between bites, Andy told me, "A pirate came to our little inn, Billy Bones. He spent most of his time drunk and watching for other pirates. A few of his fellow pirates discovered him, gave him the black spot, he died, and when they came back, they set my family's inn on fire."

I wanted to set those idiots on fire myself. "That must have been terrifying, and certainly having him die in your inn must have been scary."

"He wasn't the only death." A shadow moved across Andy's face. "My father died just a few days before. Then, after the inn was on fire, another pirate was run over by a horse."

"It's impressive that you survived the ordeal. I hope that the pirate paid you well for his stay."

Andy nodded. "He paid a few gold coins, but that was it. The pirates got away with the rest."

Either this boy didn't know anything or was a straight-up liar. Someone had gotten the map from Billy Bones. I wondered for only a second, as I sipped my tea. But no, if Black Dog and his men from the raid on the inn had the map, they wouldn't be here.

Harry returned, out of breath, and confessed that he had lost track of Black Dog in the crowd.

I sent Harry away. "I'm sorry, Andy. A town like this draws pirates."

Andy shook his head and said vehemently, "I'm sorry that he wasn't caught. He must have recognized me when I came in. Mostly, I blame Billy Bones for my father's death. But the rest of them destroyed what could have been a living for my mother."

His mother, I could relate.

"Harry, take over for me in the kitchen." Harry nodded. The customers would not be happy with their meals, but this place had done what I needed.

"Andy, finish up that breakfast. I want to walk with

you to the squire and tell him about this pirate escaping. He will want to know that he's nearby."

As we walked along the quays, I could tell Andy was interested in the ships. I shared what I knew about each one, how some were taking on cargo, and another was making ready for sea.

"How do you know so much about the ships?" he asked.

"I was a ship's cook."

"How, though? I've read a lot about pirates and ships, and many consider a woman on board to be unlucky."

"It's true. Seafaring people tend to have many superstitions. In my case, my first ship really needed a cook and was willing to take me on."

When we got to the pub, the squire was seated at a large table with another man. He was introduced to me as Dr. Dawe.

"Sirs, you should know that a pirate, Black Dog, was spotted at the tavern by Andy. The pirate escaped."

Dr Dawe shook his head. "How did he find his way here? Did he follow one of us? Maybe we should postpone our send-off."

"No," Squire Trelawney said. "If we postpone, it gives the pirate more time to stop our plans. We should leave as we planned. At four this afternoon." He stood, "We have much to do to prepare. Chen, I'd like you to come and inspect the food that's been stored and let me know if we'll need anything else. Andy, I want you to come along with Dawe and me to inspect the ship."

THE HISPANIOLA

I couldn't decide if Chen was a pirate or not. She seemed too young, only a few years older than me. At the same time, her story about being a cook seemed true enough. Breakfast was as good as my mother's cooking.

However, seeing her and a man whispering together conspiratorially when I first walked into the tavern made me suspicious, and the fact that Black Dog was eating there seemed too coincidental. And, she was very knowledgeable about ships.

My concerns about her disappeared, though, as myself, the squire, and others boarded the boat for the *Hispaniola*. There were so many ships here that we went under the figureheads and round the sterns of many other ships, and their cables sometimes grated underneath our keel, and sometimes swung above us. I was fascinated by everything.

At last, however, we got alongside, and were met and saluted as we stepped aboard by the mate, Mr. Arrow, a brown old sailor, with earrings in his ears and a squint. He and the squire clapped each other's shoulders and were very friendly.

Our ship sat low in the water, a two-masted schooner with clean lines and fresh paint that gleamed even in the waning evening sun. She looked fast—with graceful curves.

It was the crew that made my stomach tighten: rough men with hard eyes, moving about the deck with the easy confidence of those who'd spent their lives at sea. I felt like a fish out of water.

But seeing Ron on the ship made me so angry that my fear disappeared. I wouldn't fear them, and I wouldn't dare show I was scared to someone who had no courage.

We had hardly got into the cabin when a sailor followed us in:

"Captain Smollett, sir, axing to speak with you," he said to Squire Trelawney.

"I am always at the captain's orders. Show him in," said the squire.

The captain, who was close behind his messenger, entered at once and shut the door behind him. He had a pointed nose and chin, and his grey eyebrows seemed knitted together in his scowl.

Mr. Trelawney seemed unaware of his mood. "Well, Captain Smollett, what have you to say? All is well, I hope; all shipshape and seaworthy?"

"Well, sir," said the captain, "better to speak plain, I believe, even at the risk of offending you. I don't like this cruise; I don't like the men; and I don't like my officer."

I was taken aback, but more importantly, the squire's normally congenial features turned upside down.

The squire stood. "Perhaps, sir, you don't like the ship?"

"I can't speak as to that, sir, not having seen her tried," said the captain. "She seems a clever craft; more I can't say."

"Possibly, sir, you may not like your employer, either?" Inquired the squire with a sneer.

But here Dr. Dawe cut in.

"Captain, stay a bit," said he, "stay a bit. No use of such questions as that but to produce ill-feeling. The captain has said too much or he has said too little, and I'm bound to say that I require an explanation of his words. You don't, you say, like this cruise. Now, why?"

The captain looked around the room, then nodded at the doctor. "I was engaged, sir, on what we call scaled orders, to sail this ship for that gentleman where he should bid me," said the captain. "So far so good. But now I find that every man before the mast knows more than I do. I don't call that fair, now, do you?"

"No," said Dr. Dawe, "I don't."

"Next," said the Captain, "I learn we are going after treasure — hear it from my own hands, mind you. Now, treasure is ticklish work; I don't like treasure voyages on any account; and I don't like them, above all when they are secret, and when, begging your pardon, Mr. Trelawey, the secret has been told to the parrot."

"Chen's parrot?" Asked the squire.

"It's a way of speaking," said the captain. "That every man, even a parrot, knows before me. I believe that neither of you gentlemen knows what you are doing."

"That is all clear, and, I daresay, true enough," replied the doctor. "We take a risk, but we are not so ignorant as you believe us. Next, you say you don't like the crew. Are they not good seamen?"

"I don't like them, sir," returned Captain Smollett. "And I think I should have had the choosing of my own hands, if you go to that."

"Perhaps you should," replied the doctor. "My friend should, perhaps, have taken you along with him, but the slight, if there be one, was unintentional. And you don't like Mr. Arrow?"

"I don't, sir. I believe he's a good seaman, but he's too free with the crew to be a good officer. A mate should keep himself to himself—shouldn't drink with the men before the mast!"

"Do you mean he drinks?" asked the squire.

"Yes, sir," replied the captain, "and he's too familiar."

"And the rest of the crew?" Dr. Dawe asked.

"It's bad enough that we have a woman cook; some might believe this voyage unlucky because of it. I don't believe that, but I want to know that a woman can pull her weight. And we have this untried lad, who seems to be your friend, as a cabin boy. Is this cabin boy to report to you or me?"

REARRANGED

I bristled at being pointed out. I liked being part of this important group of people on the ship, but I also didn't want to be seen as lazy.

"I'll do what needs to be done," I said.

"See to it that you do." He nodded toward me.

Mr. Trelawney sighed, "Andy is indeed our friend, but as a cabin boy, he falls under your jurisdiction. As for the cook, she seems a good sort."

"Well, now, and the short and long of it, captain?" asked the doctor. "Tell us what else you want."

"Well, gentlemen, are you determined to go on this cruise?"

"Like iron," answered the squire.

"Very good," said the captain. "For some reason, the men have put the black powder and the arms in the fore hold. Now, you have a good place under the cabin; why not put them there? Then there are four men planning to berth forward. Why not put them in the cabin deck with the rest?"

"Captain, you have all the power on this ship to do what you would like. Feel free to see to these changes. Any more?" asked Squire Trelawney.

"One more," said the captain. "There's been too much blabbing already."

"Far too much," agreed the doctor.

"I'll tell you what I've heard myself," continued Captain Smollett: "that you have a map of an island; and that there are crosses on the map to show where treasure is."

"I never told that," cried the squire, "to a soul!"

"The hands know it, sir," returned the captain.

"It doesn't matter who it was," replied the doctor.

Although all of us knew it had to be the squire.

"Well, gentlemen," continued the captain, "I don't know who has this map, but I make it a point that it shall be kept secret from Mr. Arrow and me. Otherwise, I would ask you to let me resign."

"I see," said the doctor. "You wish us to keep this matter dark, and to make a garrison of the stern part of the ship, manned with my friend's own people, and provided with all the arms and powder on board. In other words, you fear a mutiny."

"Sir!" said Captain Smollett, "if I truly feared a

mutiny, I wouldn't be justified in taking us all out to sea at all."

I felt safer knowing how the captain felt.

"As for Mr. Arrow, I believe him to be thoroughly honest; some of the men are the same; all may be for that matter. But I'm responsible for the ship's safety and the life of every man and woman aboard her. I see things going, as I think, not quite right. And I ask you to take certain precautions, or let me resign my berth. And that's all."

I considered telling them about my suspicions of Chen, but would they believe me? Would they believe a woman could be a pirate?

"Captain Smollett," began the doctor, with a smile, "When you came in here, I'll stake my wig you were meaning to do or say more."

"Doctor," said the captain, "you are whip-smart. When I came in here, I meant to get discharged. I had no thought that Mr. Trelawney would hear a word."

The squire nodded. "Had my friend not been here I should have seen you to the deuce. As it is, I have heard you. I will do as you desire, but I think the worst of you."

I wanted to roll my eyes. This man was being cautious and smart and the squire was being petty.

"That's as you please, sir," said the captain. "You'll find I do my duty."

And with that, the captain took his leave.

"Trelawney," said the doctor, "contrary to all my notions, I believe you have managed to get two very honest crew members on board with you— that man and Chen."

"Chen, if you like," said the squire, "but as for that intolerable humbug, I declare I think his conduct unmanly, unsailorly, and downright un-English."

At that, I decided to keep my suspicions of Chen to myself.

"Well," said the doctor, "We shall see."

When we came on deck, the men had already begun to take out the arms and powder, yo-ho-ing at their work, while the captain and Mr. Arrow stood by superintending.

SET SAIL

The captain turned to Trelawney. "Sir, I'm making it so that Mr. Arrow and Joyce will be sleeping on deck near the companion. There would be room for two more in the berths astern with Chen, Cooper, the doctor, and you. Who would you like me to move there?"

Mr. Trelawney nodded toward me. "Let's put Andy and that young man, Ron, in those berths. Two we know we can trust."

I grimaced to be put near Ron, but it was also such a relief to me that I'd have my own space and not be in the larger room with the other men. It was still very low in the ship, of course, and my berth would be the space of a hammock.

To show the captain that I wasn't going to shirk my duties, I went to work with the other men moving the powder. It took two or more to carry one of the barrels, and I jumped in with whoever needed help. I had to hold my side up higher for the barrel to be level with the men, but I did it without complaint, even though it took all my strength.

At one point, I went to pick up a barrel and the one person who stepped up to help me was Ron.

At first, he was quiet, but when we lowered the barrel into its new place, he said, "You've grown stronger since the last time we saw each other."

"Yes," I said, and left it at that.

One more boat showed up with a few men and Chen. Instead of waiting for the boat to be hoisted up to the deck, Chen climbed the ropes as nimble as a monkey. I wasn't sure about anyone else, but I was certainly impressed.

As soon as she saw what we were doing, she asked. "What's this?"

"We're a-changing of the powder, Chen," answered one man.

"Why do this now? We'll miss the evening tide." She shook her head.

"My orders!" said the Captain shortly. "You may go below, Chen. Hands will want supper."

"Ay, ay, sir," answered the cook, and she disappeared in the direction of the galley.

The men on the boat included Mr. Blandly and a few others who were here to wish us a good voyage and safe return. While they, the doctor, and Trelawney stood toasting our voyage, the rest of us were bustling to get things stowed in their place.

A little before dawn, I was dog-tired when the boatswain sounded his pipe. The crew began to man the capstan bars. I thanked the stars that, from my reading, I knew what it was and what we were up to.

We'd take our turn pushing the capstan to pull up the anchor.

One of the men pushed me aside, "Not you, cabin boy. You need to be a little taller."

He was right, but it still stung to be told I couldn't do it. Even though I was weary, I stepped back and watched. All was so new and interesting to me—the brief commands, the shrill note of the whistle, the men bustling to their places in the glimmer of the ship's lanterns.

At the helm were the Captain, Cooper, and the squire, apparently conferring about direction. I had no idea that Cooper knew anything about navigating.

And we were off! I watched Bristol disappear behind us, and I was excited for the adventure.

I went down to the galley to grab my dinner.

As I sat down to eat, Mr. Arrow threw his plate on the floor. He pushed at my shoulder. "Pick it up, cabin boy."

I didn't know why the second mate was being a dog and I wasn't going to take that from anyone. I took a bite of fresh fish and vegetables then said, "Don't be a pig. Pick it up yourself."

I saw out of the corner of my eye that he had pulled out a knife, hidden underneath the table, but a threat nonetheless.

I started to pull the axe from inside my coat, but Dirk squeezed in between us on the bench, even though there was plenty of room. He moved my plate over, away from Mr. Arrow. Then Dirk cried out, "Now, Chen, give us a beat."

"Ay, ay, mates," said Chen, who was standing by and at once broke out in the air and words I knew so well—

"Fifteen men on the dead man's chest"

Mr. Arrow and I put away our weapons, and then the whole room, including me, sang the chorus:

"Yo-ho-ho, and a bottle of rum!"

It carried me back to the old inn, and I seemed to hear the voice of Billy Bones piping in.

The *Hispaniola* had begun her voyage to Grimwood Isle.

THE FIRST STEP

Troubled by Mr. Arrow's aggressive moves, I wasn't sure if I should talk to the captain or Trelawney. I would certainly do my best to avoid him, but I couldn't do so forever on such a small ship.

Now that it was my chance to sleep, I set up my hammock and arranged what few things I had brought into a canvas bag.

I pulled out the flask. At the last minute, I had emptied it of brandy and decided to fill it with water instead. It would be my only way of cleaning up, as fresh water was only to be used for drinking.

The thought that all the men on this ship would either wait for rain or occasionally be dunked in the sea for a rinse made me sick to my stomach. The books I had read hadn't said much about it, but it also made me wonder that maybe I shouldn't be so clean. When the ship started to smell, maybe I wouldn't notice so much. But that idea also made me sick to my stomach.

How I already missed the warm water in the fancy basin from the squire's home. I used a rag to rinse myself off, hung it on the end of the hammock, tucked away my flask, and then climbed in.

It took some practice and some maneuvering to fully get into the hammock, but once I was in, it became so comfortable. I rolled up a shirt as a pillow.

Ron came down into the berth while I was getting settled. He quietly set up his hammock next to mine, then sat in it and looked at me.

He was ready to say something to me, I was sure, but I wanted to start first.

"I'm so mad at you. You let me down. Those other village idiots, they had no courage. But you were my friend."

He held his head in his hands, and I didn't care until I realized he was crying.

I waited for his reply.

He finally looked up at me with red, tearful eyes. "I thought at first that I should listen to my father, but after we went home, all I could think of was you out there against the pirates. Father locked the door and kept the key with him. Andy, please forgive me. We've grown up together. You are my best friend."

"I'll think about it." It was the best I could do for now.

He continued, "That's why I'm here, you know. I want to prove to you that I not only have courage, but that I'm here for you."

Cooper joined us in the berth and luckily stopped our conversation. I wasn't ready to stop being mad.

Cooper nodded over at me. "Andy, make sure to practice with those weapons of yurs, and maybe we'll have some time for muh to teach you some fighting skills."

"Thanks, Cooper."

"Weapons?" Ron asked.

"Aye. He has an axe and a sickle, so don't mess with him." Cooper said that with a wink. "And Ron, you might be a good partner for him. You're just a few hairs taller, a better sparring partner than me, if you're interested."

"Yes, I think that would benefit us both," Ron said.

Someone on deck was playing the bagpipes, a comforting sound so far from home.

I closed my eyes. I was so exhausted I couldn't keep them open anymore.

The hammock swinging with the ship quickly lulled me into a deep sleep.

SEASICK

The next morning, I was up before dawn, as requested, to help Chen prepare breakfast. I peeled about a million potatoes and then helped to clean the tables afterward, stealing a short time for my own meal.

Dirk sat next to me. "Andy, there are men who like to pick on those smaller than them. Makes them feel bigger. Watch out for them."

I knew he was talking about Mr. Arrow. I had a quick break up top and saw Mr. Arrow order one of the men about, and the man completely ignored him. That didn't bode well for the crew if the second in command couldn't command the men.

The captain, seeing me taking a breath, ordered me to swab the deck. I nodded and dashed downstairs as if I was running to answer him. I didn't want to be seen as if I was disobeying, but I also needed a break. I sat down on my hammock and stretched my sore muscles for a moment.

When I felt reasonably less annoyed with the captain, I went to clean the deck. I was scrubbing near the mainmast when the wind changed from a steady breeze to a downright blast. The clouds grew heavier, and the first drops of rain hit my face like cold needles.

I looked up, and the sky had turned a dark green. I had lived along the coast long enough to know that was a sign of a terrible storm. I grabbed my supplies and put them down below.

Suddenly, the *Hispaniola* pitched beneath my feet in a way that made my stomach lurch.

"All hands!" someone bellowed from above. "Secure the rigging! Move, you dogs!"

I scrambled up the steps to the deck. Around me, sailors were climbing, running, hauling. I stood frozen, unsure where to go or what to do.

A hand shoved me from behind. Hard.

I stumbled forward, barely catching myself against the mast. When I spun around, I found myself face-to-face with Israel Hands, one of the older crew members. His smile showed more gaps than teeth.

"Out of the way, cabin boy," he sneered. "Unless you want to be useful for once."

The ship rolled hard to starboard. My feet slid on

the wet deck, and I grabbed for the mast again. Above me, thunder cracked like cannon fire.

Hands had moved on, but I wished he had fallen overboard.

"Galley," the captain yelled at me, jerking his thumb toward the stairs. "Get below for now."

The stairs pitched as I descended. Twice I nearly lost my footing, catching myself on the rail with both hands. I wanted to sit on the stairs to get my bearings just for a second, but a crew member came flying by on his way somewhere, so I had to keep out of the way.

The galley door stood ajar and swinging with the movements of the ship, lamplight spilling into the dark passageway. I pushed inside and found Chen at the stove, one hand braced against the wall, the other stirring something in a massive pot. The cook didn't look up.

The ship lurched again. The pot Chen was stirring slid sideways. The cook caught it with practiced ease, muscles flexing beneath her sleeves as she wedged it into a special bracket built into the stove.

I grabbed the doorframe to steady myself. "How many times have you been in a storm at sea?"

Chen's dark eyes flicked to me, assessing. "Long enough to know when to move and when to hold still. Think of it like a seesaw, back and forth."

For some reason, that comparison made my

stomach worse. I pushed that idea aside and held it together. "What if, what if we capsize?"

Chen shook her head. "These ships are made to withstand storms, and this crew is practiced enough to keep it upright. But just in case, do you know how to swim?"

My jaw dropped, and I didn't know what to say, other than that no, I didn't know how to swim. Then I realized she was laughing.

"I'm just kidding, Andy. It's very rare that anyone falls off a ship."

The ship lurched again, and Chen adjusted with ease.

"Are the men giving you trouble?" She asked.

I thought of Mr. Arrow. "Nothing I can't handle."

"Good. Now, do me a favor. There are dishes in the officers' mess. Go get them for me."

I tried to move, but my feet wouldn't listen.

Chen looked at me, and her eyes grew wide. "Oh."

She grabbed me around the shoulders and led me to the dining area, sitting me down on a bench. "Stay here. You're looking a little green around the gills."

I couldn't have moved if I had wanted to.

She returned with a cup of hot tea. "Drink this."

I wasn't sure I could. My stomach was sure to eject it immediately.

She put it in my hands. "It will make you mend."

The warmth from the mug somehow started to

make me feel better. I lifted it to my lips and sipped. It was a fragrant tea, and I breathed in the sweet fumes. Another sip and I could taste a touch of alcohol as well.

The next thing I knew, Ron was tapping me on my shoulder.

"Andy, are you okay?"

I nodded, "I was a little seasick. I'm okay now."

The ship had stopped rolling, and men were coming down the stairs for dinner. I went up to the deck, and the sky was dark but clear.

I stepped into the kitchen. "How did you do that?"

"Do what?"

"It's like time passed."

Chen laughed, "All I did was give you a remedy for sea sickness. If it made you lose track of time, then maybe that's what you needed. Don't just stand there," Chen said, "Go get your dinner. Then you can help me wash the dishes."

"Oh, great," I said with no enthusiasm.

Chen laughed. I liked her laugh.

At the same time, I had to wonder again if she was a pirate. Billy Bones had said, "She's got a magic about her."

Remedy or not, she always seemed to have things work around her with ease.

I'd try to keep my eye on her from now on.

SPARRING

The next morning, I practically fell out of my hammock. My muscles were so stiff from the cold air and hard work that I could barely move. I did my best to move quietly, though, and not wake anyone.

I stretched, pulled my coat on, and walked out to the deck. The sky was afire with pinks and oranges as morning approached. I stood at the railing until the sun flashed across the ocean and the sky's hues had returned to normal blue.

If only sailing were always like this. A great pleasure.

From the crow's nest, someone yelled down, "Sail ho!"

Suddenly, there were several crew members near

the crow's nest, Dirk, the captain, and Chen among them.

"Can you see their colors?" asked the captain.

The watch was quiet for a moment before answering, "I'm not sure. It could have been a Jolly Roger, but they're out of my sights again."

Jolly Roger! That meant pirates.

The watch continued, "But they've moved off. They might not have seen us."

I noticed Chen and Dirk exchange concerned glances. I went to follow them as they started talking, but Cooper stepped in the way. "Andy, 'tis time we worked on yer fightin' skills, so it is. Get yerself some breakfast now. I've gotten permission from the captain to do a bit of hand-to-hand combat trainin' for anyone who's wantin' it."

I nodded, excited and nervous, I wolfed down a small breakfast and dashed back up to the deck. Cooper had assembled several crew members, including Dirk, Ron, Billy, and Nails.

"Right, fellas. What happens when ya've lost yer blade or find someone too close to use yer good weapon? let's get to work."

Cooper would demonstrate a fighting move, then have the rest of us practice it on each other. Then we moved on to weapons. After an hour, Cooper stopped the practice.

"All right. Now, yer going into a fight. Stay in your

pairs, and I want yeh to go easy on each other. You're trying to best the person; injuries are acceptable, but remember, if they can't do their work, you get to step in for them and do double duty."

Ron and I faced each other, our hands up in defense.

"Ron, if you break my nose, I'll break yours."

"Fair enough." He grinned. "Come on then. Show me what you got."

But I wasn't falling for that. Cooper had said that step one was to keep out of their range, if you could.

He lunged forward, reaching for my shoulders.

I jumped sideways, and his hand closed on empty air.

He reached out for me again, but when I jumped sideways, he quickly moved behind me and wrapped his arm around my shoulders. He started to pull me down to the deck, but I stomped down hard on his foot. He let go immediately, hopping away on his unhurt foot.

I heard Chen say, "Well done." I felt a ping of pride.

I glanced up and realized a crowd was forming, watching all six of us fighting against each other.

Ron took advantage of my distraction. He leapt forward with his fist in the air, aimed for my face. I ducked and shoved his chest with both hands, trying to knock him off balance, but he twisted and caught one of my wrists in his hand.

He pushed me back against the mainmast, and the breath was knocked out of me.

I kicked him in the groin.

The whole of the sailors watching gasped.

Ron doubled over in pain, but stepped back as I went to kick him in the head.

As I expected, he came at me again. This time, I stepped up into his momentum, stuck my leg behind his, and pushed. He fell backwards.

I stayed on top and ended up straddling his chest, both of his wrists pinned to the deck on either side of his head.

We were close enough that I could smell the salt and tar that clung to everyone on the ship.

Ron looked up at me, eyes wide with surprise. "Way to go, Andy. I didn't see it coming."

"Yield?" I asked.

"I yield, bloody hell, Andy, when did you get so strong?"

I rolled off of him. "I have changed, or didn't you notice?"

"I've noticed," he said quietly.

Cooper walked over and raised my hand in the air. "Winner, Andy. Mind ya, lads. If you're fighting someone fer real, fight to survive."

We nodded then watched with the rest of the crew while Billy and Nails squared off, with Billy the winner.

"I want some time in this ring." Mr Arrow said. He was looking at me.

Cooper shook his head, "I don't think Andy is ready for that."

"If he isn't ready now, who says he'll be ready when the need arises?"

Mr. Arrow pushed back his sleeves. He was a little unsteady, wobbling on his legs as the waves moved the ship.

Dirk stepped up and looked at me.

I took stock of Mr. Arrow's weak condition and nodded at Dirk. He stepped back. "I'm ready."

Mr. Arrow had a sneer on his face and his hands up to fight.

I waited a wave to tip the ship back just slightly. At that second, I rushed forward and kicked him hard in the chest.

His face filled with alarm, his arms waved through the air as if he was trying to grab hold of something, and he fell back like a tree felled in the woods. A great loud thunk echoed against the masts.

"Whoa!" came the cries from the crew.

"That's enough. Everyone, back to your posts." The captain yelled.

I was going to check on Mr. Arrow, but Cooper stopped me and stepped forward himself.

"He's fine. He's going to have a hell of a bump on that noggin'."

"Does this mean I get to be second mate for the day?"

Cooper laughed and shook his head. "I dun think so, Andy."

"Mr. Cooper, see that Mr. Arrow is taken to his bunk."

"Yes, Captain."

MR ARROW

The next morning, Mr. Arrow appeared on deck with hazy eyes, red cheeks, stuttering tongue, lashing out in anger at other people besides me, stinking of alcohol, and other marks of drunkenness. The captain finally ordered him below in disgrace.

The next morning, he again appeared as if drunk, but no one could figure out where he got his drink. It was the talk of every crew member when the captain wasn't around.

In our berths, there wasn't room for much other than a stash of clothing and some personal items. Nothing large enough to hold enough alcohol to make such a large man inebriated. The ale stowed in the ship was continually checked and found to be unchanged.

When anyone asked him to his face, he would only laugh, if he were drunk, and if he were sober, deny solemnly that he never drank anything but water.

I hadn't had much to do with him since the sparring incident until one morning when I was at the port bow, staring out at the horizon. We were heading S.S.W., and had a steady breeze abeam and a quiet sea. The *Hispaniola* rolled steadily, dipping her bowsprit now and then with a whiff of spray. Almost everyone was in the best spirits, because we were now so near the end of the first part of our adventure.

I turned to go back to work, and Mr. Arrow was standing there, watching me.

I could tell he was drunk again; he couldn't quite keep his legs under him and wobbled with every movement of the ship. "What are you looking at, rat? No," he laughed, "You're the lowest thing on this ship. Lower than bilge rats. Lower than the barnacles on the hull." He was getting red in the face.

"Nothing," I said and walked away. I saw it coming; he stuck his foot out to trip me. I tried to adjust, but the deck rolled at exactly the wrong moment. I went down hard on my hands and knees, the impact jolted through my bones.

He moved to kick me, and I rolled away faster than he could move.

"What the blazes are you doing?" I yelled at him,

hoping a crew member would walk by or see the tension, but no one was near.

He sneered. "I see you looking down at me. You are lower than me!"

A mean drunk. I had seen them before, only my father or one of the villagers would have grabbed him by the arm and escorted him out of the inn.

He swung out with a fist, but I ducked it. He was so drunk that I wasn't too worried until he pulled out two knives, one in each hand.

I hoped to deter him, so I pulled out my own weapons from my jacket. The axe and sickle felt good in my hands, but I had yet to spend much time practicing with them.

I don't think he saw them. He only had eyes for my face as he leapt forward.

The knives were pointed at my chest. I swiped down with the sickle, meaning to deflect the closest blade, but I was too slow. Instead, it sliced through his wrist, and his hand fell to the ship's deck.

I gasped.

He didn't seem to realize he was injured. He raised his other arm, the knife poised above my head.

I stepped to the side and let him rush forward, then hit him with all my force, shoving him over the side of the ship.

I watched him fall into the ocean and disappear without even trying to swim. I jumped when I saw movement next to me. It was Chen. She threw his bloody hand into the ocean.

"I was coming to try and help you, but I see that you solved your own problem. I'd swab up the blood, though, if I were you. Don't want anyone slipping on that."

PORT OR STARBOARD

That day at lunch, everyone in the mess deck was talking about Mr. Arrow.

My heart was in my throat while I scrubbed pots and pans. I considered telling them what had happened, but I didn't want to be sentenced to the gallows for his death.

Finally, Chen chimed in, "That drunken idiot probably fell overboard. Good riddance."

The captain added, "Agreed, that saves the trouble of putting him in irons. Andy."

I jumped a little.

"Mr. Trelawney wants to speak with you once you've done your chores."

I nodded and wiped the sweat from my brow, letting myself breathe again.

When I walked into the cabin, Trelawney, and the doctor were waiting.

The doctor looked me over closely. "Andy, how are things going as cabin boy? You look a little thin."

I took a precious moment to sit down on a real chair, the cushions enveloping me in their softness. "It's a lot of work." Then I spied a bowl of fruit on the table and swiped a banana, then went back to sink into the cushions.

"Yes, indeed," said Mr. Trelawney. "I've heard good things about your work."

"Yes, we have. But we decided to have a council." The doctor pointed his finger at the table. "What do you make of this, Andy? This sea creature on the map?"

I reluctantly stood up to look at the map. I knew what he was talking about, the sea creature with big teeth. I sank my own teeth into a big bite of banana.

The doctor continued, "We're approaching from that side of the island and I'm wondering if it's a warning about coral reefs or some other sort of natural danger."

"Maybe we should just go around, approach from the other side?" I suggested. "I read a book from a pirate who said sea monsters exist. Maybe the map image is a warning. Plus, it says here to approach from that other island."

Mr. Trelawney waved his hand to dismiss the idea. "Captain Flint probably had the artist add that creature to scare anyone from coming to the island. Besides, it would take a full day to circle around that and approach the island. I say that we have someone in the crow's nest keep a sharp eye out just in case."

We all agreed to the plan.

"I will go tell the captain," said the doctor.

On our way out, the doctor tapped my shoulder. "Are you really all right, Andy? I think it's well that Ron is here, someone else from home. Don't you think?"

I shrugged my shoulders. "I suppose."

"I do hope that you've forgiven him," and he walked out, leaving me surprised that he knew or cared about Ron and my relationship.

Meanwhile, I kept seeing Mr. Arrow's body falling from the ship. Ron was fixing some of the railings that had come apart. He and I had had signals as kids - if I didn't want my parents to hear what we were saying, I'd wave my hands with two fingers out.

I signaled him, and he immediately followed me down to the berths.

"What's going on?" he asked.

I thought about it for a moment, but I had to tell someone. "I'm the reason Mr. Arrow has disappeared. He attacked me, and I killed him, pushed him over the side at the end. He's food for the fish now."

"Okay."

"That's it?" I had expected a lot more.

"We've both seen mean drunks. He would have kept

coming after you or someone else. Besides, the price for him attacking a fellow sailor would have been flogging at the best, hanging at the worst. We both know it was him or you."

I shook my head. "I don't think it would have come to that if I knew how to use my weapons better. I slashed out with the sickle to parry his knife, but cut his hand off instead."

"Okay. We find some time to come down here each day and practice with fighting weapons."

"Thanks, Ron."

He smiled, and I knew it was because I was forgiving him. I was happy he was here.

We stepped onto the deck and heard the crow's nest yell, "Bloody hell! Sea monster! Prepare to push off a sea monster!"

Ron and I and everyone else within earshot of the crow's nest looked forward of the ship.

"Bloody hell!" both Ron and I exclaimed.

The captain ran to the steering "To starboard!"

SEA SERPENT

The creature's head, easily the size of a longboat, swayed above the deck, making me feel like a tiny mouse. Its long body coiled around the ship's midsection, and timbers groaned in protest.

Crew members scattered as the serpent's spiked tail whipped across the deck.

Ron's hand grabbed my wrist and held on like iron, his other arm wrapped around a rope on the mast. "I've got you!"

I didn't know why he had grabbed me until a giant wave of water crashed over us. It threw my feet up into the air and pulled hard. But Ron held on, muscles straining.

That wave was followed by another from the other

direction, pulling just as hard. As soon as the water receded, we gulped for air.

The sea serpent was still hovering. Its breath reeked of brine, fish, and death.

"Thanks, Ron. The harpoons!" I shouted, pointing to the weapons mounted along the rail.

"No!" The captain yelled. "Harpoons will be useless to a dragon hide. Man the cannons!"

The crew rushed to the cannons.

Even as we moved toward them, the serpent's tail swept low across the deck. I tackled Ron, and we hit the planks hard, rolling as the spiky tail whirled overhead.

"Thanks, Andy," Ron said. He helped me up.

Someone had managed to set off a cannon. I coughed at the smoke of gunpowder. The serpent's head had moved away from the ship and all we could see was smoke. We all waited for it to clear to see if it had hit its mark.

Ron and I ran to an unmanned cannon and all the others were manned and ready to fire.

The smoke cleared, and the serpent was near the water. Its tail was still wrapped around the ship. It opened its mouth to take a bite out of the ship.

OVERBOARD

I felt bad for Andy. The look of terror in his young eyes when Mr. Arrow had his knives pointed at him. I had tried to get across to them quickly, but it hadn't been fast enough.

It was never easy to take a man's life, even if it was in self-defense. I had told my men on day one to leave the cabin boy alone. Even if we decided to mutiny, Andy would get a choice on who to join. He was young, and hopefully he'd choose wisely.

Dirk joined me in the galley. "Chen, we've had no luck searching for the map. Whoever has it is keeping it on their person."

"I was afraid of that."

"What's the plan now?"

"We wait until we get to the island, then we figure out who we can talk into our cause."

"Israel, and some of the others, are talking about murdering the doctor, the captain, and some others in their sleep tonight."

"You tell them if they so much as harm a hair on their head, I'll tie him to the mast and let him rot. Not one of us is a master at sea navigation. If we lose that advantage, we might as well sink the ship and be done with it. We need them to take us to the island."

"Yes, Chen. I'll make sure they understand. I'm in the crow's nest next. I'll get to them after my shift."

How I longed for my new crew. Meg, Ty, John, and the rest of them. I hoped all was working well with them.

I opened a cabinet and pulled out the drawings of the people I had lost. Father, the captain, Ben Gunn, and the Chinese woman. I was going to speak with them when I felt a presence behind me.

I whirled around.

"Oh, I didn't mean to startle you."

It was the doctor. He stepped forward, staring at my drawings. "These are amazing. Are these of real people?"

I folded them up and put them back in the cabinet. "Yes. Friends and family who are no longer with me. How can I help you?"

"They look so real. You have a rare gift, Chen."

I had never thought about my drawing. It was just

something I did. I smiled at the compliment. "Thank you. Can I help you?"

"Yes, Mr Trelawey is feeling under the weather. I'm here to get some tea."

I gave the doctor two cups of tea and peeked outside. The sun was high, and the sea breeze drew me to step out further.

I started to walk back down to the galley when I heard yells of "sea monster." Curious, I stepped back out to the deck. Certainly, there was no monster, but the captain ran past me yelling for the ship to turn starboard.

The next thing I knew, a sweep of water crashed onto the deck. I was being tossed and couldn't tell which way was up. For a second, I spotted the deck of the ship just a stretch of the hand length, then I was whisked up and away.

The next thing I knew, I was in the sea, a wave curving up over me, nothing but dark ocean below me. I spotted the ship, moving away. I couldn't see any way of getting their attention; they were already too far away, and next to the ship was the largest creature I had ever seen in my life.

Everything I had ever wanted was floating away, and from the looks of it, about to be crushed.

My clothes were pulling on me, and my boots felt like bricks. I tried to swim toward the ship, but they were in a battle against the monster, sending large waves of water that pushed me farther away. There was nothing around me but the ocean.

I heard cannon fire, but I was too busy staying afloat to watch what happened. If this was the end, I was glad I had at least gotten to see my mother recently.

Another wave crashed over me, and I fought to the surface. It was taking too long, but I finally made it, bursting to take a breath.

If only I could take off my boots!

Another wave came. My arms and legs felt like lead.

Then, something wrapped around my arm. I fought back, but it was pushing me up. I broke through to the air, gulped for breath, and found it was the purple octopus, its tentacles wrapped around me.

It reshaped its body and became a seat for me as it pushed us towards the ship. The ocean around me still made me nervous but when a large wave came over us, the octopus would pull me back to the surface, shape itself into a seat, and continue the journey.

But as we got closer, I realized that was a bad idea. The creature, long like a snake but with a head like a dragon, was now taking a bite out of the gunwale. I wasn't sure we could win a battle against a sea monster.

"Hey, my friendly octopus. I think we should not get involved in this. Perhaps we wait to see what happens."

It obviously didn't understand me. It kept moving

faster and faster for the ship. But then I realized that it wasn't moving toward the ship. It was moving us toward the sea monster.

I tried to step out of the seat, but the octopus kept reshaping itself to fit around me. I tried jumping out, but it wrapped its tentacles around my ankles and wrists, holding me in the seat as we went straight for the monster that was now spitting out wood from the ship, even holding some pieces of wood in one of its claws.

Was I some sort of sacrifice to the monster? Was the octopus his friend and offering me as lunch?

I struggled and screamed but stopped when the monster turned to look at me.

THE OCTOPUS

The octopus stopped swimming and it felt like it was waiting for something. The monster to bite off my head, perhaps?

The monster sank down into the water until its eyes were in line with mine. I tried to lean away as much as possible.

I heard someone on the ship yell, "Hold your fire!"

The monster sniffed at my wet clothes and my hair, then blew out a long, warm, stinking breath that dried my clothes.

A thought occurred to me. "Are you a type of snake?"

It didn't answer, but seemed to smile. The octopus allowed me to pull a hand free, and I reached out to the monster. It let me run my hand across the thick, soft, yellow scales along its wide nose.

"Okay, so you're not going to eat me?"

The octopus lifted me up higher and tossed me onto the snake's head. I landed on my knees with a thunk. "A warning would have been nice."

I didn't know if the sea monster would actually understand me, but I asked, "Any chance you could lift me up to the ship?"

I slipped and held onto one of its ears as it lifted out of the sea.

The look on the crew's faces as I came up over the gunwale on the monster's head was full of wonder, and a few of fear. I hopped off the snake and turned to pat it.

"Thank you. If you'd let us continue our way, that would be very much appreciated."

It nodded its head, then turned and dove down into the ocean. The whole of the crew rushed forward to watch it disappear.

"All right," the captain yelled, "Let's get this ship to rights. Andy! Take a count, see if we lost anyone. Israel, check over the ship, let me know what damage we have. Everyone else, back to your stations."

I looked back out to the water. There was the octopus, below the surface of the water, following us. Following me. It went deeper and deeper until I couldn't see it anymore.

"Chen! That was a feat fit for a song!"

"Chen! Why didn't you stop it sooner?"

"Chen! How did you do that?"

They came from everywhere at one time.

The captain walked up, scowling. "Don't be derelict in your duties. Get back to your stations."

The crew reluctantly moved away. To me, the captain said, "Chen, I've never in my life seen such a monster. Perhaps every ship should have a woman on board."

Then he turned and yelled at more of the crew to move along to their work.

Back in the galley, Dirk came to report.

"We've lost two of our men and one of theirs, I think it was that first wave of water that hit us. That leaves us with our nine to their fourteen."

I felt guilty about being rescued while they were lost at sea. I could imagine them feeling helpless, lost, and unable to reach the ship. For a moment, I couldn't breathe.

Dirk put his hand on my shoulder, and I looked up from the stove.

"Chen, that was— lifesaving."

I smiled and put my hand on his shoulder. "I'm not quite sure how I did it, but thank you."

A few moments later, several crew members, including Andy, overtook my galley and insisted I take a seat. They were going to finish cooking dinner and serve the savior of the ship.

I laughed and took a seat.

The captain came in and sat with us, which he'd normally be in his own mess or cabin for dinner. "Crew!"

There was a grumble as if he was going to send everyone to work.

"The grog is open. One glass per crew member, and no more."

Andy was handing out glasses of ale to many waiting hands. When everyone was seated, Andy yelled from the galley.

"All right, Chen, I had to listen to a pirate every night at my inn tell me stories about the sea. Now, it's your turn. Tell us about the monster."At the opposite end of the room were a few of the men, some of them from the old Flint crew like Israel, some of them not, who looked at me like I was poison. They got up and left as I started to speak.

The rest of the room was all eyes on me.

YEAR OF THE SNAKE

"I was born in the year of the snake. For most Chinese people, it tells of that person's personality and fortune. For my family and me, it meant much more."

"It is believed that I'm related to the White Snake. She was a ..." I started to say demon, but didn't want to scare anyone who wasn't already afraid of me.

"She was an angel in the form of a snake that could change into a woman. She fell in love and became a woman forever. It seems that I have inherited some things from her."

"I was swept overboard and fought to swim, my clothes and boots dragging me down. I was sure I was going to die when I was saved by an octopus. It lifted me out of the water and carried me over to the sea monster."

"I didn't know why it saved me. I thought the sea monster was going to eat me."

The crew laughed, and I had to smile as well. My heart felt a little lighter.

"When it didn't eat me, the octopus set me on the sea monster's head, and it carried me up to the ship. It is some form of snake, I suppose. You know the rest."

Andy raised his glass. "To Chen!"

And there were mirrored responses throughout the room, "To Chen!"

I waited until I could leave the galley and went straight to my berth. Alone, everyone else celebrating, I let the tears flow. I had never in my life been so afraid, not of the monster, but of the sea.

I got a hold of my fear and pushed it aside, just in time to hear someone yell down to the hold, "They are calling land ho!"

There was a great rush of feet across the deck. I joined the rest of the crew, where all hands were already congregating.

A belt of fog was moving away, and there was a full moon. To the south-west of us were two low hills, about a couple of miles apart, and rising behind one of them a third and higher hill, whose peak was still hidden in the fog. All three seemed sharp and conical.

Now this was a sight I remembered. We had arrived at Grimwood Isle.

Then Captain Smollett issued orders. The *Hispan-*

iola was laid a couple of points nearer the wind, and now sailed a course that would just clear the island on the east.

"Who knows this island?"

"I've once weighed anchor here," Israel said.

"What is the history of this place. Locals?"

"It's believed to be haunted," Israel said with a seriousness. "It was once a place known for pirates, but the English decided to build a garrison here to entrap pirates. The garrison was abandoned."

"Why?" Asked Andy.

Israel leaned toward him and said in a dark voice, "Because their men were disappearing, never to be found. It's said the ghost of the pirates took them."

Andy smiled, "I'd like to meet that ghost."

Israel smiled and turned back to the captain. "That hill to the north they call Fore-mast Hill. There are three hills in a row running south. Fore, main, and mizzen, sir."

"But the main hill- that's the big one, with the cloud on it—they usually call it the Spy-glass, by reason of a lookout they kept when they was in anchor."

"I have a chart here," said Captain Smollett. "See if that's the place."

I leaned in to look at the chart and tried not to show too much excitement at what might be the map, and I know Israel's eyes brightened as he took it, but when I saw how fresh the paper was, I knew we were out of luck.

This was not a map that would have come from Billy Bones. It was probably a copy with everything but the crosses needed to find the treasure.

Israel did well to hide his annoyance. "Yes, sir," he said. "This is the spot to be sure."

"Ay, here it is: Grimwood Isle—just the name my shipmate called it. There's a strong current that runs along the south, and then away northward up the west coast. Right you are, sir," he said. "To haul your wind and keep the weather of the island. Leastways, if such was your intention as to enter and careen, and there isn't any better place for that in these waters."

"Thank you, Israel," said Captain Smollett. "I'll ask you, later on, to give us a hand."

Exhausted, I went back to my berth. Soon we'd find the treasure, we'd make our move, and then be on our way. I just hoped we could make this as bloodless as possible.

THE ISLAND

I stepped out onto the deck as the sun broke over the island trees. There was only a skeleton crew working, as the Captain had given many of the men a break, handing out another glass of ale last night, and giving us all a handshake for a job well done.

We had moved into a cove, much the same shape as my cove at the Inn. Only here could I look at the strange trees that crowded the island and came all the way to the edge of the water. They were very tall, some having leaves at the top, others covered top to bottom in branches, thick leaves, and plants crowded onto the limbs of trees, but not a leaf stirred. The wind had died down, and the sun was already beating hot.

The hills on the island were tall and rose above the tree tops in spires of naked rock. All were strangely shaped, and the spy-glass hill, which was by three or four hundred feet the tallest on the island, was by far the strangest, running up sheer from almost every side, and then suddenly cut off at the top like a pedestal to put a bust on.

I couldn't imagine someone climbing up that formation to spy at the top, but I could see that it would be a great vantage point for the whole island.

My excitement built as I realized this was my very first land that wasn't England!

A shorebird flew by, dove into the ocean, and then soared with a fish in its mouth. I wished I could fly over the island to see it entirely.

Doctor Dawe came to stand beside me.

"It's amazing that this little island, of no known repute, could have a great deal of gold hidden amongst its hills."

I nodded.

"Andy, if you'll come with me. The captain, Trelawney, and I want to have a meeting to discuss our next steps."

I followed him in. I glanced back to see Chen standing out on the deck. She had seen us go into the cabin. If we were plotting, so was she, I was sure. I was more sure than ever that she was the Chinese woman who had frightened Billy Bones.

It occurred to me that facing a pirate that could command a sea serpent was not a good opponent to have.

The captain was saying, "Let's allow the men an afternoon ashore. We can make a plan to retrieve your treasure."

"Andy!" Squire Trelawney called. "It's good to see you, lad. Such a terrible couple of days to reach this sight. At least we now know that we should have gone around the, what did you say they might be, Doctor? A coral reef? Quite a reef."

The men laughed. I, for one, would look carefully at maps in the future and heed whatever warnings that might be laid bare.

Trelawney waved at the captain. "Certainly. A day off, and tomorrow we hunt for treasure."

I stepped forward. "What if. Well, what if there were pirates aboard our ship? Pirates from Flint's crew. How would you change your plan, Captain?"

Trelawney shook his head, "Balderdash, there are no pirates here."

The doctor's eyes widened. "What makes you think there are pirates here?"

The captain nodded. "I have my suspicions about a couple of the men, like Israel Hands." The captain sat down and rubbed at his chin.

I answered the doctor's question. "At the inn, Billy Bones was terrified of a Chinese woman, a pirate from Flint's crew. I'm sure that Chen is that woman."

Trelawney laughed. "I say again, balderdash. She's as innocent as a butterfly. Mr. Bones was more than likely mistaken. Besides, a woman pirate? I've never heard such a thing."

"I've heard of a Chinese pirate," the captain said from his thinking position. "She's known as the Sapphire Siren. They say that she lures ships in and murders all of their crew. Ruthless. If that's Chen, she's doing a great job hiding it."

Doctor Dawe sat down next to the captain with a thud. "Whether or not Chen is a pirate, I think we should plan accordingly. Reduce the opportunities for anyone to mutiny or take the treasure for themselves. Even good men will find gold hard to pass up."

Trelawney leaned back in his chair. "The deuce! I suppose a plan would be a wise move."

A NEW PLAN

The captain stood. "I would clap Chen in irons, but there are a lot of men who look up to her, consider her a good luck charm. Pirate or not, they wouldn't look kindly at that. Besides, a woman in irons? It could cause a mutiny just for the suggestion. If I only put Israel, that still leaves any others that could cause trouble."

I leaned forward, glancing over the map that Trelawney laid out, looking at the location of the treasure. "What if we send everyone on shore as planned. We warn the men that we trust that we think there are pirates. They can keep an eye out and listen in on conversations. By the time they return from shore leave, they should know at least more of the pirates, and we can put them in irons. And, if we must put Chen in irons too." I thought it was silly to leave Chen out of the plan just because she was a woman.

Trelawney nodded, his wig and hat moving with a bounce. "Let's start with step one of our plan. Besides, what better way to discover the dangers of this island than to let the crew explore?"

And so it was decided. Cooper, Joyce, Ron, and Hunter were taken into our confidence and received the news with less surprise and better spirits than I had expected. They were handed loaded pistols.

"Be sure to tuck those away, men." The captain warned. "I don't want anyone getting an idea that we know something is up."

Then the captain, Trelawney, the doctor, and Cooper would stay on board to ensure we kept the ship.

Then the captain went on deck and addressed the crew.

"My lads," said he, "it's going to be a hot day, and you're all tired and out of sorts. We survived a sea monster and some dashing storms. A turn ashore'll hurt nobody. Take the gigs, and as many as please may go ashore for the afternoon. I'll fire a gun half an hour before sundown to call you back."

The men gave a cheer that started an echo on a faraway hill. Birds that had been hiding in the trees were sent flying and squawking around the anchorage. For a moment, it gave me the shivers, but then my worries passed as I thought about my own chance to explore.

I wanted to survey the island without boundaries, without orders. I slipped onto a boat with men that I didn't know well.

Ron, Chen, Dirk, and Israel were all in other boats. Away from me so they couldn't tell me what to do.

Chen called from the other boat. "Andy, when we land, you should stick with me."

I wanted to trust her, but knew I couldn't, not if she thought I knew where the treasure was.

The men quickly dropped the gigs into the water and raced for the beach, but the boat I was in, having an early start, shot far ahead of the rest. The second the gig was among the shoreside trees, I caught a branch and swung myself out, and plunged into the nearest thicket, while Chen and the rest were still a hundred yards behind.

"Andy!" I heard her shouting.

But I paid no heed; jumping, ducking, and breaking through, I ran straight before me, till I could run no longer. I finally stopped, laughing and excited about breaking away from everyone.

Just in case anyone decided to follow my broken path of branches, I walked carefully for at least another mile in a different direction. That's when I found the pond.

It sat in a hollow with a rocky hill and a short

waterfall on one side and dense trees on the other. Dark green ferns crowded the tree side of the pond. The water itself was so blue and so clear that I could see to the bottom. A small group of fish congregated at one end.

One tree had fallen over the pond, its top hanging just above the surface, as if it were looking at its reflection.

As I stepped closer, I could feel that the air was cooler here. The chance that someone could find me here was still possible, but I didn't care. I threw caution to the wind and undressed.

I walked into the water and kept going until it enveloped me. I rinsed out my hair that had grown out a little. I would grow it out long, just like the men, no one would know the difference.

I floated on my back, then realized I could maybe swim. It didn't seem that hard. I dove into the water and then surfaced with a laugh.

With my newfound courage, I walked out onto the tree that created the bridge over the water and jumped into the deepest part of the pond. I surfaced with another laugh. I had to do it again.

On the way to the tree, I grabbed a white flower from a nearby vine and put it in my hair, and was ready to jump in again when I heard a sound of branches breaking. I ran to my clothes.

I had thrown on my undershirt when I saw a

shadowy figure jerking back and forth among the trees and then disappearing. I dressed quickly and climbed up on the rocks for a vantage point.

There was no one at the perimeter that I could see. Maybe they wanted to follow me to see if I'd lead them to the treasure, but my plan today was to simply keep an eye out for the landmarks mentioned on the map, and explore, of course.

I smiled even in spite of someone spying on me. I hadn't felt so clean in weeks, and my skin still tingled from the cold water. I moved through the rocks, intent on continuing my adventure.

Whoever had seen me hadn't moved like one of the crew. Maybe it was a local? or maybe it was the ghost?

COOPER

Istopped to look closely at a green bird pecking at the ground when I heard three voices speaking softly. I moved as stealthily as possible to get closer, to figure out who they were.

My face flushed as I realized it was Cooper and Israel. Israel was trying to talk Cooper into their side.

I heard Israel say, "We paid for this treasure in our own blood, sweat, and tears. It belongs to us."

Cooper was angry. "And who paid for this excursion, and who put together a fine crew, and who found the map?"

"We would have done just fine had the lad at the inn left things well enough alone. We have our own crew and would have had the map ourselves." Israel said, his voice deep and dark.

I got down on all fours and slowly crawled close

enough so I could see them from my vantage point. I also drew out my weapons.

"But ya didn't, did ya? Ya were outsmarted by a lad and his mother. Great pirate, ya must be."

Israel had been pacing, and at this, he pulled out his knife.

I almost gasped aloud, but put my hand over my mouth.

Cooper pulled out the pistol. "I'm taking you to the ship. The captain will want to speak to you. Drop your knife, you blaggard."

Israel dropped his knife with a sneer.

Then everything happened at once. I stood up to join Cooper, and Israel pulled another knife from his boot and threw it at Cooper.

Cooper fired his gun, but the bullet hit a tree behind Israel. Then Cooper fell back into the grass, his hand on his chest where the knife had entered.

I yelled and threw my axe with all my strength. It struck Israel so hard in the shoulder that it made him step back, and it stuck. Blood began to trickle down. I rushed forward and sliced the sickle through the air to warn Israel back from Cooper.

Israel pulled the axe from his shoulder and hacked it toward me. I hopped back out of the way.

My shirt got caught on a branch, and I ripped away from it, only to have my shirt pull open in the front. I pulled it down, but not fast enough.

Israel spat on the ground. "Witches, all a ya."

He lifted the axe as if he was going to throw it at me, then changed his mind and sprinted into the woods.

I dropped to Cooper's side.

"Cooper?"

His eyes were open, and he blinked at me. "Andy. Ya silly lad. What are ya doing, challenging a pirate?"

He coughed, and blood spilt from his mouth.

"Oh my god. We have to get you back to the ship!"

Cooper smiled. "I wasn't so sure that Mr. Trelawney should have brought you in the beginning. Now I know he made a good choice. It's time for you to head back to the ship, lad. Without me."

He coughed again, bubbles and blood coming up through his mouth. Then his whole body sagged with his last breath.

"No!" I screamed, a primal scream.

Cooper had deserved so much better in life. If I met up with Israel again, he'd be dead.

There was no way I could carry Cooper's body. We'd have to come back later and bury him appropriately.

I grabbed his gun and headed back to the ship.

ISRAEL

I blew the whistle and waited. This was a good opportunity to talk to all those from Flint's crew and get a plan together.

Dirk and Novak were already there, Nails and Gibbet showed up next, then Iron Tom. Ezra showed up a few minutes later. Then Weasel Fitch came into the clearing, supporting Israel Hands, whose shoulder was wrapped in a dirty cloth, more than likely Weasel's missing shirt.

The crew gathered around Israel and helped him sit.

"What happened?" I asked. Full well knowing this couldn't be good.

"I tried to talk Cooper into joining us. He seemed a good sort. He refused. I've taken care of him."

I held back my urge to stab Israel. "You were

supposed to hold off doing anything. And we definitely don't want to kill any of their members."

He laughed. "I don't see any reason ta be a swab."

"It's not a swab to be smart. Israel, who's the navigator for the *Hispaniola*?"

"Cooper had a hand in it, but Captain Smolett has been navigatin'."

"And can anyone in this crew navigate?"

He looked around at our ragtag group and shook his head.

"By killing Cooper, you've left us with one more person. How cooperative do you think Captain Smolett will be now that you've killed one of the crew?"

His left eyebrow rose.

"That's right. We don't have anyone who knows enough to get us to anywhere. If you kill the captain, if you kill his employer, he might refuse to help us. You strand us here." I didn't want to tell him I had some knowledge, but that would give him and the others full tilt on killing everyone who stood in their way.

"Start using your brain for God's sake."

Israel stood, shaky, with a sneer on his face. "I'm tired of your lip, devil woman."

"And I'm tired of you not listening to me."

The sound of hissing drew both of our eyes to the ground. A nest of snakes was facing and advancing toward Israel.

"Is that the only way you can take me? Using your devil snakes?" He drew out an axe.

I took a deep breath and did my best to send a message to the snakes to move away. It worked; they scattered and disappeared.

I moved away from the other men to give Israel and me some room. I pulled out my own knife. "That's Andy's axe."

Israel spit. "That lass's going to get hers soon enough."

"Lass?" I asked. he didn't respond, and I didn't need him to. Andy was a girl. I was happy to know Andy was okay and that she was probably the reason Israel had a hole in his shoulder.

Israel made the first move. He swung out with the axe, and I was easily able to jump back out of range.

He snarled and rushed forward. I used my knife to parry the axe, but the weight of the axe pushed the knife out of my hand. It went flying into the vines, hidden from view.

I heard a few quick breaths from the men.

I jumped back, a longer distance than I meant to. It seemed that I could leap farther than I thought.

On the ground was a thick, long branch. I picked it up and rolled aside just as Israel came at me again.

He was letting his guard down and slowing. I swung the pole and smacked him in the head. He screamed in anger and rushed toward me, the axe held high.

He threw it hard. I used the branch to catch it, the crook of the axe circled around the branch and then dropped to the ground. I didn't bother to pick it up.

He came at me with his bare hands and I used the end of the branch to bash him in the forehead. It knocked him back a step and probably down a few pegs as well.

"Israel, it's time to stop," Dirk warned him, but I wanted Israel to try again.

This time, Israel came at me at a run.

BEN

I dropped the branch, used my foot to lift the axe's handle to my hand. I whirled in a circle and chopped his head off. His body stood there for a second then dropped with a thud.

While I had been fighting a few of the men had left together - Weasel, and Gibbet, obviously afraid of me, the devil woman. That only left the six of us.

"Right." I took a deep breath, anger dripping from me like the blood from the axe. I chopped it into the sand to clean it, then set it aside.

"Here's what we're going to do. We'll go back to the ship, take it from the captain and put him and the rest in irons. Right now, there are only a few on the ship, and we should have a chance. We find the map on the ship and liberate our gold."

A wail came from the trees. "Yooooouuuuuu llllleeeeffffftttt mmmmmeeee!"

We all looked around for the source of the mournful sound.

A man, all sinew and sunburned leather skin, stepped from the shadows. He repeated his cry.

One of the men moved to cut him off with a knife, but I stopped him with a hand raised.

The voice, the face. There was something familiar.

His clothes hung in tatters - what had once been a sailor's shirt was now little more than strips of cloth hanging from his shoulders. His trousers were nothing but ragged tears. His feet were bare. On his shoulder was a terrible scar, obviously made from a sword.

"Ben?" I asked gently.

"You left me," he said in answer to my gentle question.

"Ben, we didn't know. Captain Flint told us you were dead. My friend, I'm so sorry you've been alone here."

His hair was a salt-stiffened tangle that hung past his shoulders. His beard was trimmed somehow, but not evenly. It was his gaunt look that distressed me most.

I was carrying provisions, so I pulled out some dried fish and moved to hand it to him. He grabbed it from me and ate it so fast, I was afraid he wouldn't be able to keep it down.

"That's Ben Gunn?" Dirk asked.

Ben looked up at Dirk and asked with all the anger he could muster, "Dirk, where's Captain Flint?"

"He's dead."

That seemed to satisfy Ben, he went back to eating.

"What a right mess this is," I said. I turned to my men, "Let me ask you a question. Who do you respect more, the captain on the *Hispaniola* or one of the two who left while I was fighting?"

"Oh no," Dirk said. "We can't answer that question out loud, Captain. The pirate code requires us to answer it anonymously."

I nodded. "Okay. Your choice. We rejoin the Captain, help them get the gold, and get our normal share for joining this crew. Draw an X on a leaf. Or, we take the ship, fight the fellow crew that have hightailed it somewhere else, and take the gold for ourselves. That's half an x."

Each member grabbed a leaf off a tree, used their knives to mark it, and handed it to me.

I counted them out loud, "X. X. X. X. half an X."

Iron Tom raised his hand. "That were me, Captain. If it's all the same, I'll change it to an X. It would be nice to have all that gold to ourselves, but we need a good navigator like the captain, and we need a full contingent to get to our next station. Besides-" he looked around at our deflated group, "we're in no shape to take on anyone."

"Right you are, Iron Tom." Besides, at this point, there were better ways to steal the gold.

I turned to Ben, but he was gone. He had disappeared into the jungle.

"Ben, come back! We want to take you with us!"

But there was no answer.

WARNING

Ithought I was walking in the right direction, but soon found myself completely lost. I could feel panic rising in my chest. Somewhere out there, Israel was killing, and I had to get to the ship to warn them. I prayed that Ron was okay.

To my left, I spotted one of the tall hills. I fought my way through branches and thick vines, then climbed up the hill until I was well above the trees. It made me nauseous to realize how high I was, but too many lives were at stake for me to get sick.

I sighed in relief when I saw our ship in the cove, but something didn't look right. No, the cove was the wrong shape. It was almost square. And the ship, it was flying the wrong flag. It was a Jolly Roger!

I looked in the opposite direction, and there was my

ship, the English flag, the rounded cove. I had to get there quickly.

I noted several landmarks along the way to my ship. I also looked back at the other ship and noted what they were up to.

Climbing down was harder than I thought. Foot holds were hard to find, and I was still fighting my stomach flipping every time I looked around.

I finally made it to the ground, exhaustion trying to overtake me, but I ran. I found each landmark and moved on to the next, and finally, I stepped out to the beach along the cove.

There was only one gig sitting on the beach; everyone else must have already returned to the ship. I stepped into the boat, and Chen and a few men stepped out to the beach.

Were they going to kill me?

Chen smiled at seeing me, "Andy, I'm so glad you're okay. Israel attacked us. I had to kill him." She reached out and handed me my axe.

Chen certainly looked like a death's head upon a mop-stick.

I heard a familiar voice call, "Andy!"

I turned to see Ron on the ship, and it made me so happy. He gave me a signal that meant he was glad to see me.

I waved back at him, then turned to Chen.

"We have no time to waste. There's a pirate ship on the other side of the island."

Chen's face fell, and she turned to the men with her. "Let's get this boat back to the ship, now. We have work to do."

They listened to her like she was their captain, jumping into the gig and setting us off quickly.

"You are a pirate, aren't you?" I asked her.

A few of her men looked over at me. It probably wasn't the smartest thing for me to say at the moment.

Chen leaned toward me, "You keep my secret, and we'll keep yours."

My jaw dropped. Of course, she had fought with Israel, and he had let my feminine cat out of the bag.

"We're in this together, right?" I asked.

Chen nodded.

That would have to do for now.

As soon as we reached the ship, Chen climbed the ropes so quickly that it looked like she was shot out of a cannon. The rest of us had to wait as the boat was hoisted up.

THE PIRATES
ARE WAITING

I climbed up the ropes and found the captain, doctor, and Trelawney were out on the deck.

"Gentlemen, we have no time to waste. Andy has reported a pirate ship on the other side of this island."

Trelawney froze in his tracks and seemed not to know what to do next.

The doctor looked at the captain. "What should we do?"

"You have two choices, the way I see it," the captain answered, "leave and forget your treasure, or we go get your treasure now. We can keep a small team on the ship, and use everyone else to guard the group getting the treasure."

The Squire nodded. "Indeed, we should heave ho back to Bristol immediately."

"That's not the way this works now," I told him. "Every man on the ship knows you're looking for treasure. When it comes to treasure, the rule of the sea is that you have to call a vote."

The captain nodded. "She's correct."

I organized the vote as quickly as possible. When the captain counted the votes, it was two for leaving and the rest for going for the treasure. I knew one of those votes would be Trelawney, but I wondered who else was willing to sacrifice all that gold. I knew it wasn't Andy; she was chomping at the bit.

The doctor brought out the map and laid it on the deck so that all could see. "There are two stashes of treasure, but close together. Ten paces says the map."

TAKE HEART

I stepped forward. "I know that map by heart, and I've seen the landmarks it mentions. I can lead us there." I didn't mention that I had also gotten lost yesterday, but I was quite marry that I could find my way.

The captain nodded. "I suppose that could work, lad. Men, grab shovels and weapons, anything we might use to carry treasure, and get loaded on the gigs."

As the captain boarded a boat, he said, "I need a few men willing to stay on the ship and protect her."

Trelawney raised his hand, I think to protest, but the captain acknowledged it, "Thank you, Mr. Trelawney. You will be most helpful here."

Joyce, Novak, and Hunter also stepped forward.

I pointed toward the south. "You should all know,

the pirates were moving along the coastline. They'll be coming from there."

Trelawney nodded, as if he had finally caught up to what was happening. "Cooper. Cooper knows how to set traps. Where is he?"

I felt the tears in my eyes and forced them away; I didn't have time. "I'm sorry, Squire. He was killed by Israel Hands."

The squire's eyebrows seemed to droop, and then he was looking around the ship.

"Israel was taken care of by Chen."

He nodded and then shook his head. "Cooper was a good man." He stood up straighter and looked at the group that was staying. "We should lay traps on the island while we still have time. And we should make sure the cannons in that direction are ready to fire."

Novak tapped Hunter in the chest. "I set some good traps when the Navy was chasin' a crew and me across Jamaica. I've got some ideas."

The two of them looked at each other and grinned. "We'll be back. We're going to make a welcome for our new friends." And they joined the boats.

I jumped into a boat and found Ron right at my heels.

I took my place at an oar and was still blinking back tears for Cooper. It was welcome to have Ron with me.

"Going to stick with me?" I asked.

He smiled, "I would go to the ends of the world with you."

I couldn't help but smile. "Really?"

"I left that comfortable village for a cold, damp ship. We've weathered a storm, a sea serpent, and now we face pirates. Of course it's about you."

I laughed as the boat touched down in the water and I pulled on the oars in time with the rest of the crew. "Ron, I know you also love the adventure."

"I love many things."

His innuendo intrigued me. Did he mean he loved me? I pulled hard on the oars.

I just hoped that we'd be able to defeat the pirates and survive so I could find out exactly what Ron meant.

FACE OF THE CANYON

I didn't know how to get directly to the canyon, so I decided to follow the map directions. I could see the words floating in front of me as we made our way through the jungle.

COMMENCE *at the tall tree atop the Spy-Glass shoulder.*

From the wood, take the South-East course, but mark this well: once you descend into the canyon, the black sand is the only honest ground.

Come at last to a black crag, with a face wore into it by wind and years. It keeps watch o'er the pass.

From the gate, proceed ten strides hence. There lies the first cache.

The silver bars lie another ten fathoms beyond.

· · ·

GETTING to the tall tree on the "spy-glass shoulder" was easy enough. We could see the black hill from almost anywhere on the island. The tall tree was standing on an extension of the hill, which could be described as a shoulder. Although I didn't think the tree would be here much longer. It was dead, some of its branches lay on the ground, and it looked like the whole of it could fall in a strong wind.

"From here we head southeast, which I think is this way." I stepped in that direction.

Chen pulled out a compass and checked it. "You've got it."

We trudged through thick vines, and strange birds cawed overhead. Finally, we came to a path of black sand; the black walls of a canyon were beginning to form here.

Here, I knew we just followed the canyon, but I wondered for a moment about *"the black sand is the only honest ground."*

I stepped into the black sand, which was soft, making it hard to walk in. It felt like it was taking all my energy to continue.

Stones were scattered on the bottom of the canyon. It was strange, though; they were brown, like other parts of the island, but the canyon was all black.

For a moment's rest from the sand, I stepped up to a stone. I heard a click, and the stone began to sink.

I threw myself backwards into the sand. The rest of the crew was still catching up. Above me, a boulder swung hard and raked my waist. I cried out in pain and quickly scurried back just as the rope holding it broke, sending the boulder crashing onto the stone.

I lay in the sand as everyone came running.

I raised a hand. "Stay on the sand! There are traps otherwise."

Ron and the doctor rushed forward to help me up.

"Are you okay?" The doctor asked.

"I'm fine." I looked down, rips in my shirt exposed bloody scrapes, but I wasn't badly injured. "Let's keep going."

We climbed over the boulder, and then I could see it. It was unmistakably the face in the canyon.

Along the wall of the canyon was the twisted and smooth surface of the sentinel. The left eye socket was higher than the right, a deep hollow with a dark shadow. The right eye was a shallow depression. Between them, a ridge of stone formed a crooked nose.

The mouth was a horizontal crack, deeper on the left than the right. It gave the whole visage a lopsided, leering quality. When the pirates had found this, they must have thought it a sign, certainly.

From the distorted face, I took eleven long strides, certainly the same as a man's ten. "We dig here."

The men rushed to my feet. I leapt back as they started.

A whistle overhead made us all stop, our hands on our weapons.

PHANTOM TREASURE

I had my hand on my sword as the whistle bounced through the canyon. We all looked up.

There was a man standing above us, and he was looking at me. He had a knife pressed against Caitiff's neck. What was Caitiff doing here? He and the crew of the *Night Sky* should be far away.

The man with the knife, obviously from the pirate ship, smiled. "We've been lookin' everywhere for ya', Chen."

I climbed up the side of the cliff in haste and anger. A pirate who wanted to see me. I'd show him!

When I reached the top, I pulled out my sword.

"I would na move any closer," the pirate said.

Poor Caitiff was wide-eyed and so much thinner than the last time I had seen him.

"Say what you came to say," I said.

"Captain Crazy Eye will gladly take any treasure you find in exchange for your crew. He will, however, keep his ship that you stole."

My heart sank. The ship that had been following us had been my own. I would save my crew no matter what it took.

"Anything else?" I asked as I figured out the quickest way to kill him. Most of his strength was being used to hold up Caitiff; he was weighed down.

"You have till sundown to bring the booty to the *Black Heart*. That's all, Chen."

I reached back and thrust my blade through the air. It flew true and went right between his eyes. His body fell backward. Caitiff fell to his knees.

"That's Captain Chen to you."

I pulled my sword from the pirate's body and then helped Caitiff up.

"Are you okay?"

"I will be Captain. It's the others I'm worried about. They're in the hold of the ship and have had naught to eat for days."

I glanced down into the canyon and was surprised to see a line of holes dug in the black sand.

"What's going on?" I called down.

The captain looked up. "We're finding nothing but bones. Someone's turned this into a burial ground."

"What the devil!"

I needed that treasure to at least appease Crazy Eye,

up until I killed him. These bones, though, probably belonged to the men who had been killed by Captain Flint. Who knew how many times he had come here to bury treasure and leave his own crew behind?

Ben. Ben was the one who survived. All this time on the island, what else had he had time to do but to carefully bury the bodies of his fallen crew members, and more than likely, move the treasure?

I looked around at the woods. Was he here somewhere, watching? If not, where would I find him?

"Stop digging. Throw some sand back over those bones and get up here."

A cannon shot echoed over the island, sending birds flying in all directions.

Some of the pirates were at the *Hispaniola*. We had to move faster. Hopefully, the crew would be able to hold them off.

I turned to Caitiff. "I won't leave you or the rest of my crew to suffer, but I need to move quickly." I handed him an apple from my pocket.

He greedily bit into it.

Ben stepped out from the shadows. "You won't leave your crew behind?"

"Ben, I won't leave you behind either." I pulled the picture I had drawn of him the day he had disappeared from my life. "I appreciated all the help you gave me. I drew your picture when I thought you were dead so that I'd have you with me."

He took the picture, and the difference between it and this emaciated man was tremendous. He brushed his hand over the image, and tears rolled down his cheeks.

"I thought about you," he whispered. "You were kind."

Some of the *Hispaniola* crew were beginning to reach me, and Ben looked around nervously. I signaled them to stop approaching.

"Ben, we need to save my crew. Can you tell me where the treasure is hidden?"

DETERMINED

I pulled the banana out of my other pocket. "I don't know if you like bananas as I do. Would you like it?"

Ben yanked the banana out of my hand, but then seemed to think better of it. He put it back in my hand and said, "Yes, thank you." Then took it slowly.

He stepped back near Caitiff. "I'll keep an eye on your friend here. You can find the treasure under the waterfall."

Andy ran past me. "I know where that is. Come on!"

Everyone followed at a run. I glanced back to see Caitiff leaning on Ben. I hoped we all survived this, and I could get them off this island.

It wasn't long until we found the waterfall. It was so small, I couldn't imagine there was anything underneath it. Andy and several others dove into the water and approached the rocks.

Andy took a shovel and shoved it into the rocks, parting the falling water so we could see a cave, part above and part below the water. Even from here, I could see the sparkle of treasure in the light.

Cries went up from the men and they ran out into the water. As they worked to gather the coins, bars, jewels and other glittering items, I took a bag from Dirk. "I can lighten your load." He nodded, then went back to work filling another bag.

I climbed the rocks, up to the top, over ten men high, where no one could reach me quickly, and waited for all the treasure to be gathered. As everyone began to leave to take the *Hispaniola* back, if necessary, I called out to everyone below.

"Crew! The pirates that are hunting us have stolen my ship and imprisoned my crew. I am Captain Chen of the *Night Sky*. I won't abandon my own. Those men and women on the *Night Sky* - they're not just my crew, they are my brothers and sisters, who have stood by me.

Crazy Eyes thinks he can trade lives for gold like they're nothing more than cargo. I intend to take him and all of his men to Davy Jones locker.

I know what I'm asking. The *Night Sky* isn't your fight, and these aren't your shipmates in chains. You signed on for treasure, not a rescue. But I'm asking you to stand with me anyway. If you'll join me, bring your loot, and let's make history as those who killed Crazy Eyes the pirate."

I walked away without looking to see if anyone would follow me. I hoped they all would, but I didn't know what else to say.

COURAGE

I watched as Chen moved away from the top of the rocks and disappeared into the woods.

Dirk and a few others stepped toward the rocks, following her. I also stepped forward but realized everyone else was standing around, unmoved.

It reminded me of the village, and my anger burst forward.

"I'm a 16-year-old girl, and I've got more courage than all of you. I'm not gonna let those pirates murder Chen's crew, and I'm not gonna let them get away with even one piece of that treasure. It belongs to us.

"Even if we still have our ship under our control, that pirate is going to chase us down. Better to face him on land than at sea! I won't let her do this alone. Up your mettle and join me!"

Ron and the doctor started climbing, then a few

more, and a few more. The captain joined them, and finally, there were only two left.

I turned my back on them, ripped a hole in the potato sack full of treasure, and hung it over my wrist. The weight of the coins was heavy, but I was determined to make it up. To go around would take too long.

From the sounds of grunting below me, it seemed the last two had decided to follow.

Ron was waiting for me and pulled the sack up. I climbed over the top, grabbed my bag from him, and ran. Those who had slowed down sped up to keep up with me.

I figured Chen would wait for us before she started something.

CRAZY-EYES

The closer I got to the cove, the slower I went. The last thing I needed to do was blunder into any of Crazy-eye's men.

I could start to see the ocean in the distance, and then soon I was able to spy the cove below me. What I saw made my blood boil.

My father's flag was tied across two trees; underneath was a pyre of wood, waiting to be burned. Around the pyre, tied to stakes, were my crew.

But there were no pirates in sight. A perfect trap for me.

I didn't know if anyone was coming to join me, but if it were a trap, now would be a good time to spring it, so that not everyone was caught in the middle. Besides, I knew some of his men were attacking the *Hispaniola*, how many could be left?

I slung the bag over my shoulder and walked down the hill, my hand on the hilt of my sword. I walked across an open field and sauntered up to Meg; her mouth was gagged. I began to untie her, but slid my dagger out of my sleeve and put it in her hand.

"Wait a minute, Little Miss. I hope you received my message. Gold is required for the lives of your crew."

Those words again meant to disrespect me. I couldn't wait to cut this man down.

I stepped back and held up the bag. I couldn't see who was speaking, but the voice had come from the other side of the pyre.

"I have gold, and the crew of the *Hispaniola* is not far behind me, bringing more."

"Really? They're willing to give up their gold for you and your crew? That seems very unlikely, Little Miss." He stepped around the pyre. He had a lit torch in his hand. His eyes bulged out of his face and looked in two directions.

Around me, I saw others step out from behind trees. I was surrounded by at least fifteen men.

I wanted to get the attention away from the pyre so I walked toward the beach and the ship. I upended the bag and let the treasure of coins and jewels fall into the sand.

A few of the men ran, grabbing the jewels.

"Captain, it's real!"

Their captain smiled. "It's too bad the rest of them aren't coming. We'll have to go find them. In the meantime..." He threw the torch onto the pyre.

BLACK HEART

I stepped towards the pyre, but the two men near the gold leapt in front of me. I cut down one before he could lift his sword. The other was ready and snarled as he parried my blade.

I knew there were too many of them. I backed up to the trees.

I raised my sword and swung hard at two coming from my left. My blade was deflected by the second.

I stepped back further.

They both swung their swords at me, I stopped the first sword. The second was aimed at my face. I closed my eyes and heard the sound of it clashing with another sword.

A jolt went through me as I realized I had just been saved by Renard, the card player from Bristol. He was wearing a dark blue vest and a white shirt that looked too clean for a pirate. How had he gotten here?

Both my attackers seemed as surprised as me.

I took advantage and cut down another pirate. Renard continued to fight against the other.

A yell from the hill gave me hope. I glanced for a second and saw Andy running, her sickle and axe in each hand, looking like a vengeful sailor. She might make a good pirate.

My masculine friend and I moved back-to-back, taking on the men who were coming at us. Some had moved off to greet Andy and the other men as they came down.

I glanced at the pyre, Meg and the others were almost done breaking everyone off of the stakes.

There were too many men between me and the flag, but I couldn't bear for it to be burned. The flames were on the top of the pyre, about to touch my precious flag.

I moved to climb up the nearest tree and found myself flying through the air up to the highest branch that would hold me.

I didn't know how I did it, but I had to keep moving.

I leapt over to the tree holding the flag, cut the rope, took hold of the flag, leapt to the other tree, and cut it as well, just as the fire began to lick at the tree tops.

I threw the flag around my shoulders, tying it with the rope ends like a cape, and jumped back down. My crew had joined the fray against the pirates.

They were holding their own. Andy and the *Hispaniola* crew were splitting the pirates into two fronts, a good sign. But I didn't see the captain anywhere.

I suspected he had gone back to the ship while I had been distracted. If he had any plans of escaping, I was going to put a stop to it.

BLOWS

I thought I'd try my hand at flying again. I pointed my sword toward the ship, but my feet were still firmly on the ground. I glanced around to make sure no one was watching me.

I reluctantly took one of the boats on the beach and rowed myself to the anchor rope. I climbed up, touched her hull and asked her if she'd accept me again.

I peeked over the gunwale at the deck. The captain was standing at the capstan with several others, ready to pull up the anchor.

He had his sword out and was tossing it in the air, catching the handle and repeating.

I climbed over the gunwale and asked him. "You don't seem very concerned about your men on the shore."

He turned and smiled, his men stayed at the

capstan, possibly ordered to stay if they needed to heave ho quickly.

He stepped towards me, well taller than me. He now twirled the sword in his hands. "Did you think you'd get away with it? Stealing my ship? The whole ghost thing was impressive. Those guards swore up and down that my ship was taken by the spirits. I, of course, wasn't buying it."

"Well, I'm taking it back. You should have left it to the ghosts. But I'm glad you didn't. One less pirate in the waters will be fine with me."

He laughed deeply. "Oh, Little Miss, you think you have a chance at besting me?"

He turned away from me and twirled his sword behind his back.

The second I stepped forward, he whirled around, stepped to my left, and struck downward with his sword.

I parried, pushed his sword back, and thrust my sword tip towards his face.

He jumped a step back, his eyebrows shot up. Was he really surprised that I'd be aggressive, or was he feigning?

I rushed forward, wary of any traps.

I swung at his legs, and he came at me with a downward strike again.

I danced away from the strike, turned in a circle, and cut into his leg. He leaped back again.

His back was against the gunwale at the stern; he had nowhere to go.

"Don't just stand there, you lubbers! Come get this girl." He called across the deck.

I glanced at the men watching from the capstan and was struck on the temple. I put my hand up to find I was bleeding. On the deck was a dagger. Crazy-eyes, he had taken that moment's distraction to throw it at me; he had only gotten me with the hilt.

It hurt like hell, though.

The men at the capstan now moved to fight, but not with me, instead at the rush of my crew coming over the side.

Now I knew there were no traps, no feigning. He had thought me inexperienced.

I whirled in circles in and out of the range of his sword, cutting him on his hands, his feet, his legs.

He finally jumped over the side. I looked down, and he was swimming to shore, away from the fighting.

A cheer arose from the beach first, and a wave took it up to the ship.

We had won! But what was the cost?

RENARD

My crew got *Black Heart* ready to sail while the *Hispaniola* crew climbed on board. Bags of treasure were being piled up near the mast. Except Nails, who was carrying a bag around like it was a baby, stroking it once and awhile.

It felt right to be a captain again; I had the ship and my crew back. But as the wounded were helped on board and set up in a space the doctor prescribed for a ward, my excitement waned.

Ron, Dirk, Will, and Micajah were sitting down, being looked at. I searched for Andy but didn't see her.

"What's the plan, Chen?" Captain Smolett asked.

"I'll sail around the island to your ship. If it's been taken, we'll take it back. Then, we can split the treasure and move on from there."

He clapped me on the shoulder. "I don't like pirates.

But you've been a damn fine cook, and I like to see you keep your word."

I nodded. "Captain Smolett, please check on your crew and let me know if we're missing anyone."

I kept looking for Andy, and instead found Ben and Caitiff joining the doctor's group of wounded.

"Ben!"

He nodded, helping Caitiff to sit. "We may be wounded, but we're still sailors." Ben sounded almost like his old self.

John approached me, and I was so happy to see him, but I didn't see Cuddy anywhere. He wasn't with the wounded, and if he wasn't standing next to John, then he...

"John, I'm so sorry."

That weighed on me.

"Andy!" Ron was calling her name and being held down by the doctor. Ron's leg was cut open to the bone.

"Did anyone see Andy?" I asked.

I looked out over the beach. Nothing was moving. I was going to look among the bodies, but Captain Smolett stopped me with a gesture.

"I'll go. He, I mean she, is my responsibility."

I paced the deck, and I didn't think I could stop until I saw Renard.

No one but me would know he didn't belong to either of these groups. I walked across the deck to where he stood, waiting, it seemed, for me. His eyes were a darker blue than I remembered.

I asked, "How did you get here? You weren't with the pirates, were you?"

"I have my own mode of transportation." He waved at me, and suddenly his arm was a long, purple tentacle. "I cannot hold this shape for very long. Until next time."

He bowed to me, then jumped over the side.

I rushed forward and saw a few purple tentacles rise from the water. They were waving at me. Then disappeared into the ocean.

"You tried to feed me to a sea serpent!" I yelled after him, but he didn't respond.

A man who could also be an octopus? I would have so many questions for him the next time we met.

DARKNESS

I lay on the dark, rocky floor of the cave and assessed myself. I was alive, that much was good. I heard no movement in the cave; the man I had been fighting had fallen in with me. Perhaps he was assessing as well.

One minute, we were fighting above the cove; the next, we had fallen through the earth. Above me, I could only see a small slit of sky; the rocks were being held on by the roots of plants.

It would probably be a good idea if I moved away from possibly being stoned to death.

I cried out as I leaned up, my right shoulder sending shots of pain through my body. I reached up my left hand to hold my right arm and found my shirt covered in blood.

I heard no other movement in the cave. I could see a

dark form next to me, but I didn't bother to check him. If he were alive, he was on his own.

I grabbed my weapons and moved away from the dangerous location. I tore off my sash and used it to bind my arm to my torso.

But now what? I was trapped in a cave. Was there another way out? I couldn't see climbing with my arm in this shape, and if I didn't get out of here, no one would ever find me.

I could see some light up ahead, so I went to investigate. From the light, I could see there was water ahead, a small pond it appeared. Lighting up the water were five small serpents.

I sat on the edge of the water and watched them for a moment. They seemed to be playing, touching each other with their snouts, running away, then rushing back again.

Were these luminaries? Their brightness illuminated many strides away in the cave. Around me, there were no other lights, but if there was water, could it be open to the ocean somewhere?

I stepped in the opposite direction that the serpents were playing and found that within a few steps, they were following me.

"You're not going to eat me, right?"

They didn't answer and I was glad of that. But I was in a hurry. Might they be able to help me?

They scurried as I stepped into the water. Then they

hurried back, checking out my boots by touching them with their snouts. They had sharp barbs at the end of their tails, and I was sure had teeth like a barracuda, but I needed to get out of here.

I kneeled down and put my hand in the water. The largest of the serpents swam over my hand, letting me touch it. When it came back, I tested out the idea of picking it up.

It curled around my wrist but did nothing else.

"I just need help finding my way around."

It stayed where it was, so I walked forward into the water. I hoped I was heading toward the beach, but then a shine of gold caught my eye. Off to my left, there were three sea chests and a pile of treasure!

I dashed over, careful not to jar my new friend. So many beautiful things. I picked up a necklace of red jewels and gold, put it in my pocket, and turned away. It wouldn't do me any good if I could never get out of here.

LUMINARY

Finding the treasure meant there had to be another way out of this cave. With newfound determination, I stepped into the water in the direction of what I hoped was the cove.

The other serpents happily twirled in the water around my feet. In front of me, all I found was rock walls, but I could hear the ocean! I followed the sound. When I started to see daylight, I put my arm back in the water to let the serpent go.

"You can go, my friend, you helped me find my way."

His friends poked him with their snouts, but he stayed snuggled around me.

"I hate to take you, friend, but I need to keep moving."

I walked out onto a beach and turned toward what I

hoped was the cove. When I came over a rise, it was unmistakably the right place. There were bodies everywhere, but the waters of the cover were empty!

I had only one opportunity. If the *Hispaniola* were still here, I would have to get across the island.

I ran past the bodies, not looking in case one of them was someone I knew. I didn't want to know, not yet.

With every step, my shoulder sent waves of pain, and my midsection ached.

I ran past the pond and wished dearly that I could soak in its waters. Past the canyon entrance, past the spyglass hill. And then I ran right into the doctor.

"Whoa! I have her, fellows!" He yelled.

My momentum gone, I collapsed to the ground.

DECISIONS

I lay on a makeshift bed of potato sacks on the deck of the *Black Heart*, next to Andy.

The doctor explained, "We couldn't leave without one last check. Truth be told, Ron wouldn't have let us leave unless we had you with us."

Ron was sitting up, watching the doctor bandage my shoulder. Everyone was giving my left hand plenty of room; the serpent's head was lifted up and was curiously watching everyone. In the sunlight, it had a beautiful purple sheen to its body.

Chen stepped up to my left, unafraid of my new friend, and cast a shadow over my eyes. "Andy, we leave shortly for shores unknown. I want to invite you to stay on board and join my crew of the *Night Sky*."

The doctor shook his head. "She needs to come back with us to Bristol. Her mother will be waiting."

My mother and nothing else. Mother and I had enough money to be comfortable for the rest of our lives, but I wasn't hungering after comfort. I wanted adventure.

"Doctor, make sure my mother gets the money from my share."

He looked stricken, but nodded.

Besides, I had that beautiful necklace I could sell. I'd have plenty of money when needed.

"I'm in, Captain Chen."

"Welcome aboard. Now, Doctor, we need to move the *Hispaniola* wounded over."

"Except for me," Ron said. "Where she goes, I go."

I reached my hand out to him, and he took it, serpent coiled around my arm and all.

"Doctor," I said. "What about the *Hispaniola*? Is everyone okay after the pirates attacked?"

The doctor smiled. "Apparently, Squire Trelawney is more cunning than we know. The lot of them that we left not only kept the pirates at bay, but sent them scurrying for their lives."

"Thank goodness. Then please tell the squire that I shall miss him."

The doctor nodded. "We will see you again, Andy."

He helped Micajah to his feet, and they moved away and off the ship.

"All hands to launch!" Chen yelled.

After feet scrambled and hands rushed to stations,

and we were on our way, Chen continued, "I have new plans, all. Think on this. We have enough money to live comfortably. But what about adventure? I propose that we become something new. Pirate warriors that protect the innocent and take from those we see fit."

I looked around and saw smiles from some, confusion from others. I was wondering, how did we know one from another?

"and, I want to go after that Aztec gold that's sunk to the bottom of the sea."

At this, the whole crew was enthusiastic.

Then all movement on the ship stopped when the giant sea serpent rose out of the ocean, its head hovering over the ship.

"Don't harm it!" Chen yelled to her crew.

My heart was going to burst from my chest as it came to hover over me and sniffed at the serpent on my wrist. I reached out my hand. The serpent poked its nose into the giant sea serpent's face, but didn't move from me.

The sea serpent nodded and recoiled back into the ocean.

I whispered, "You're not going to get that big, are you?"

It didn't answer, but coiled up on my chest.

Join Andy and Chen on their next adventure, *Treasure of the Golden Sun*. Sign up for my email list for free short stories and to know when the next book arrives! http://eepurl.com/cAzV5v

You can also go to my website to find the link. https://sonjadewing.com/contact/

PART THREE

READ MORE ABOUT REAL WOMEN PIRATES

 List of books to read:

I did a lot of research about women pirates while I developed this novel, so I thought you might like some of the books I read (although I didn't read all of these).

1. *The Republic of Pirates: Being the True and Surprising Story of the Caribbean Pirates and the Man Who Brought Them Down* by Colin Woodard - covers the golden age of piracy and includes Anne Bonny and Mary Read.

2. *Pirate Women: The Princesses, Prostitutes, and Privateers Who Ruled the Seven Seas* by Laura Sook Duncombe, et al - focuses specifically on historical women pirates.

3. *A Pirate's Life for She: Swashbuckling Women Through the Ages* by Laura Sook Duncombe - Stories of 16

women who came from all walks of life but had one thing in common: a desire for freedom.

4. *Bold in Her Breeches: Women Pirates Across the Ages*, edited by Jo Stanley - a collection of essays about women pirates throughout history.

5. *She Captains: Heroines and Hellions of the Sea* by Joan Druett - about women who went to sea, including pirates.

Also, the series with only one season on Disney, "Pirates".

INTERESTINGLY, there are no English-language books about the most successful woman pirate, Ching Shih, a Chinese pirate who commanded a massive fleet. I did a lot of online research about her.

Historical figures you might want to research: Anne Bonny, Mary Read, Ching Shih (Chinese pirate who commanded a massive fleet), Grace O'Malley (Irish pirate queen), and Sayyida al Hurra (16th-century Moroccan pirate queen).

I ALSO SUGGEST *Black Hands White Sails* by Patricia C. McKissack and Frederick McKissack - this book shares the history of runaway slaves becoming members of whaling ships during colonial times, including a story of a woman who goes to sea as a man

About the Author

Sonja Dewing is an award-winning author of fantasy adventure and thrillers. Get her complete fantasy series that starts with *Toy of the Gods* today.

Toy of the Gods

An ancient god. A deadly jungle. A tour they'll never forget.

When a mischievous Inca god traps a group of unsuspecting tourists deep in the Amazon, it's up to former adventurer Leslie Kicklighter to get them out alive. But survival won't be easy. Between ruthless mercenaries, hostile villagers, a shady plantation owner, and even a troop of drunken monkeys, danger lurks behind every tree.

And the god isn't done playing yet.

Toy of the Gods is the pulse-pounding first book in the award-winning *Idol Makers* series—a wild mix of mythology, mystery, and mayhem. If you love the high-stakes action of *Indiana Jones*, the clever twists of *Repairman Jack*, or the bold heroines of *Tomb Raider*, then dive into this jungle adventure today.

"This story has the charm, the humor, and the

thrills that readers will love." – *Five Stars, Readers' Favorite*

Buy *Toy of the Gods* now and join the adventure!

Follow Sonja Dewing on:
Instagram: instagram.com/sdewing_author
Facebook: facebook.com/AuthorSonjaDewing
Tiktok: tiktok.com/@sonjadewing_author

www.ingramcontent.com/pod-product-compliance
Lightning Source LLC
Chambersburg PA
CBHW070236200726
48293CB00005B/1646